TALES

OF

SOUTHERNERE

VOLUME 1

TALES

OF

SOUTHERNERE

VOLUME 1

INDRA ZUFAYRI HAMDAN

LitPrime Solutions
21250 Hawthorne Blvd
Suite 500, Torrance, CA 90503
www.litprime.com
Phone: 1 (209) 788-3500

Published by LitPrime Solutions   02/05/2021

ISBN: 978-1-953397-88-1(sc)
ISBN: 978-1-953397-89-8(e)

Library of Congress Control Number: 2021901621

CONTENTS

All praises to Allah for giving me the inspiration to write this story. An inspiration received through playing soft toys with my two sisters. A story I am elated to share since I was ten. And of course there were changes along the way, all with intention to make the story more interesting and logical.

(THIS STORY COMES IN SERIES)

PART 4

MAJUZA'S AVENGER

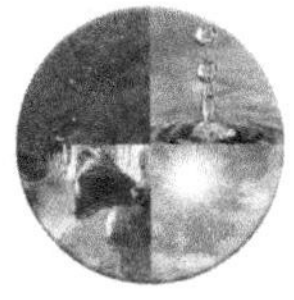

BATTLE AT THE ACADEMY

Powers were thrown everywhere. All the elements, common spells, or even the rare Gratultyn magic. Sprites showed their nature power, Helazes threw fireballs, Ardnis deflected them with the atmosphere, and Winterains conjured streams of water from in between their fingers in defense.

All SHAW masters' strength were just enough to prevent the huge group of avengers continuously coming down to attack. They came down from the sky, transforming back from a big black bird to their usual self. It wasn't a fair fight. The avengers outnumbered the masters five to one. If the ratio changes, the lower the chances become for the masters to defend the school.

Master Jackenzie, headmaster of SHAW Academy. He was the strongest of them all. Three avengers were facing him alone. And he defeated them with ease. His close companions were also all around the school field fighting whoever they came across with. So were the other masters and some head students. Master Widow, Jackenzie's mother was fighting near the school. She and a few others were shielding the building and preventing the avengers from trying to get past. So they thought they wanted something inside the school. But they were wrong. None of the avengers were fighting them to get into the school. Most were fighting other masters at the centre of the field, where Jackenzie was. And those who went near the school were just fighting the other masters for fun. If only the masters knew their actual motive, what happens next won't happen, possibly.

Then, came a few horses with armoured riders on them. A handsome man in his thirties got off the most armoured horse and drew his sword. Happy expressions came from the masters who caught sight of him. The king and a few of his men were here to help.

Avengers came to attack them. The soldiers drew their swords and prepared to defend. But the king had defeated them already with a few wind tricks and a swing of his sword.

'King Henry, should we go ahead with the accustomed plan?' one of the king's guards, Bobby (also his royal butler and head of squires and castle servants), said.

'Yes, drive every last of them out of Combination. And ensure everyone's safe' King Henry replied. All of them got to work. And the horses as well, kicking the avengers with their hooves or running them over. Henry cleared his way to the centre of the field to join Jackenzie.

'My king, you have arrived!' Jackenzie said.

'Focus on your opponent Jack'

An avenger faced the king and conjured a flame on his palm. He sent it speeding towards Henry. Henry caught the flame in his own hands and made it vanish. The avenger became more angry. Now was Henry's turn to return. He conjured a small tornado on his palm, moving it onto the ground and made it man-size. He then sent it towards the avenger. The avenger wasn't an expert in wind so he was easily swallowed by the tornado before it vanished.

While that happens, another avenger came to face Jackenzie. He continuously conjured fireballs and threw it at the master. Jackenzie blocked and blocked. The avenger was feeling very satisfied, at least he gave the master no chance to counterattack. Jackenzie continued the rhythm but suddenly the ground beneath him cracked. The crack made its way up to the avenger who was already shocked. Jackenzie made that happen with his mind. A lot of tasks he could do at once, so continuous fireballs can't stop him. Goodbye to the avenger. The shock made him lose concentration and the fireballs stopped. Jackenzie moved up his hands and at the same time, the ground beneath the avenger moved up, devouring him and bringing him back underneath, burying him deep inside.

Master Mousy, a mouse the size of a small cat, also one of Master Jackenzie's closest companions, faced two avengers trying to get past her to Jackenzie. A man and a woman.

'This isn't fair, you know that right?' Mousy said.

'Who cares you ugly rat!' the man said. He formed rocks from pieces of the ground and threw it at her. Mousy stopped them and sent them back, half of them towards the man and the other half towards the woman. The woman crushed them all. Mousy controlled the soil near where they were standing. She made them gripped onto their shoes hard. They both exclaimed in anger. The man transformed into a bird which set him free from the grip and flew past her towards Jackenzie. But Henry killed him with a swing of his sword. Bird feathers spread all around. Mousy focused on the woman now. She destroyed Mousy's bond on the grip and came running at her. Mousy formed a shield just in time before they collided. But the woman overpowered it. The shield broke and Mousy stumbled on the ground with the woman now on her. Both started punching and blocking each other's offenses. Mousy narrowed her energy into a force she was planning to let out. The woman was hurting her fur so badly. Finally Mousy pushed the woman away with all the force she narrowed. The woman was flung violently upwards. And before she landed back onto the ground, Mousy formed a huge spike from the soil in the woman's landing position. Few seconds later, the spike went through her body. Mousy deformed the spike and returned the soil back to its place. The woman's body lay on the ground motionless. A big hole in her back with blood spilling out.

'That's not appropriate, Mousy' said a white cat who just came up to her. Master Kitty, also one of Jackenzie's closest companions, and Mousy's best friend.

'Come on Kitty, this isn't training' Mousy replied.

'That is why what I said counts even more!'

'Mercy Master Mousy' Jackenzie said. He was standing behind them for quite some time. And he noticed Mousy's actions.

'Yes Master Jackenzie'

The three of them went back to fighting. By this

time, there were no more new avengers coming down. The ratio was now seven to one. And the avengers were winning. Many masters and soldiers were passed out or dead. The avengers were blocking the centre in a huge circle. That means, no escape for Jackenzie, Henry, and the others. Unless they turn into birds and fly away. But the avengers would still manage to catch them.

The powers slowly stopped and so did other attacks. Everyone in the centre was looking cautiously at the avengers surrounding them. The avengers were looking back at them with anger. The masters outside the circle could only wish that all this had never happened. A flash of lightning lit the darkening sky. Heavy rain was about to shower on the city. Another black bird appeared in the sky and landed in the circle, transforming into another avenger. But he was not like the others. He was the leader and has this aura around him that proves so. And another difference was that he was bald.

'Morgan' Jackenzie uttered, loud enough for Henry to hear. And the bald guy heard it too by some hearing enhancement he did towards himself.

'It's Lord Morgan to you young master' Morgan said. He smirked. 'I respect you by addressing you with your title so be polite and address me with mine!'

'What do you want Morgan?' Jackenzie said.

'No respect indeed. Even towards the king'

'Jackenzie is one of the most respectful people I've ever met. Now you and your army get out of our city' Henry said, defending the master.

'Have you forgotten?' Morgan was being cocky. 'Oh, I just remembered! You Inlanders have thrown us out, look down on us like wastes! Your stupid ancestors changed what truly happened. You and all your snob brothers and sisters have been brainwashed by false information'

'We all know clearly who was the enemy' Jackenzie said.

'Oh no, not her. Majuza has always been like us, the one who was looked down upon. But still, she has never done something so wild as your hypocrite great mother Sofya, burning children to death'

'Oh stop it toe-head, we have discussed this before. You people are the one with the false information' Mousy said.

Morgan exerted a forcefield that flung Mousy backwards a few metres. She landed near to the other avengers standing in the circle. She got up immediately and stood in a ready position to strike back.

'Go home Morgan' Jackenzie said.

'Not until I finished what I came to do'

'What do you want?'

'Your blood'

There was no warning. Morgan immediately sent the ground shaking and breaking apart in the direction of Jackenzie. And he threw a few fireballs in the same direction as an additional attack. Jackenzie defended all the attacks with the help of Henry, Kitty, and Jenny who were all very near to him. Morgan sent another wave and this time adding a wild tornado bigger than the one Henry conjured earlier. Jackenzie dealt with the ground, Jenny dealt with the fire, and Henry dealt with the wind.

'Go home Morgan' Jackenzie said again.

Morgan quickly moved his hand up to the sky then downwards. A bolt of lightning zapped an area near them. The grass caught fire and started burning, slowly spreading.

'Magic involving the weather is forbidden in this land' Henry said. 'The punishments to be placed on you has just got worse'

'We don't care' Morgan said. And immediately, the whole field got noisy again as the avengers all at once started attacking again. It was like they planned all that together very well. The next few moments were filled with magic and screams. And Jackenzie was facing Morgan alone. They have not enough men to have backups facing an enemy. In fact, most of them have to face more than one person continuously.

'Now this is a very important task entrusted upon me. So come now, don't make my life more difficult' Morgan said. Jackenzie formed rocks from the ground, mixed it with the fire from the burning grass, and sent it towards Morgan. Morgan formed a black hole in front of him. The rocks went in and Jackenzie realised that he sent it somewhere else when he saw another black hole appeared a few distances away. The rocks hit a master who was defending against an avenger's attacks.

'Another forbidden magic' Jackenzie said sternly.

'Again, I'm the one with manners. I speak to you with respect, but you don't return it' Morgan said. He was already moving his hands around in circular motion. The fire around rose following Morgan's directions. They went continuously in circular motion in the air just like Morgan's movements with his hands. They were ready to attack anytime Morgan ordered so. Jackenzie wasn't backing down. He also did something. He clenched his fists. The ground vibrated.

'Fire versus rock, who do you think will win?' Morgan smirked. 'You can't possibly think you can stop me, plus if I add all my ultra magic skills'

Jackenzie again did not say anything. He just stood with his mind all ready to defend and attack whenever needed.

Morgan sent a few waves of fire. Jackenzie blocked them and returned a few waves of rocks. Morgan blocked them. Jackenzie formed a huge boulder and flung it at Morgan. Morgan stopped it, changed it's form into a bear. Morgan transferred some of the fire to the rock bear and added some skills that were unknown to Jackenzie. The rock bear was now a burning bear like a magma cube, only it's a bear. And it was alive.

'That's forbidden as well!'

'Snap out of it headmaster, you're not fighting with your students, you're fighting one of the greatest SHAWs of all time!' Morgan boasted.

The bear came charging at Jackenzie. Jackenzie jumped out of the way, at the same time, moved his hand up, bringing the soil around the bear to go up, gripped it and dragged it inside. But the bear's resistance was very strong. The soil forming the grip around the bear was losing to the fire on its body. Morgan did not waste his opportunity. He sent fireballs at the master. Jackenzie was unable to concentrate on that and a few fireballs hit him, burning the part where he got hit.

Jackenzie divided his focus, his hands on the bear and his mind on Morgan.

'Give up master' Morgan said. Jackenzie pushed his hands down, the soil continuously reached out to grab the bear, pulling it down. With his mind, Jackenzie sent a quake in Morgan's direction. Morgan took control of the force and pulled apart the crack all the way up to Jackenzie. The ground opened, Jackenzie lost his balance and his focus. The soil gripping the bear stopped pulling. The bear hopped back out. Jackenzie fell on the ground, just beside the small crack that leads down into no one knows how deep. Morgan walked to him, the bear was also near. Any movements Jackenzie made now can be easily countered. The bear let out a loud growl like it was screaming in pain. Morgan looked up, King Henry had stabbed the bear deep with his sword.

'Step away from him' Henry said, pulling the sword back out, the bear fell down, dead. Henry advanced towards Morgan, but Morgan sent the waves of fire continuously towards him. That got Henry busy defending himself. Morgan now focused on Jackenzie. Jackenzie looked at him, his eyes filled with knowledge. Like he already knew what's gonna happen. Jackenzie breathed in deep, like he was preparing. Morgan quickly took out a knife from his black robe. And he went down swiftly, stabbing the master in his chest. Jackenzie let out a soft cry as he breathed out. Henry saw what just happened and exclaimed clean shouts of anger towards Morgan. Morgan pulled the knife back out and transformed into the bird before flying up and far away from the school. The other avengers followed immediately, knowing their task had been accomplished. The surviving masters and Henry threw quick shots of magic towards them. Some got hit and fell but most of them escaped. Everyone's attention was now on the dead master at the centre of the field. Master Widow, who was at the building's side entrance, came rushing towards her son. The other masters came as well.

King Henry searched for Bobby. He saw him with some of his men and walked to them.

'Bobby, I need you to send a message to the queen, she'll know what to do' Henry said. Bobby briskly walked to one of the horses that survived the battle. He got on and rode away.

All the head students involved survived. Mousy went to one of them and asked to check on all the students hiding in the school building.

The field was very quiet now. The sky became brighter as the rain had stopped. All the masters, King Henry and some of his men stood in respect. Only the cries of Master Widow could be heard, even from the edges of the field.

THE PRINCE'S THEORY

Before you start reading the next chapter, finish what you're supposed to do first. Done? Carry on!

The entire city of Combination was quiet. The busy streets were now empty. Everyone closed their shops for the day. Most people were going to the city hall where Master Jackenzie's farewell was being held. The entire Inland had received the terrible news. The royals from the other cities and towns, who knew the master, were coming. Southernere is a big plot of land surrounded by the ocean, and two small islands in the south. Due to the far distance between Combination and the farthest city in The Inlands, the royals of that city will take about a day to reach. Arstar is the farthest city. The king of Arstar would need about twenty-two hours of travel by horse carriage. So Arstar only sent a letter to pay their respects. A raven reached the castle six hours later.

However, the gathering has already started an hour after the battle. The city hall has already been filled with rows and rows of chairs. Majority of the people who came were citizens and students of the academy. The masters sat in the second row while the first was reserved for the royals. King Henry has brought his family since the start of the gathering. Queen Dorothy and Prince Edward sat in the front row on the right of the centre aisle, occupying the second and third seats from the edge. Henry was busy communicating with the masters or greeting his citizens. He was indeed a very friendly king. Everyone knows him. Literally knows him. He is always welcoming anyone into the castle. They don't have to sneak in the gardens just to get a view of the beautiful interior. Because every month, King Henry would plan a ceremony and invite everyone in the city. Everyone looks up to him like a model friend.

About an hour after the gathering had started, the royals of White Shore arrived. White Shore is a small town towards the northeast of Combination. In fact, it is a town fully under the orders of Combination that it does not have a king but only a lord to protect. A lord chosen by the king of Combination years ago and the roll has been passed on to their descendants since then. The lady is King Henry's half sister. So they're all a big family actually. Lord Adam arrived with his wife Lady Matilda. She was pregnant for about four months now. Her shape was obvious to tell. The two families greeted one another. The ladies pulled into a hug, beginning with the right, then the left, and back to the right again. Their beautiful long scarves moved with their movements. The ladies in Southernere generally cover every part of their body, except for their hands and face. They cover their modesty. So you could say, every lady has long dresses and scarves over their heads. The animals are in their normal selves, not wearing any fancy clothes. They don't have to, their fur or feathers or any other kinds of skin is enough to cover them. Except for some like the royal horses who have armour on them.

'How's my growing nephew? How are you?' Lady Matilda said, bending down a little to hug her eight year old nephew. Prince Edward hugged her.

'I'm great. Bobby taught me a new trick with a sword!' Edward said excitedly.

'He did?' Matilda replied, entertaining him. 'Why don't you tell me more later, I'm staying at your castle for the week!'

'Really?' Edward's eyes were filled with excitement.

'Alright let's go sit down' Queen Dorothy said, smiling the whole time.

Soon the royals from the city of Barenge arrived and they greeted one another again. The royals of Barenge are Dorothy's family. The king and queen are her parents, and Princess Darleen is her younger sister. Their ages are quite far apart for being the only children in the family. Darleen's twenty-five whereas her sister is ten years older. Princess Darleen was overly excited to see her nephew that she forgot she was at a farewell. She just loves to see children. And she gets very excited especially when the child is related to her.

The event started. Master Jenny went up the stage on behalf of Master Widow who was supposed to go up because she was the assistant head of the academy. Jackenzie's body lay in a casket on a stone table at the centre of the stage. Jenny greeted the royals, individually, and then everyone and proceeded with the royal speech which she invited King Henry on stage.

'We are gathered here today, because of our own will to pay the highest amount of respect for the passing of our grand master. A son, a friend, a soldier, a husband, a father, and a master. And he's legacy will continue to provide assistance to all of Inland. We wish this farewell to you as a reminder for us as well, that we will be in your place one day. And your spirit will always stay with us' King Henry said. The whole hall was very quiet. Master Jenny proceeded back up as Henry went to take his seat beside the prince. Prince Edward was a bright young boy. He may be eight but he understood whatever his father had just said. In fact, he was multitasking, listening while looking around at all the other guests. Everyone behind him thought that he was just being a normal kid when he kneeled on his chair and peaked at everyone behind. But he was listening. Edward looked at all their faces that were filled with tears. Edward has a special gift. He has the ability to read people through their facial expressions. He's not right all the time, but most of the time he is. And to him, many people were faking. They were not crying out of genuine sadness for the loss. But they were just trying to show that they care. Edward was sad. How could he not be, Master Jackenzie was one of his personal mentors. Edward doesn't go to the academy like the other kids. He learns what they learn but his lessons are at the castle. Masters Jackenzie, Mousy, and Kitty will come to the palace taking turns, teaching him whatever magical subjects appropriate for his age. Other mentors like Bobby, is Edward's personal teacher for swordfighting. The prince is very close to Master Jackenzie, even not during lessons, Jackenzie spent quite an amount of time with him. Edward was like his own son. Lillain is Jackenzie's only daughter. And she too is very close to Edward. She was like a big sister to him. Because almost every time Jackenzie went to the castle, Lillain would follow and play along with Edward and his friends. Since he doesn't leave the castle much, Edward has not many friends. In fact, the only human friends he has are those who frequently visited the castle, and they are his masters and Lillain. So he would proudly call the castle staff as his friends as well. It makes him happy to have people around him that he would call friends even though sometimes some of the workers at the castle are new and he had never met before. But he does have real friends though, animal friends from the small forest, Combination Woods, just beside the castle grounds. Captain, and Bale, are two chipmunks, and Oliver, a cat. And they always play together with Lillain all around the castle and the gardens. However, Edward wasn't feeling like crying. And he wouldn't fake something just to show others. He was sad, but if he's not in the mood to cry, why force?

His eyes moved to the second row on the other side. Master Widow was the first person that caught his eyes. Lillain was sitting beside her, crying and wiping her tears. Master Widow was doing the same. But Edward saw something that surprised him a little. Lillain was crying for real, she wasn't faking. She was really sad. But Master Widow was not. She was faking. Edward squinted a little, trying to read her more.

'Edward, how long do you want to look at everyone behind you?' Queen Dorothy's voice entered Edward's ears. The prince turned immediately, losing his focus on Widow. But he kept on thinking, why the mother of the dead master was faking her tears? He bent again, looking past his father to see the second row. Master Widow was not there anymore. He looked behind again. Widow was walking down the aisle and she exited the hall. After the speech that seemed to take ages for Edward, he got up and rushed to Lillain's row as his parents were already busy communicating with the other royal guests. Lillain was still crying. He stopped in his tracks. Took a few steps back. He thought, maybe he should give Lillain some space for the time being. He looked around, Masters, Mousy and Kitty were standing together at one side of the hall. Edward ran to them.

'Master Mousy! Master Kitty!' Edward called as he came closer.

'Hey Eddie!' Mousy said, opening her arms to accept the hug given. Mousy is a tough and fierce character, but she was very much loved by the prince. She was very supportive of him and always listened to him even when he was speaking plain nonsense. Kitty on the other hand is very quiet. It may get awkward when a random person has nothing to talk about and Kitty's just standing there looking at everything around him.

'I have something to share' Edward said.

'What is it?' Mousy replied. The two masters looked at him attentively.

'It's just one of my theories. But I'm afraid this is not a joke'

The two masters processed his words and it increased their curiosity.

'It's about Master Widow'

'What about her?' Mousy asked softly. She got excited by the name. It's not like she noticed there was something strange but maybe it is strange in the eyes of the prince. And Mousy trusts Edward's instincts whenever he is being serious. And Edward definitely sounded serious.

'I saw her earlier. She was crying, with Lillain beside her' Edward said. 'But when I looked at her and I looked at Lillain, her tears were not as real as Lillain's. She was faking her cry, just like almost everyone else in this hall'

'What do you mean Eddie?' Mousy asked.

'What if... Master Widow wanted her son dead? What if she asked the avengers to kill him?'

'I think that's too far, are you sure?' Kitty asked, he was already uncomfortable with the conversation. 'I mean, Master Widow has been fighting the avengers and enforcing the law to banish them for years! And why would she want her own son dead?'

'I don't understand. I just told you what I saw and I am sure that her cry was fake'

'Maybe she wasn't in the mood to cry but she doesn't want people looking bad on her so she faked it' Kitty suggested.

'I believed you Edward' Mousy said simply.

'Really?' Edward's face brightened.

'I'll try to figure it out'

'Thank you Master Mousy' Edward said, and hugged her again. The prince went to rejoin his family.

'You really believed him?' Kitty asked, feeling a little disbelief.

'He was getting very disappointed after hearing what you said' Mousy replied.

'You can't always make him happy. He's growing up and he has to know that the world is not as joyful as every child thinks'

'He'll learn that alright, but not from me. And think about it, a mother who lived for fifty years with her son, has to fake a cry when her son was murdered? I really meant what I said to Eddie. I'll look into it'

Mousy walked away, joining the crowd who were walking out of the hall. Kitty stared at her, thinking back on the entire conversation they just had.

EVENT PREPARATIONS

Before you start reading the next chapter, finish what you're supposed to do first. Done? Carry on!

Everyone went back home. The streets remained quiet for the rest of the day. Many were not in the mood either to buy or sell anything. The only busy place was the castle. They have a preparation going on. A royal birthday celebration that has been announced for weeks. Tomorrow it'll be the first birthday celebration for Princess Erieka, daughter of King Henry and Queen Dorothy. The royals went back to the castle along with Lord Adam and Lady Matilda who will be staying there for six more days. The castle got even more busy the minute they returned. The royal chefs one by one came to ask the queen's final opinion on the dishes they prepared. The royal dressmaker came to ask both the queen's and the lady's final opinion on the dresses that they'll wear tomorrow. Bobby repeatedly came to the king to give a report on the number of men who will constantly guard the halls and patrol around the castle. And Lord Adam assisted the royal butler with decorations.

As for Prince Edward, he went to visit his sister in her chamber. Princess Erieka was lying in her crib, her eyes wide open.

'How long have you been awake dearest sister?' Edward said. Erieka responded with the cute baby voice of hers saying something no one can understand.

'I don't understand you. But I'll act like I do' Edward said again, smiling at her as he stood on his toes to look into the crib. Their eyes connected. Erieka made another sound of happiness.

'You're so good! Lying down in here all by yourself! Where's Annie?'

Annie is the head of the royal maids and handmaidens and Queen Dorothy's personal handmaiden. But she spent most of the time with Erieka, queen's orders.

Erieka made her baby sound again.

'I shall pretend that you said she is busy helping the preparation. Oh, really? Okay, let me be the first to wish you! Happy birthday Erieka! In seven years time you'll be as big as me! And I'll be bigger, like Lillain!' Edward said, laughing at his imagination.

'Are you happy? Are you excited? Let me read you' Edward said, standing on his toes as long as he could, he looked into Erieka's eyes. He saw the high energy that she has. He could feel her energy around him running in all directions, excited and ready to roar.

'You are powerful' Edward said, amazed by what he felt. Erieka opened her mouth and to Edward, it looked like she was smiling.

'You wait, I'm going to tell mother' Edward said, running out the doors. Edward found his mother with his aunt, Lady Matilda, sitting at the tea table in the gardens, still discussing on the dresses.

'Mother! You have to come and see! Erieka's energy, I could feel it around me when I'm near her, she's very powerful!' Edward said excitedly. The ladies looked at Edward, adored by his cute excitement.

'I know Edward, I gave birth to her' Queen Dorothy said, smiling. Edward replied simply, "oh". He didn't think about that.

'But was it a surprise to you when you first felt it?' Edward asked.

'Honestly no, because I know someone related who has that energy as well'

'Father?'

'Yes! Clever boy!' Dorothy clapped. Edward went nearer to her.

'Do I have that energy?' Edward asked. Dorothy shook her head gently. Edward's face saddened.

'But I've never seen anyone with so much spirit before except you' Dorothy said.

'I don't quite understand the difference between energy and spirit' Edward said.

'Energy you can feel it, but spirit, you have to see it. I see and know your spirit since the day you learn who your parents are. Yes energy will seem powerful and intimidating to anyone. But spirit is the real reason that someone is very powerful. Because of spirit, all the great masters you know master a more complicated magic such as Gratultyn magic and those with higher spirit master light magic or if the opposite, dark magic'

'That's a long explanation, but I understand mother'

Dorothy smiled at her son.

'Okay then, I'm going to go and play again!' Edward said. He ran off.

'Don't forget, you have sword training lesson with Bobby later at six!' Dorothy raised her voice loud enough for Edward to hear as he went away.

'Yes mother!' Edward replied loudly. He went into the fountain gardens on the east side of the castle. A big sculpture sits in a big stone bowl in the centre of the gardens. Water rippling inside as holes around the sculpture shoot water out of them creating a peaceful waterfall fountain. This is Edward's most favourite spot outside the castle. He plays here, studies here, trains here. All because of the fountain. He's a Winterain, SHAWs that are born in winter and have the specialty of water. SHAW is the acronym of four words which are the names of groups of magic wielding people. S stands for Sprite, the group that is born in spring and has the specialty of nature. H is for Helaze, the group that is born in summer and has the specialty of fire. A for Ardni, the group that is born in autumn and has the specialty of air. While W as explained, stands for Winterain, the group born in winter and has the specialty of water. Together all of them are called SHAWs, that differs them from those born without magical abilities. An example of someone who is not a SHAW is Bobby. So because of the fountain, this is Edward's favourite spot to train his specialty and other elements and magic will tag along. But his intention to have fun and play with water was changed because as he reached, there were his three best friends, Captain, Bale and Oliver, on the wide seating area around the fountain.

'Guys! You came to play?' Edward said.

'You're right we did' Captain said.

'What do you wanna play?'

'Hide and seek?' Oliver suggested.

'In the gardens again?' Captain asked, annoyed.

'What's wrong with that?'

'Can we play somewhere else? Like in the castle?'

'That is not possible today, we have preparations going on inside. And I think why don't we play some magic this time!' Edward said.

'Have you forgotten again? Bale and I don't have magic!' Captain said.

'Oops, yep, sorry again'

'Hide and catch?' Edward said.

'That's fun for a change. Let's play that!' Captain said. 'Okay we hide and you seek'

'Why must I seek?' Edward said.

'Because you suggested it'

'Okay then, seeking you in twenty seconds!' Edward turned to a nearby flowery column, closed his eyes and started counting loudly.

'Hurry hide!' Captain exclaimed in excitement. The three animals ran to different parts of the garden. Captain reached the edge of the fountain garden, he went into the hedge, he could see the queen and lady of White Shore chatting at the tea table.

'Did he say we cannot go to other gardens, aside the fountain one? I think not' Captain said gleefully as he made his way into the main gardens, north of the castle.

Meanwhile, Edward had just finished counting down, he went looking, excited to find everyone. It was easy to find Bale and Oliver. He found them both together hiding under a bench behind some bushes. Captain was not easy. They went across to the main gardens but still could not find him.

'Do you think he might have gone inside the castle?' Oliver asked. They went inside through the main gardens entrance that led them to the main ballroom where the heart of the celebration is going to take place. Everywhere servants and temporary hired staff worked on getting the place ready with the finishing touches. Edward noticed Jordan, the assistant royal butler, and Lord Adam at one of the buffet tables, and went to them.

'Jordan, have you seen my friend Captain?' Edward asked.

'My prince, is it the mischievous one? Better not he be in here' Jordan said. 'Nope, have not seen him'

'Thanks Jordan' Edward said. They went out of the ballroom into the main hall. Walls on both sides of the huge ballroom double doors, curving around to the curvy stairs on both sides that leads to the second floor. Walking straight ahead will lead to the entrance hallway and to the castle main entrance. Just behind both of the stairs are smaller hallways with rooms on its sides.

'This will take forever to find him' Oliver complaint. 'Such a cheater'

'I know what to do' Edward said.

'What?' Oliver and Bale asked together.

'We just wait until he got tired of hiding and comes out of his hiding place!' Edward said.

'You want us to wait and do nothing? That's even worse than searching!' Oliver exclaimed.

'No, we do whatever else we want, he'll get bored, we don't' Edward grinned. The two animals looked at him with a cunning smile. They agreed to the idea.

A servant came to them.

'Your highness, the queen has requested me to summon you'

'Alright, thank you' Edward said. The servant walked away.

'Sorry guys, I guess time has passed so quickly. I have sword fighting lesson with Bobby. You guys can do what I suggested, or you guys want to find him' Edward said, then walked back into the ballroom to head into the main gardens.

Aside from the queen, lady of White Shore and the dressmaker, now the king, Lord Adam and Bobby were there too.

'When will you be back?' Queen Dorothy said.

'As soon as possible' King Henry replied. He turned to walk away with Lord Adam following behind.

'Where are you going?' Edward asked, he was already standing in his father's way.

'To White Shore. We received urgent news'

'Can I come?'

'Sorry Edward, I can't bring you along this time, and don't forget, you have lesson with Bobby' Henry said.

'Alright'

Henry and Adam walked away.

'Your highness, are you ready for your lesson?' Bobby said. Edward nodded.

THE STRANGER FROM
THE OUTSIDE WORLD

Before you start reading the next chapter, finish what you're supposed to do first. Done? Carry on!

It took King Henry and Lord Adam around one hour to rush to White Shore on their horses. The White Shore palace entrance was wide open, ready to welcome the king and lord.

'Your majesty, Lord Adam, the guest has awoken' the butler said, gesturing with his hands the way, and led them. They passed the entrance hallway into the main one that has rooms on each side facing one another. The butler led them into a room on the right. It was a small guest lounge. It was a very cozy room, anyone could just sit here and fall asleep within seconds. The couches in one corner, a fireplace by the side. A small counter with jugs and cups for water. And potted plants decorated every empty corner of the room. A young lady sits on one side of a three-seater couch. She looked different than most people anyone had ever seen in Southernere. In fact, she looked different than everyone. Her skin was a little bit darker. She wore an unrecognisable long blouse and the bottom part was like a cloth, all with unique pattern designs. And she also wore a headscarf, longer than those in Southernere that it was a bit loose. Basically her appearance was different than all, but her style was mostly the same, she covers her modesty like the other ladies. The lady flinched as she saw the three men entered.

'Greetings miss' King Henry began as he sat on the couch opposite her. She seemed to pull herself back, looking very uncomfortable.

'Do you need some water? Fetch her some water please' Henry said. The butler took the jug from the counter and proceeded out of the room.

'You don't have to be in fear of me or any of us, we're not gonna hurt you. The Inlanders are civilised people. I'm King Henry of Combination, my family and I help one another to maintain the peace'

The lady remained quiet, refusing eye contact.

'You are not from around here' Henry said. The lady still gave no response. So Henry got up and pretended to leave the room and that caught the lady's attention.

'Where am I?' she said. Her accent was very different as well. Clearly, she doesn't always speak English although she understands and knows what to say.

'You're in White Shore, a town located northeast of Southernere. The whole land we are on' Henry said.

'I never heard about that before' she said.

'Where are you from?'

The lady was conversing but her words were coming

out slowly, as she was still uncomfortable and processing the words in her mind properly before saying.

'Indonesia' she replied simply just as the butler entered with the jug filled with plain water. Henry thought about what the lady just said. He turned to the butler as he was pouring the water into an empty glass.

'How did she end up here again?' Henry asked.

'We found her in a boat at the shore. She was unconscious at that time, your majesty' the butler said, excusing himself to deliver the glass of water to the lady. She accepted it gently.

'And what makes you think this is a big matter for the king?' Lord Adam said.

'Everything we found on her or on the boat were just rare items, in fact we had never seen them before. Unless some were similar to the artifacts that our famous explorers brought back from the outside world milord'

'That's what I thought as well' Henry said in agreement. 'I read in some of the books on voyages by our explorers. Indonesia is one of the nearest world to ours'

'Indonesia is not a world. It's a country' the lady interrupted. Henry was a little surprised by her attitude. He was not used to commoners correcting him without the proper address and etiquette. But probably because the lady was a stranger and does not know the ways of the people here.

'My mistake, yes, a country. That's the exact word used in the book' Henry said, giving a smile. 'May I know your name?'

'Dewi' she said. 'Dewi Binte Omar'

'You have a long name! Something we people of Southernere don't have. You know mine already. Just plain Henry, the titles in front are what made our names long' Henry said, laughing at the last part.

'Omar is my father's name. In my family culture, we have our names, some have more than one. Then our father's name follows after' Dewi said.

'That's interesting. So if I were part of your family, my name would be Henry Harry!' Henry laughed.

'Something like that'

There was a pause for a brief moment.

'Now, on a more serious note. Do you happen to know how you ended up here? Because I think you still don't realise that you are not in the same world you were from' Henry said.

Dewi thought about the sentence, her expression was obvious that she was confused.

'Have you ever heard of a land, or you call it country, that is called Southernere?'

Dewi shook her head.

'That's because you are not in your own world right now. Now with your arrival here, I believe all the explorers that returned from their journeys to your world and shared in their books that we learnt in school. I used to think those were just stories. Then I started believing them when an old famous explorer during my early twenties came back from your world with an item he brought back as proof of its existence. Now, with you here, whatever doubts I have left are no more. The only thing I'm still curious about is how those explorers got to and from your world. Because in our world, there is only the huge island of Southernere and two small islands in the south. The rest are ocean going on from the north and soon will end up back in the south, because our world is a globe. That is why I am excited to learn from you, how you came here. But it seems like you don't know it yourself. Given that you were unconscious when they found you. Can you recall, what exactly happened before you became unconscious?'

Dewi tried hard thinking back what she had been through. But her description was not really answering Henry's curiosity.

'I was on the boat...' Dewi said. '...a larger boat. In fact it was a ship. It was my dad's. We were venturing the seas. It was the third day we were on that ship. It was just me, my dad, and a few members of his crew. He's a businessman and he's very busy. That trip was supposed to be a vacation for us both. But on that day, the weather was bad. The storm was very wild. The waves were crashing onto the sides. I was sitting in my room below the main deck. That was when I saw the lightning zapped the ocean a few metres away. And then there was a deadly hurricane, we called it a cyclone. I was uneasy, so I left my room. The crew was very busy working hard to steer the ship out of the storm. I heard my dad called me from the captain's deck. I wanted to turn, but something hit me on the head, I remember the pain was intense for a short while and I don't remember anything next, except that I woke up in this room and I was worried, I searched for my father in the halls but then the butler came and told me no one was with me. I thought, maybe my dad and the rest of the crew didn't survive. But I also wondered how I did. The boat you found me in, that might be one of the small boats we had on the ship in case of emergencies for us to escape'

'I'm sorry to hear about your father, the crew and your ship' Henry said. 'Would you follow me and Lord Adam here back to Combination? We'll take you to the palace, my wife would be delighted to welcome you as our guest. And we could learn a few things from one another about our worlds'

Dewi nodded gracefully. Henry smiled, the lady was not royalty or maybe she is in her world, but she has polite manners. Though, she still has to learn to stop interrupting anyone, especially the king next time. So King Henry and Lord Adam proceeded back towards Combination. The butler prepared one of the royal horses of the palace stables for Dewi to ride as she followed the two royals wherever they went. Surprisingly, Dewi seems to be good with horses as well. Not that you need any skill in Southernere to ride a horse because the horses here are more intellectual. Because the animals and creatures here are very much alive. They could talk. So getting a horse to let you ride on him is much easier.

THE ROYAL CELEBRATION

Before you start reading the next chapter, finish what you're supposed to do first. Done? Carry on!

Another hour taken for their journey back to Combination. It was already dark outside. The lights from houses, buildings, schools, streets, the castle and the gardens brightened the area around. It definitely is magical here. Dewi was very attracted to her surroundings. She admired its beauty. The whole land of Southernere is magical. But like everything else, there are beautiful places in this land, and there are also places where people will never wish to go.

King Henry's words were accurate. Queen Dorothy was very delighted to see them return, and her face got even kinder upon seeing Dewi. Henry introduced her. And Dorothy was very welcoming.

'How was the preparation dear?' Henry said, embracing his wife.

'All is well, just a few more checking routines tomorrow and we're ready. Alright, enough about our family matters' Dorothy said. She turned to look at Dewi.

'How are you dear? Let me help you inside'

Dewi was surprised to see her. She wasn't expecting her to be covering her entire modesty. She had never seen anyone aside from her race covering before, and looking very stunning. She was touched even more by her kindness. Dewi smiled in return and followed her along with the handmaiden accompanying her.

Dorothy led her passed the entrance hallway into the main hallway and into the smaller hallway behind the stairs on the right. They stopped in front of one of the rooms. The handmaiden opened the door.

'This will be your room' Dorothy said, inviting Dewi inside. Dewi felt good. She felt like she was being treated like someone important. She loves this place already. The guest chamber was not as big as the other royal chambers. It only has what is essential for a royal bedroom to have. Which are the bed, two armchairs, carpets, lamps, paintings, bookcase, the bathroom, a closet room, and a table of refreshments.

'This is my room?' Dewi asked, feeling very honoured.

'You have nowhere else to stay, this will be your room. All our guests are part of the family and treat it like your own home' Dorothy said kindly. 'Of course there are rules in every home, so whenever there is a need for advice, anyone of the castle staff can guide you, there's a button with the crown symbol beside the bathroom door, just press it anytime for assistance'

'Thank you very much your... queen' Dewi said, not sure how to address her.

'It's your majesty' the handmaiden helped her.

'Thank you, your majesty' Dewi said. Dorothy smiled.

'It's my pleasure Dewi. Did I pronounce correctly?' Dorothy said.

'According to your accent, yes you did' Dewi replied.

'Get some rest, there's a big celebration tomorrow, and you can be one of our guests as well' Dorothy said and left the room with the handmaiden following behind.

Queen Dorothy went to visit her daughter in her chamber. Annie was there sitting on the armchair by her crib. She immediately stood up in respect as the queen entered.

'How is she Annie?' Dorothy asked.

'She's just fallen asleep after I gave her a warm milk' The milk bottle was on the refreshments table.

'Thank you Annie' Dorothy said, as she smiled, then went to give Princess Erieka a kiss on the forehead.

She went to visit her son next. His chamber was on the second floor a few rooms away from hers. Prince Edward was still awake, he was sitting on his bed comfortably reading a book.

'Mother' Edward said affectionately as he looked up. Dorothy approached the bed and sat on it.

'What book are you reading?' she asked.

Edward turned the book around to the cover page and handed it over to his mother.

'"The Adventures of Galliver in the Outside World"' Edward mentioned the title. 'So the stranger is staying in our castle?'

'Yes Edward' she replied, returning him the book.

'And it's late, it's time for you to sleep' she got up and tucked her son before kissing him on the forehead. She left and headed to her chamber. Dorothy dismissed the handmaiden before she entered. King Henry was already sitting in bed, legs straight and his back leaning on the headboard. He was half asleep.

'If you're tired, you could have just gone to bed' Dorothy said.

'Then I'll miss our daily discussion' Henry said.

'Your health is even more important'

'My wife is important to me as well'

Dorothy smiled, touched by her husband's sweetness. She changed into her nightgown and sat beside him.

'Alright, you first' Dorothy said.

'The battle just now afternoon drained most of my energy. I was so close to helping Jack. Then at the farewell, it was difficult speaking for someone I was close with since I studied at the academy. The preparations were great. Halfway I have to leave for White Shore. Dewi didn't want to share anything at first. But she opened up. And it seems she was really from the outside world. But I'm still figuring out how she ended up here. There could be more of our race out there. Because she looks like us. Only a bit different in how she speak or how her appearance is'

Dorothy held her husband's hand.

'It's okay dear, you did your best today. If you couldn't have saved Jackenzie, no one else could have, because everyone else was much farther. Everything has been completed for the preparations. We just need to do the final checking routine tomorrow and we're ready to start'

Dorothy kissed her husband on the forehead.

'Goodnight dear. Rest well' she said, getting under the covers and lying down to sleep. Henry did the same.

The next day arrived very fast. Everyone was already up and ready to start the final checking routine. While the adults are already working, Prince Edward and Princess Erieka are still getting ready, assisted by their squire or handmaiden. That is a young man named Jeff and Annie. Queen Dorothy visited Dewi's chamber and found that she was already wide awake and was studying the books that were present on the bookcase.

'You're an early person?' Dorothy said.

'It's my daily routine to wake up early and pray. But I called for assistance earlier, no one knows what I'm talking about' Dewi said.

'Pray?'

'I thought the people here knew because the way everyone dresses is like me, covered. But when I saw the sun rose, I estimated the direction for me to face'

Dorothy smiled.

'There's definitely a lot we can learn from one another. I never heard of that word before, pray'

'It's in my religion, cause I'm a Muslim'

'That word, religion, I read it somewhere before. Among the strange words I found in the books the explorers shared, about their adventures. Words like culture, tradition'

'Your majesty, you have no other races in Southernere? No other methods of celebration?'

'I have no idea about the Outlanders but we Inlanders all usually come together whenever there's a celebration. What is races?'

'It's plural, your majesty, so it's "what are". It's different kinds of people, like me and you, we're definitely different races. I'm Indonesian, and judging by your looks, you're Caucasian'

'No, I'm CombiNation' Dorothy replied simply.

'Isn't that the name of this city?'

'Yes and no, I meant CombiNation, with the capital N. Everyone in Southernere and even in The Outlands are The Nation of Combi. Combi is our very first ancestor that started life on this land. We don't know how he got here or where he was from but he and his wife Mayang and their two daughters, Sofya and Majuza, are our ancestors. But, I read before about theories that might be true or might not, Combi might have originated from your world'

'I see, your majesty, that's an interesting story as well. Mayang is a word familiar to my people or generally in the Malayan Peninsula'

'That's fascinating, maybe we're connected somehow? So there are different types of people in your world'

'Your majesty, from reading some of the books just now, I think my world and yours are not different'

'What do you mean?' Dorothy asked, getting curious.

'I think, we are all in the same world but only in a different way. What I mean is, maybe your world is in another dimension. But it's still part of mine. Our world is called Earth. And although I can't remember how I got here, but, it can't be very difficult since I was nowhere near any sort of portal when I'm on that ship yesterday. What I'm saying is, I think, your world is part of mine but it exists on a different plane'

Dorothy listened attentively before she smiled at the last part.

'That's a lot to take in, I am very much confused and I don't want today to be ruined by my brain telling me all sorts of things I don't understand' Dorothy laughed. Dewi laughed as well.

'Alright your majesty, that's just what I thought. Go ahead and enjoy the day!' Dewi said.

'Come and join us! We're having a quick breakfast before the celebration. You can meet my children!'

'You have children? Young prince or princess?' Dewi was excited to hear.

'Both' Dorothy smiled. 'I see that you love children'

'I do very much actually! I was a teacher back at my hometown'

'How old are you?'

'Twenty-one' Dewi replied.

'So young. I feel so old already!' Dorothy laughed again. 'Come and join us?'

'Sure!'

'You can change to any of the clothes in the closet if you want' Dorothy said, looking at Dewi who was wearing the same clothes. 'You'll draw less attention later at the ballroom. After you're done, press the crown button I told about yesterday. Someone can guide you to the dining hall. If you go alone, you'll get lost in this place'

Dorothy left as Dewi went inside the closet room to

change. Dewi entered the closet for the first time and was amazed by all the beautiful dresses and gowns, suits, coats, vests and scarves. There were also shelves with pieces of jewellery. She thought if the guest chamber has all these, the king and queen's chamber would have more. Dewi picked a decent dress that attracted her, and a scarf to match it. She looked at herself in the mirror to straighten everything before pressing the crown button beside the bathroom door. A few seconds later, a handmaiden arrived. A different handmaiden than the one who assisted her earlier that morning. She brought her to the dining hall, passed the main ballroom door to the other side of the castle. The doors here are tall. The walls are even taller. Dewi entered the hall to find another room to be amazed. The room was very big. A long dining table, like the size of four dining tables placed together, sits in the centre. A fireplace in the middle on one side. A warm fire burning wood inside. The royal family were already seated at the table. King Henry and Queen Dorothy at one end. Lord Adam and Lady Matilda to their right. Prince Edward to their left. And Princess Erieka's mobile crib, by the side of Queen Dorothy.

'Dewi! Come and join us, you may sit beside Edward' Dorothy called excitedly, gesturing to the empty seat beside the prince. One of the royal waiters helped Dewi to the seat. She was feeling a bit shy and awkward.

'I am very honoured to be here. I feel like I don't deserve all this' Dewi said shyly.

'You are our guest Dewi, and all our guests deserve a place to stay and food to eat' Henry said, smiling. The other royals were also smiling along. It was kind of funny but it was very joyful as well.

'Hi!' Edward said cheerfully at Dewi. He was happy to meet someone new.

'Hi!' Dewi replied, a little surprised by his cheerfulness.

'I'm Edward, Master Mousy calls me Eddie. Sometimes my mother calls me Ed. What about you?' Edward said.

'My name's Dewi. You can call me Dewi because everyone calls me Dewi' Dewi said, releasing a short laugh. Edward laughed as well. He laughed even harder actually.

'You just repeated how I said it, that's funny!' Edward laughed.

The breakfast was very delicious, eggs and toasts with some potatoes. But Dewi did not straight away touch her plate.

'I'm sorry to bother or interrupt your majesty, but may I know, are there any ingredients in the food that contain alcohol?' Dewi asked cautiously.

'It's just plain eggs and toasts and the potatoes are fresh! Best of Southernere' Queen Dorothy replied.

'Thank you' Dewi said, and then started to eat.

'Is there a problem?' Dorothy asked.

'It's just something I practice' Dewi replied simply. Her reply was obvious to Dorothy that it was unclear. But she let it go.

'That is something your world has? The ingredient you mentioned?' King Henry asked.

'You don't have alcohol?' Dewi asked back in surprise.

'Yes the one you mentioned. Never heard of that except probably in the books' Henry said.

'Sorry your majesty for interrupting' Dewi said, realising she had just ignored the king's question and asked hers instead.

'That's alright. It's wonderful you are learning our ways' Henry replied. They finished their breakfast with different topics for conversation.

Soon, it was noon and time for the celebration. The sun shone brightly over the castle. It was a wonderful summer afternoon, and the streets were already back to being busy today. But most people were heading towards the castle. The castle was even busier. Soon the ballroom will be filled with guests in beautiful gowns and suits. The final checking routine had been carried out and the servants were already in their positions to carry out their assigned tasks for the day. The castle soldiers guarding the entrance greeted everyone who came. A servant stood just behind to guide the guests to the ballroom. As the servant went, another servant came to guide the next group. The castle was never short of workers. Everyone was happy to be working there and even when the staff is already full, there are still people who wants to get a job there. The royal men were in the men's restroom, a room in the castle just for clothing and a small bathroom. They were waiting for the right moment to enter the ballroom. There was no right moment or anything, it's just the way royals of Southernere enter after their guests arrived. But if they want to enter now is also up to them, no one can stop them from breaking their ways, they're royalty. So that was what King Henry did. He entered the ballroom early, when the room was only occupied by the waiters, servants and a few guests that had arrived. The announcer at the door announced the king's arrival. He will do the same for every royal entering the room later on. The royal ladies were in the women's restroom. And they were ready since they first got dressed earlier that morning. So they were just waiting to be invited by the servants. Princess Erieka, was the star of the day, lying down quietly in her mobile crib. Her white velvet dress and her two centimetres brown hair made her look even more beautiful.

'It's your birthday celebration Erieka! Many people are going to see you turn one year old today!' Queen Dorothy said happily, smiling at her daughter.

'Your majesty, shouldn't I be entering the ballroom now with the other guests?' Dewi asked.

'Nonsense. You'll enter with us. Like I said, treat this like your own home'

Dewi smiled. From she was conscious until now, she has never stopped being amazed by the kindness of the people here. She wondered if everyone in Southernere is as nice as those that she had met.

Fifteen minutes passed, and the hall was already filled with guests. And there were still people expected to arrive, like Queen Dorothy's family, royals of Barenge. But Lord Adam, Lady Matilda, and Prince Edward already went ahead and entered the ballroom first. Dewi followed Matilda timidly. The announcer announced all the royals name. Everyone turned to acknowledge them amid their conversation with one another or admiring the food served. King Henry was seated at one of the tables reserved for the royals, he was already eating while chatting with a commoner sitting beside him. Again Dewi was impressed that the king was like any normal person, don't mind sitting with anyone even in their own home.

She was even more attracted to the ballroom, its atmosphere and the decorations. The high ceiling was decorated with golden patterns that seemed to be sparkling. Dewi still doesn't know that this place was magical for her logical mind to accept. The huge majestic chandelier hung to the ceiling in its centre. The end of the ballroom, tall windows reached from the base to the top. Its wide length made it look majestic as well. On the other side, anyone can see the main gardens. Only the centre has no window, because there was the door to the gardens in its place. The smell of the different varieties of food at the buffet table made her want to find the eggs and toasts she ate earlier that morning again. But she was cautious of course, as she mentioned that she practices. The labels placed for each serving was very helpful for her. Now she could easily choose what she was sure she could eat. Like she took the bread for her first plate. Then she went to try the fish.

'Announcing the arrival of King Jonathan, Queen Alice, and Princess Darleen from the city of Barenge' said the announcer. The door had already opened before he spoke. In came the royals of Barenge. They proceeded to the royal tables. A few seconds later, the door was opened again. It was most of the masters from SHAW Academy. Master Widow was among them and Lillain was with her too. Among the rest were Masters Mousy,

Kitty, Jenny, and Asher the blue wolf. Everyone mixed around with one another or just stayed with those they are comfortable with. A few minutes later, the announcer began to speak again.

'Announcing the arrival of Queen Dorothy and Princess Erieka' he said. The doors opened after he spoke this time. Queen Dorothy entered with Annie pushing Princess Erieka's mobile crib beside her. This time everyone turned to watch. The star of the day came in with her mother and head of the handmaidens. People looked in awe at how adorable the baby princess is. They admired her.

'Thank you Annie, I'll take it from here' Dorothy said softly. Annie walked gracefully to join the other servants working in the ballroom as Dorothy took over her. She strolled with the crib around the room for everyone to see. People looked at and admired the baby as she passed. Some spoke a few words of respect. Others could only see from a distance due to the large crowd in front of them. Dorothy made her way until the royal table where King Henry and Prince Edward were sitting. Everyone resumed what they were doing. And the celebration went on with short speeches by the king, games that were planned by Lady Matilda, and more food served at the buffet tables.

Everyone was having so much fun. The sun has already begun proceeding downwards. That was when everyone heard a blasting sound from outside the ballroom. All eyes turned to the door. The announcer was the closest. He was about to check when the door burst open and the soldiers that were guarding it, were thrown into the room. The announcer was thrown as well. Their unconscious bodies slid across the floor and stopped a few steps away from where most people were. There were gasps of fear and surprise among the crowd. King Henry and the soldiers guarding inside the ballroom led by Lord Adam went in front of the guests to protect them for whatever is incoming. The masters all joined him. King Jonathan and some of his men stood by Henry as well. Morgan and a pink rabbit named Alphaga came in. The masters ready their powers at the tip of their fingers, knowing very well who they are facing.

'This is the greeting we received?' Alphaga mocked.

'I know, the descendants of Sofya are the worst. They have to learn some manners' Morgan said.

'Whatever you do, make it an effort to seize them. Their crimes are too much to ignore' King Henry said sternly. He glanced at his wife who immediately understood what he meant. She directed everyone to exit the ballroom from the garden entrance. They followed obediently and in fear.

'Now this is gonna be fun' Alphaga said. He charged a continuous line of black current from his eyes towards any target in front of him. The masters put up a shield. Their strength combines to create a strong forcefield which they exert towards the rabbit. He stopped the current and deflected the forcefield to other targets with his back feet. He resumed the black current. Master Mousy took his challenge and sent her own green current. Both currents collided, forming an impact around the point of collision. Zaps of current occasionally attacked any objects around the point's small danger zone. Few other avengers came into the ballroom. A battle began between the soldiers, the masters, and the two kings, against the avengers. While that happens, everyone outside was calming themselves down. Some had already left the castle. But others felt rude to leave when the celebration was not over yet. Prince Edward was trying to get a good view of someone inside. He peered through the window.

'Edward, get away from the window!' Queen Dorothy exclaimed. The other royal ladies were by her side trying to calm everyone down. Dewi was beside her too, looking very shocked. She had never met someone causing mischief before back in her village, let alone an evil person. And they got magical powers. Edward kept looking and he found her. Master Widow was at one corner, fighting with one avenger. He paid close attention and noticed that she wasn't fighting the avenger alone. Another master and a soldier were attacking him. Master Widow was actually just releasing some powers periodically. It was like she was not putting any effort to help. Leaving the job to the other two. Edward placed his palm on the glass and searched for Mousy. He closed his eyes, doing something with his powers. Inside, Mousy was fighting Alphaga with Masters Kitty and Asher. She stopped and turned to look at the window. She felt Edward's signal to her. She reacted in amazement at Edward's abilities and focused her eyes on him from that far distance, trying to find out what he was calling her for. Edward opened his eyes, and looked at Widow, his palm still on the glass. Mousy captured the information.

Edward was trying to signal Mousy about Widow. She looked at the direction Edward was directing her to. And she saw the old master. Exactly as how Edward saw it. Widow's effortless attacks were proving Edward's theory to be true.

THE STOLEN ARTIFACT

Before you start reading the next chapter, finish what you're supposed to do first. Done? Carry on!

I t was weird, Queen Dorothy thought. The avengers came into the ballroom to attack but who was their main target? Most of them had already left the ballroom but they were not in any harm. The only battle going on was inside the ballroom. Dorothy became more afraid as the thought of King Henry being the next target disturbed her mind.

'Darleen, please watch over the children, can you?' Dorothy said, feeling very worried.

'Of course Dorothy' Princess Darleen replied. Dorothy went back inside to join the fight. The battle went on for the next few minutes. There were casualties. Soldiers got injured by the avengers' strong magic. Fortunately, no one died. It was like the avengers had some sort of secret powers that only they could hear, like someone calling them. Because immediately, they all stopped the magic and retreated out of the ballroom very quickly. King Henry and some of his guards went to chase them but they were very quick. They went back out of the castle. And just like how they always came, the same way they transformed back into bird-forms and flew into the sky.

'What was that for?!' Queen Dorothy asked, feeling very annoyed that the celebration that was going very well was disrupted.

'That was most probably a diversion, your majesty' Master Mousy said, still observing Master Widow very closely.

'A diversion for what?' Lord Adam asked.

'Perhaps is there, or, are there something valuable to the eyes of the enemy?' Mousy said. King Henry immediately rushed to the right wing hallway upon realising Mousy's point. A few of the king's guards including Bobby and Lord Adam followed. At the centre of the hallway, onto the left, a stairway leads downward, where the dungeons, treasure rooms and huge empty spaces are. The nearest door to the stairway was a strong defensive blockage to unauthorised persons, guarded with enchantments. But it was broken. Someone broke in. Inside was another metal door that was guarded by two soldiers who were now unconscious on the floor. The metal door has a huge hole in it, like it was blasted with dark magic. Henry rushed inside. The octagonal room was like a small vault, full of treasures, jewels, rare items, and sacred items. In the centre was a small stand with nothing on top. A glass case lay unstable on the floor.

'Those rebels are up to something big' Henry exclaimed in frustration. The rest looked at him and at what he was looking at. Bobby's expression became shocked as well. He knelt down on one knee in front of the case to pick it up.

'They have been ignoring Majuza's amulet for a long time, what for, are they needing it now?' Lord Adam said.

Queen Dorothy, Masters Mousy, Widow and Kitty arrived through the door. Dorothy also had the same expression. So did the masters. The object that is missing is a very precious artifact. It is not as important to them as it is to the avengers but it is very important for them to keep it away from the enemy. Majuza's amulet was one of her own deadly weapons, both for attack and defense. A weapon she crafted herself through the years she spent in The Valley of Sorrows, formerly known as The Valley of Dreams. The amulet held a very special place among Majuza's precious objects, that before she died, she sealed the powers in the amulet and enchanted that no one can unseal the powers within except by someone as similar to her in abilities and the person must be of royal blood, a direct descendant from Combi.

'I know what they're up to' Henry said.

'Your majesty!' Mousy exclaimed, almost cutting his last words. She was struggling to choose her words properly. 'The guests first'

'Yes! That first, thank you Mousy' Henry rushed back outside.

Mousy breathed out calmly, glad that nothing was awkward or strange. She did that on purpose. One purpose alone. Master Widow cannot hear and find out whatever knowledge the king has on the enemy.

Because she already believe hundred percent whatever Prince Edward's suspicion was, is true.

Everyone except Bobby and the few king's guards, who stayed to clean the mess up, proceeded back to the ballroom. All the guests were still hanging around outside, no longer in fear since they saw the fight inside had stopped. Instead they were busy looking through the windows, very curious to know what's going on or what had just happened. King Henry went through the garden entrance and addressed his guests. He told them that the celebration was over but everything was fine and they need not worry about anything. The guests listened obediently. Some were reluctant at first, they had such a good time before they were interrupted. But they all just left with their mind still curious, questioning themselves a lot about the incident. Sooner or later, word will spread about the disaster that happened at the princess' birthday celebration.

The royals went back to their respective cities and kingdoms, except royals of White Shore, and Princess Darleen who volunteered to help King Henry regarding the crime.

The next two days went by very slowly. King Henry led a group of masters and some of his men to investigate the matter of the stolen amulet. Everyone else resumed their daily activities as per normal. A lot was going on in many of their minds, but they cannot keep on entertaining those thoughts. Everyone has to move on. Prince Edward's lessons at the castle also resume the day after the incident. Henry had told him that Master Widow will be taking over his lessons with Master

Jackenzie. Edward was shocked. He tried to convince his father that that was not a good idea.

'Father, please. I don't mind anyone else but please don't let Master Widow teach me' Edward said.

'I'm sorry Edward, I'm too busy at the moment. A lot of meetings to conduct, a lot of matters to discuss. I don't have much time to talk longer. But what's wrong with Master Widow?'

'I… I don't trust her' Edward tried to find a valid reason that does not give away his suspicions. The moment his father takes his theory into consideration, Master Widow would be more careful and tends to not expose herself as a threat.

'Why not? Master Widow is the most senior SHAW master we have. She's the mother of your previous master. I don't see any valid reason why she should not be your master' the king said. 'I know you are still sad by Master Jackenzie's leave, I'm sad too Edward. But you can't let that emotion take over you. The mind has to be strong. Be a good boy, listen to your new master, lessons start tomorrow. I love you'

Henry kissed his son's forehead and walked away.

Edward's lessons continued. Master Mousy's SHAW lesson was the first in the morning. Then came Master Kitty's Common Magic in the afternoon. Bobby's Sword Fighting was late afternoon. And Advanced Magic was in the evening with Master Widow. The lesson was as normal as it was supposed to be with Master Jackenzie. Widow was not so different from her son in the ways they teach. For the whole lesson, Edward kept forgetting that Widow was the enemy. The lesson ended well with

Widow complementing Edward before he made his way briskly back to his chamber. He did not stop for even a short moment to realise that Widow was not leaving the castle as how all SHAW masters did after every lesson (to get back home and change before starting another activity even if the activity is at the place where they are now). With her long black dress and headscarf, she dragged them with her into the castle.

At the main entrance, Master Mousy had just reached the main doors. She was there for a meeting with King Henry regarding the stolen artifact. The royal guards greeted her and opened the doors. Mousy stumbled upon the old master in the main hallway.

'Master Widow! You are still in the same dress since morning?' Master Mousy exclaimed, not actually surprised. She already believed Edward's theory and always knew something was up whenever she stumbled upon Widow.

'What's wrong with that?' Master Widow asked innocently, like the question was the most ridiculous thing she had ever heard.

'Usually human masters go home after lessons to change before anything else. Especially you, but you are still in the same dress now even after your lesson with Edward'

'Why must I be the same all the time? And can't I be early for the meeting?'

'The meeting doesn't start until half an hour later. Your house is just down the street after the castle gates, you have plenty of time to go and come back and given the powerful magic you have you have more than plenty'

Mousy noticed Widow's expression changed. She clenched her fists from under the long sleeve dress. Mousy was getting on her nerves.

'You don't decide for me Mousy. I am your head and you're disrespecting me. I have the choice to do whatever I want. Excuse me' Widow said calmly and continued walking to the other side of the castle.

'I have my choice as well' Mousy muttered to herself. She wasn't satisfied with Widow's response. She followed her secretly. Widow scuttled with intent. Like she knows what she was looking for. But if it was the meeting room, it is on another side of the castle. Widow knocked and entered a chamber when there was no reply. It was Princess Erieka's. The doors closed immediately afterwards.

'What is she doing in there?' Mousy's curiosity was bothering her. She partially closed her eyes as she shrunk to a smaller size, like the size of a piece of cake. She pushed the door open with a little extra force and magic for the knob since it's impossible for her to reach it now that her size is that small. Trying her best as possible to not waste her energy to be invisible but just hide from Widow's sight. The princess was not in the chamber. Probably somewhere else in the castle with the queen. Widow did not care for the crib. She went to the window, opened it for a while then closed it back. And then she left. Mousy was confused. What was Widow intending to do? What was all that for? Mousy went out to continue following her after a few seconds. But Widow was nowhere to be seen. Like she had suddenly vanished. Mousy grew back to her normal size. Suddenly, a glowing translucent sphere of energy appeared around her. The sphere rose bringing Mousy along with it. Mousy tried to break it but it won't obey her powers. A lady suddenly appeared in front of her. All black, controlling the sphere. Grinning at her was Master Widow.

'Spying on me Mousy? You do not understand my instructions to not bother me. I purposely came here not for any particular reason but to catch you in the act I thought you would do and you proved me right. You went against my command. And I don't like it' Widow said with emphasis on the last part.

'I knew you were up to something. You are an avenger!' Mousy shouted. But her voice only sounded like normal volume from outside the sphere.

'Now that's a harsh accusation Mousy. You are a master, you should be smarter than that' Widow said in a teasing way. 'Out of curiosity, who else has been spying on me?'

'No one!'

Widow took a good long look at her before deciding that she was most probably telling the truth.

'You have satisfactory powers Mousy. Only satisfactory because you are obviously incomparable with me. You can't even break out of my energy sphere'

'Let me go you old stick' Mousy said with controlled anger.

'You shall not see the light of true land until my mission is over. To the other dimension you will go, alive not dead because you are no use to me either way. But you are certainly useful to the royals by being here.

Indeed, my powers are greater than you, with that, I am confident in this curse to be obliged. I seek your permission Lord Grindel of The Northern Kingdom, protector of Forges of Beasts, keeper of beasts and curses. Approve my wish accordingly with its condition, with the price of sparing this animal's life' Widow spoke with intense energy. Her voice changed a little. Her black eyes glowed and black fog spun slowly around her controlling hand. Mousy had never seen such magic before. She heard of curses but never thought that it works. The fog grew thicker and began to spin around the sphere. It passed through the layer and spun around Mousy. Silently, Mousy vanished together with the sphere and the fog. Everything else went back to normal. Widow smiled, a wide evil smile.

THE MANIPULATION

Before you start reading the next chapter, finish what you're supposed to do first. Done? Carry on!

K ing Henry's meeting had already started. Lord Adam, Master Kitty, Bobby, Annie, Master Jenny, and Princess Darleen were present. Two seats remaining for Masters Widow and Mousy. But they seem to not be arriving anytime soon.

'I shall assume their absence is because there are other more important matters to deal with than the safety of the city' Henry said with annoyance. He carried on with addressing the attendees first. Then he started off with stating the main issue. The safety of Combination and in fact the whole of The Inlands are at stake. The chaos that will occur when the avengers manage to unseal the powers within the amulet. Henry guessed the motives of the avengers and he had done some preparations to prevent the occurrence of such chaos.

'Only a person of royal bloodline and has Majuza's specialty can unseal the powers within the amulet.

That's the curse Majuza placed on her amulet. And the person to match the description right now is my daughter, Princess Erieka. She was born last summer. Her energy is proof that she wields powers. That made her a Helaze, just like Majuza. The royal bloodline had never had a Helaze in a very long time. The last prince born in summer, son of King Billy The First, wielded no special powers. I'm afraid, the avengers' next motive is to kidnap my daughter. Which is why, Queen Dorothy and Lady Matilda are staying with the princess and also the prince at all times. We must be prepared to expect the avengers coming to attack the castle again. This time, it won't be merciful, they will kill if they have to, to get what they want. I need every master of SHAW Academy to protect the city. Master Jenny, please inform Master Widow. Bobby, gather the knights and elite soldiers, give the instructions to protect the city. The king's guards shall protect the castle. Annie, I need you to inform all handmaidens and castle staff to ensure all windows are shut and locked. Close all curtains. Only leave the castle entrances to be guarded by the guards. Later the masters shall seal all possible entrances with a layer of anti-magic. No SHAW can pass through once that is up'

With that the meeting was over. Everyone was dismissed to perform their assigned tasks. King Henry and Lord Adam stayed behind to continue planning on war strategies and tactics, believing that a war is coming. That was when Bobby entered the meeting room again with a young castle servant who held a small piece of paper, the Combination sigil (the crown) is visible in one corner, bearing a message from White Shore. King

Henry stared at the paper for a while feeling a sense of dread. He then accepted it from the boy.

'Your majesty, it's an emergency, White Shore is surrounded by Lord Morgan's army. Our forces are not enough to defend the city. Seeking reinforcements' the message read.

'Oh dear, the avengers are up to a lot more than we think' Henry said. He passed the paper to Adam for him to read.

'Bobby, change of plans, you shall lead the elite soldiers together with me and Lord Adam, we shall proceed to White Shore immediately. The king's guards shall remain here to defend the castle as planned'

'Yes, your majesty' Bobby said, before backing out of the room.

'Thank you young boy for the message. What's your name?'

'David, your majesty. Thank you, your majesty' David smiled.

'You are dismissed'

David nodded and left the room.

'We have to leave now' Adam said, hurrying out of the room. Both of them headed to the stables to get their horses. Just as Henry was about to mount his horse, Queen Dorothy came running down the castle steps, calling after him.

'Where are you going? You're not planning to tell me are you?' Dorothy said.

'I'm sorry honey, I forgot to tell you. A lot is going on right now. Where's Erieka?'

'She's safe with Annie and Matilda'

Henry nodded.

'I'm going to White Shore, bad news, Morgan' Henry said briefly.

'Be safe' Dorothy said, kissing her husband.

Bobby came up to them with some other horses with no riders.

'Sire, all the elite men are lined up at the edge of the city, ready to ride upon your command' Bobby said. King Henry mounted his horse and they rode off into the night.

White Shore was very quiet. Everyone stayed indoors. No one dared to even peak behind their window curtains at the army that was gathering around the west perimeter of town. The small group of soldiers assigned to guard White Shore were trembling. They are sure that they're going to lose this one. Without any warning, Morgan led his army into the streets and started causing terror. There were screams, sounds of explosion and swords clashing. The soldiers mercilessly broke into innocent people's homes and killed everyone inside. Some brave citizens came out of their houses armed with cheap swords but they were easily defeated. Many of White Shore soldiers also went down fighting alongside them. Morgan proudly walked past the dead bodies after his elite soldiers cleared the path from all those who opposed him. Any spots that were still clean and did not satisfy him enough, he threw fire at them and they exploded from the impact and started spreading, joining with the other fire which had been burning longer before. Some buildings collapsed with who knows how many people inside due to the pressure of the forces applied. Minutes later, Morgan reached the centre where the palace stood. He went up to the last level and admired the horrifying view of the dying town. He sent more fire from the tower towards more corners that were still untouched to him. But by now, about ninety percent of the town was in flames.

Across the buildings, at the entrance to the woods heading south, King Henry's army had just arrived. The view was overwhelming. The king and the lord were devastated to see so much destruction. How many innocent lives were taken away. Henry firmly commanded "CHARGE!" and they all rode in fast. Many of Morgan's soldiers that were near the edge of the city were easily struck as they did not expect that to happen. Towards the middle, the soldiers were more focused and it was tough to bring them down. Henry reached the palace grounds and killed one soldier before glancing up at the tower. Morgan stood there watching, smiling. A very evil grin.

'Fools' Morgan said to himself before transforming into the big black bird and flew into the sky. His laughter trailed behind. Henry realised that he had been tricked. This whole attack no matter how real was just a distraction for the real prize.

Combination was also very quiet that night. The streets were filled with SHAW masters roaming around. The castle was well guarded with the king's guards and some masters. Master Kitty was in charge of whatever magical activity happening there. Master Jenny took charge of the streets. She could not find Master Widow anywhere earlier, nor can she find Master Mousy. Lillain too had no idea where her grandmother went.

The royals were staying together in the lounge. Both children were asleep in their mother's arms and lap. Princess Darleen paced back and forth in front of her sister. Lady Matilda sat on one couch, holding her bulging belly with affection. And Dewi was there too, sitting nervously on an armchair.

'Darleen can you please sit? Your pacing is making me more nervous as well' Queen Dorothy said.

'This is bad, this is bad! How can you ask me to sit? Anytime, the avengers might come and attack us! The attack on White Shore is just a distraction!' Darleen exclaimed, full of worry.

'If what you are saying is true, calm down. We have enough defense to prevent the avengers from taking over the city. The other soldiers haven't been deployed yet. Relax Darleen'

'I am going to the kitchen' Darleen sighed. She strode out of the lounge. The hallway was quiet. It definitely was way past working hours. The castle servants are probably at home right now, with their family, and most importantly safe. But there are still those who are full-timers. They sleep in the castle. And occasionally Darleen would notice a few handmaidens, maids, cooks and other servants walking about the castle. The kitchen was empty. The door to the storage bay was open but the next door in the storage bay leading to the east gardens is locked. Annie had done her job, all possible entrances must be locked and the main entrances to be guarded. Darleen opened one cabinet and there were packets of homemade snacks. She grabbed a few and headed back to the lounge.

'You need to eat when you're hungry' Darleen said as she entered.

'In your case, I think it's nervous' Dorothy replied, laughing a little.

The atmosphere outside was mysterious. It was very quiet. But everyone roaming around could feel that something was not right. Suddenly, the fountain at the castle's main entrance behaved strangely. The water twirl up majestically and froze. The roundabout around the fountain started to crack. The tiles cracked all the way to the stairs. Master Kitty and the four guards guarding that entrance looked with confusion. It did not take Kitty long enough to think because he immediately conjured a shield covering the whole entrance door and the guards standing in front of it. The guards drew their swords automatically. The second the shield went up, a fireball blasted it and dissolved. A few seconds later a black bird landed in between broken tiles of the roundabout and transformed into an old lady. Several other birds landed around and transformed into random avenger. Morgan and Alphaga were amongst them. Kitty stared at the old lady in anger. Clearly Edward's words were true. Smiling up at him in her usual black dress and headscarf was Master Widow.

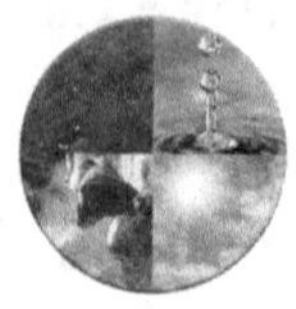

THE AVENGER

Before you start reading the next chapter, finish what you're supposed to do first. Done? Carry on!

'Traitor' Master Kitty said angrily. His voice was loud enough for Master Widow to hear. And she laughed.

'I'm not a traitor Kitty. I have always been an avenger. The avenger. I am Marcala'

That was even more shocking news. Even all the guards stared in shock. Marcala is a very famous name, belonging to the worst avenger to ever live. She had been causing troubles for many years since the time of King Billy The Second, King Henry's grandfather. She's probably more than a hundred years old now. Marcala did a lot of bad things before she started to pretend as Widow. She kills without mercy, uses her magic extremely and she doesn't even care about her own blood. That is why killing Master Jackenzie so that she can be the royal master of Combination was not difficult for her. Then when King Harry was gifted with a son, King Henry, she disappeared. No one knows what happened to her until now she revealed herself again.

'Then you should go back to where you belong, The Outlands' Kitty said, charging his shield with electric sparks. Widow stood her ground ready to block and attack, knowing very well what Kitty was trying to do.

'Inform the royals, then everyone else. Send a raven to White Shore, we need backup, quick' Kitty ordered one of the guards. He rushed inside to do as he was told.

Kitty increased the power and electric currents were occasionally zapping the perimeter around the shield.

'Your power cannot match mine Kitty' Widow said.

'I know it can't, but it can hold you for some time'

Kitty released the currents and at a fixed rate, large electric currents zapped the areas around the roundabout, reaching out as far as the castle gates. Tiles were heavily damaged upon the impact. By now, the masters and guards tasked at the gate realised what was going on and moved in to attack. The other five avengers aside from Widow, Morgan and Alphaga got busy with the new opponents. Kitty's electric currents zapped two of the avengers to death. But the others easily avoided them. Widow suddenly disappeared. And Kitty knows she went invisible. But she still cannot pass through the shield. She's probably going for another entrance. And there will be guards and masters waiting at those entrances. And the layer of anti-magic will make her job to enter the castle even tougher. Hopefully the royals and everyone else had been informed of the attack. Kitty focused on the other two.

'Your shield won't last long for any of us' Alphaga smirked.

'What if it does?' Kitty snapped.

'Then there's plenty of other entrances for us to go through. I see you have sealed the castle with smart magic. But any magic can be overpowered. Dark magic can easily destroy that seal' Alphaga said, like a nerd from SHAW Academy.

'Enough talking Alphaga' Morgan scolded. He glared at the rabbit. The electric currents were still reaching out from the shield but none hit them both. One time the current zapped Morgan but it did not affect anything. It bounced back a few times hitting magic layers that it cannot penetrate before destroying something else. Morgan had conjured a personal shield around him. And he was proud of it.

'I told you Kitty' Alphaga said. A ball of fire appeared in between his bunny ears. Morgan formed the same thing floating above his palm. Both of them sent the burning flame at once. Dividing his concentration as much as possible, Kitty conjured another layer of magic in front of the shield that absorbed the fireball before vanishing totally. The next current attempted to zap Morgan but he seemed to know that it was coming. He caught the current in his hands, taking over the force. The current resisted for a few seconds, creating sparks all around. But it bowed down to Morgan afterwards. Kitty increased the voltage and the shield illuminated very brightly. But that one current was now under the control of Morgan. It moved in zigzag on the spot while Morgan held it stationary. Morgan pushed a force through the current. The current did a zigzag wave towards the shield and the shield exploded, throwing Kitty and the three guards backwards. The guards slid backwards into the entrance hallway. Kitty was bounced back from the entrance due to the anti-magic layer and fell down the stairs before landing a few feet away from Morgan.

'You can't even enter the castle that you were supposed to protect' Morgan laughed. He raised his hand, palms facing the castle. Very translucent cells of magic came out of his hands and floated towards the entrance. A few seconds later, the cells turned red and started burning red and blue flames. The cells filled up the entrance space, spreading all around the castle. Slowly, the anti-magic layer became visible. Kitty was still unconscious, the two impacts he had were very bad. Morgan peacefully carried on what he was doing. Balls of fire now left his hands and joined the trail of cells spreading all around on the layer. Morgan added more force and the fire started burning fast. Slowly, the fire devoured the layer of anti-magic until there was none. Morgan tested the path ahead by throwing another fireball, and it was as big as himself. The fireball crashed through the entrance, burning the curtains on the front side windows. Now there is a bigger hole in the main entrance. Big enough for a house to pass through. Both avengers walked up the stairs proceeding inside. Behind them, the other avengers who were still surviving were still duelling intensely with the other guards and masters. Morgan smiled with satisfaction as he entered the entrance hallway. The three guards were also unconscious. Lesser job for them. They walked past the guards into the main hall. There were guards around the corner guarding the path leading towards both east and west wings. Morgan took the east and Alphaga took the west. The guards had already unsheathed their swords the moment they saw them. Alphaga sent a chill wind towards the guards. One of them is a SHAW. He quickly pulled the ground in a straight line in between them upwards. The tiles broke apart as the soil took its place, hardening into solid rock. The chill wind touched the rock, enclosing it with a thin layer of ice. Alphaga sent a forcefield which broke the whole wall down, broken rocks were thrown backwards, hitting some guards, while others were already thrown back by the forcefield. Morgan again did not have a hard time, none of them he was facing is a SHAW. He swung his hand over their eyes and they all fell unconscious to the floor in a deep sleep. At the end of the east wing, the entrance was well guarded by two masters and two guards. And they were battling something unseen. Magic came out from their hands but another magic returned from nowhere. It appeared in front of them and charged towards them. Morgan smiled knowing very well that Widow was the one, still invisible. He walked in that direction. At that very moment, a glowing silver sword suddenly appeared out of nowhere and was swinging towards Morgan's face. He managed to stop it just in time. The sword was still struggling to move against the resistance. Morgan swiped his hand just below the weapon and two figures appeared. Princess Darleen was the one holding the sword. A master was beside, slightly behind her. She had made both of them invisible.

'Nothing hides from me princess' Morgan said. He sent the princess backwards with a forcefield. Alphaga charged black electric current towards the master who replied with her own, green coloured. And they both got busy with duelling. Morgan continued ahead letting them finish on their own. Darleen got up and was ready to strike again.

'You don't have magic, princess. Your sword won't do you any good' Morgan laughed.

'Her sister will' the queen's voice came from the side. Instantly green fog made its way towards Morgan. Dorothy came from a smaller hallway on the right and she ran to her sister to check on her while Morgan went busy with the fog. The fog touched Morgan's skin and he started feeling burns on that spot. His skin turned white and watery and circles of it bulged out. He screamed in agony. With a panic swipe of his hands, the air around him pushed the fog away. He got control of the fog and channelled it towards the queen and the princess. Dorothy held it back a few steps, the fog stuck in between Morgan and her. Seeing that Morgan wasn't going to let it go, she dismissed the fog into thin air. Morgan sent magic sparks to a nearby potted plant. After a few shakes, the plant grew, smashed the pot under its weight and transformed into a leafy beast. It still has its original shape, the stem, the few branches but now it has a face at the top and more leaves covering its body. The roots grew wider and became stable enough for it to stand. The stem grew as thick as a tree. It stomped towards Dorothy.

'Run Darleen, let me handle this'

'No! You're coming with me' Darleen exclaimed,

pulling her sister's hand with her. Dorothy reluctantly followed. She glanced back, the plant was gaining speed fast. Its loud steps were scary enough to convince a herbivore's mind that eating plants is a bad idea. She also caught a glimpse of Morgan who walked into the small hallway she was from earlier. They both turned a corner and Dorothy pulled back.

'Morgan's after the children. They all are' Dorothy said. Darleen was about to reply but the leaf monster had just turned the corner and was a few steps away from them.

'You can't do anything if that thing kills you!' Darleen exclaimed in panic.

'Then destroy it' Dorothy said, turning her full attention towards the beast. It stood still scowling at the queen. Dorothy has to be good with her magic because if she fails, the plant only needs a few steps to get to her and end her. Dorothy tried to control the plant but failed. The plant is now bearing a soul of itself and can't be easily manipulated. She intended to burn it but there's no fire around for her to use. Unless she mastered the skill of fire, she cannot exert it from her own self. The beasts growled. How plants possibly growl is unimaginable but it did. Dorothy decided to just focus on what she is good at, nature. She stomped her right foot on the floor and the tiles broke apart all the way towards the plant. It watched in confusion at first. But then its roots started expanding. Digging into the broken tiles. Dorothy could feel the ground below vibrates as the roots reached deeper inside, gripping hard onto the rocks. Dorothy's minor quake did not affect it at all. The plant roared in anger. Dorothy had just annoyed him.

'Darleen, if you can, create fire' Dorothy said quickly, starting to panic.

'How?'

'Friction, just try anything!'

The plant moved forward with slow and very heavy steps now that its roots are so deep underneath. Dorothy strengthened her powers, reaching deep into the soil, feeling every bit of sand, clay, rocks and any ground material she can control. She moved them all at once. The castle shook with that. The ground trembled like an earthquake was about to happen. The plant looked around in fear. Dorothy could feel its roots continue growing and gripping every hard soil it can find. Dorothy increased the vibration. Slowly she felt the roots losing their grips and torn from their main body. The plant bellowed. She glanced back to check on her sister, Darleen was still rubbing two rocks together with no luck. Dorothy moved upwards, feeling her way through the soil towards the plant. She felt the roots and quickly, she ripped the roots apart using the pressure and friction of the soil. The plant was getting weaker. Dorothy pulled the soil upwards. All around the leaf monster, soil shot upwards, breaking through unbroken tiles, jumping over the plant and heading back down inside. Then they started pulling it down. Branches breaking as the pressure of the soil was too strong. Eventually, the plant sank. The soil devouring it until there were only twigs left on the tiles before hardening back to its normal state. Dorothy let go of the force and fell to the floor.

She used too much energy for all that. Darleen dropped her rocks and went to her sister's side.

'You shouldn't have wasted that amount of energy for a plant' Darleen said.

'That monster was harder to fight with than Morgan' Dorothy said, breathing in and out.

'But the person who created it certainly means that he's harder to defeat'

Dorothy stood up.

'Quick, they're after the children' Dorothy said. They both ran heading towards the lounge.

The violence in White Shore had died down since Morgan left. Many of Morgan's men had left since then. King Henry's army had wiped out all of those remaining. They were now searching through the rubble and burning buildings for survivors. King Henry and Lord Adam looked around them with grief. Hundreds of innocent lives were taken. Bodies littered the streets. Young men, soldiers, elderlies and children. The king wandered around a narrow alley. This part of town suffered less damage. Then he heard the sound of children crying. Two voices. He walked further into the alley. Behind some stacked crates and trampled boxes, two very small boys were sitting very close to each other and hugging their legs. Their cries hurt Henry so much. Tears rolled down their smooth cheeks. They flinched as they noticed Henry approaching. Henry got a clearer view of them. Their faces were covered in black and red smudges. Their blonde hair covered in dust. Henry kneeled down in front of them, full of concern.

'Hey' Henry said, his voice full of affection. 'Are you both alone?'

The boys continued sobbing.

Henry looked around. That was when he realised a body lying in one corner further into the alley. It belonged to a woman. Her skin has very bad burnt marks. Her legs suffered several strokes of the enemy's sword. She was dead. The two boys cried and Henry noticed they were looking longingly at her. She was their mother.

'Come, I'll bring you to a safe place' Henry said looking affectionately at them. They were still crying and won't be stopping anytime soon. 'I am King Henry, from Combination Castle. I'll bring you there. I'll keep you safe, I promise' Henry said extending his hand. The boys were still crying but they looked at the king's hand with interest.

'You'll be safe. Come' Henry said, hand still extended. Slowly, one of the boys wiped his tears and gently gripped Henry's hand. He was a little bit taller by a few centimetres. He was probably the older brother. His other hand extended for his brother. The smaller boy followed and Henry got up. He carried the two of them in his arms. One on each side. The elite soldiers came running out of a sudden. They were relieved to see the king. They probably thought he was dead, suddenly disappearing into some random alley. Lord Adam came and had the same expression. His face became concerned for the boys. Adam went to help carry one of them. That was when the raven from Combination arrived. It landed by Henry's feet.

'Urgent message from the castle, your majesty' the raven said, dropping the small paper he had carried on the ground. The raven flew away. One of the elite soldiers picked it up and read.

'Your majesty, urgent news. Avengers attacking the castle. Master Kitty requesting for backup' he said.

'Five men stay behind and look for more survivors. The rest, follow me' Henry concluded and rushed back to where he last parked his horse.

They're gone. Neither Lady Matilda nor the children were in the lounge. Dewi was nowhere to be seen either. Queen Dorothy and Princess Darleen searched around in panic. They went all around the east wing, first floor to the second but none of the rooms had anyone inside. They ran towards the bridge connecting the second floor's east and west wing. On the right, the doors leading to the main ballroom balcony had fallen. Someone crashed their magic inside. On the left, the railings of the stairs by the side of both wings leading down to the first floor were damaged as well. On the bridge, Matilda was lying on the floor with her hands on her stomach. She was in pain. But there was no physical injury. They ran to her side. And overlooking the main hall to their left, on the first floor was Morgan forcefully dragging Prince Edward with him. Alphaga pushing the mobile crib with his magic. And Princess Erieka was inside, sleeping soundlessly.

'Mother!' Edward cried, resisting Morgan's grip. He tried to break free and run to his mother but failed.

The water magic he exerted from his hands was easily countered.

'Let him go!' Dorothy shouted pushing her palm forward. The magical force flew through the air and slammed the ceiling of the main entrance. The walls collapsed and blocked the avengers from leaving.

'Let them all go!' Dorothy shouted. Morgan and Alphaga found the command amusing. They kept holding on to her children. They grinned, purposely intending to mock her. That caused the queen to burst into rage. Her brown eyes changed colour to emerald green. She opened her arms wide, releasing her magical force. The entire hall vibrated violently. Cracks appeared on the floor, the walls, and the ceiling. The huge chandelier hanging over the main hall started to swing around. Only a bit more force and it will crash onto the floor. Princess Darleen looked nervously at her sister getting out of control.

'Dorothy' she called. 'Dorothy!'

The queen was not stopping. She did not even realise her sister calling. The cracks opened up. The ones in the floor leading deep into the unknown. The walls showing the other rooms behind it. The ceiling showing pipings, more ceiling and a few showed the night sky. Morgan was starting to be afraid. He immediately sent fireballs towards the queen. But the fireballs became rogue. It turned back around like it was not interested in the queen and charged at Morgan. He stared in shock. Alphaga vanished them for him.

'You must have forgotten to think twice before attacking someone in a rage outburst' Alphaga said.

He looked above towards the angry queen, then at her sister. He stared at her with power in his eyes. Darleen staggered backwards holding her head. Her head was throbbing. Alphaga was causing pain to her brain. She screamed holding her head with both hands. That angered Dorothy even more. The green fog appeared again in front of her and charged towards Alphaga. The pain caused on Darleen stopped as he was distracted by the pain he felt from the fog. Darleen fell down unconscious. Alphaga's pink fur turned white with spots just like what happened to Morgan. Suddenly, everything stopped. The walls stopped shaking and the fog disappeared. Dorothy was still standing there, eyes wide open. But they're back to its normal colour. She has a shocked expression on her. Master Widow was standing very close to her. One hand was gripping her shoulder, the other holding a knife pressed into her waist.

'No!' Edward screamed. His brown eyes turned sapphire blue. Frost covered his entire body. Morgan pulled his hand back as quick as a flash. The frost spread around his hand, very cold and biting. Morgan shook it in annoyance. He heated it up and the frost went away. Edward ran up the stairs towards his mother. Widow pulled the knife back out. Dorothy's blood dripped onto the floor. Widow stepped back as Dorothy fell and Edward went to her side.

'Mother!' Edward exclaimed in sadness.

Widow reached into her black dress side pocket and took out a plain silver bracelet.

'I did not expect to use this but you are dangerous

without it. You are still young and naive. You have a lot to learn from me' Widow said. She sent the bracelet floating towards Edward. He was too concentrated on his mother to realise what was happening. He was still crying, his tears turning ice cold upon contact with the frost. The bracelet fixed itself on Edward's left wrist and instantly, the frost melted away. His eyes turned brown again and his tears fell onto his mother. Princess Erieka had woken up from all the noise and she was crying very loudly. Edward looked up and glared at the old avenger. He pushed his right arm forward intending to release a force but only managed to send a chill wind, blowing Widow's long scarf back a little.

'Your powers won't work as it should be. It is set to its minimum. You bear the cursed bracelet of Gratultyn' Widow said.

Edward tried pulling the bracelet away. He tried different methods to take it out but it won't come off.

'Only I can remove that from you. No one else has more knowledge than me. You won't find anyone in Southernere able to remove that from you'

Edward glared at her again. Widow walked to him and grabbed his arm firmly. Edward resisted but Widow was so much stronger. She dragged him along with her down the stairs.

'Please, leave them alone. They're innocent children' Lady Matilda said, getting up.

'Silence pregnant woman. Because you bear a child, we'll spare you. Majuza won't kill an innocent child without valid reason. Value your life given' Widow said, continuing down the steps.

'Please!' Matilda shouted in agony.

'Push the crib' Widow told Alphaga. He obeyed and pushed the crib with his magic. Erieka was still crying inside. Morgan raised the fallen ceiling and threw it aside for them to step out.

Master Kitty, Dewi, Annie and other castle servants were standing there with candlesticks and knives. And Lillain was there too. She was in disbelief when she saw her grandmother.

'You're not going anywhere' Kitty said.

'You kind of remind me of Mousy. I cursed her to another dimension. If you don't want the same fate, step aside' Widow said. Kitty sent a forcefield towards them but Widow countered it with her own. The two forcefield collided exerting powerful force, throwing many of the servants backwards.

'You are not smart for a master with a smart reputation. I am holding the prince and you still attacked me' Widow said. 'I don't need to step aside. You do'

Widow sent a continuous zigzag line of blue electric current towards Kitty. The other two avengers got busy with the others. Lillain stepped back, not wanting to fight. She was still in shock that her grandmother was not who she thought she was.

Kitty caught hold of the current in his eyes and they stayed like that for a few seconds, pushing forces back and forth within the current. Black current started going out of his eyes, pushing the blue one back towards Widow's hands. But it did not even make it halfway. The blue current was much stronger. Because Widow was very powerful. Widow pushed her blue current forward. Kitty's black current retreating back into his eyes. Then she sent a last zigzag wave of current towards Kitty, flinging him back towards the frozen fountain at the roundabout.

'Go now!' Widow commanded. She touched Edward with her free hand, sending a magical force inside him. He had been resisting her grip since just now but failed to escape. Edward transformed into a blue bird. Widow transfigured herself into the black bird. Casting another magic, a thin rope exited her claws and tied around Edward's body. And she carried him with her into the sky. All that was done in a few seconds. Morgan carried Erieka who had been transformed into a small red bird. Alphaga carried the crib which had been shrunk to the size of a worm, fitting nicely in his bird claws. Three black birds flew far away, leaving behind a huge mess.

THE AFTERMATH

Before you start reading the next chapter, finish what you're supposed to do first. Done? Carry on!

T he moment King Henry saw the roundabout, he knew that the avengers succeeded in whatever they came to do. The moment he stepped into the castle, through the large hole in the main entrance, he dropped on his knees. The castle servants were carrying Queen Dorothy's body onto a wheeled table. Henry stared at his wife, having mixed emotions. Princess Darleen stood beside the table, wiping her tears with tissues. Master Kitty was ordering men to gather all the other dead bodies. Lady Matilda was sitting on a chair that was taken from the dining hall just for her. Dewi was assisting Annie and the other maids cleaning up the mess. There's a lot to clean up. Lillain sat crossed legs on the floor beside Matilda, staring into nothing, still shocked after knowing the truth of her grandmother. Bobby stopped a few centimetres behind the king. He looked down, respecting the moment. The other soldiers followed him. Lord Adam walked past them to his wife. They shared a moment.

Queen Dorothy's farewell was attended by every kingdom in The Inlands. Silverside, Trisnarim and Arstar. Even minor royals from small towns under the ruling of the other kingdoms came. King Jonathan and Queen Alice of Barenge made it first. Seeing their daughter in the casket made the king sad and very angry. He went to King Henry and told him a tough decision he had to make in order to maintain the safety of his own.

'I shall summon Princess Darleen back to Barenge. From this day forth, Barenge will have no relation with Combination. I am sorry Henry. I am doing this for the safety of my people and for the good of my kin. I can't lose another, knowing that Combination is a high target for the avengers, letting her come here will result in me losing another daughter. Farewell Henry' King Jonathan said. Henry was very sad for losing the alliance with one of the cities with a mighty army. But that did not bother him much at the moment. There are other more important matters. Like his missing children. Earlier, after staring at his wife for quite some time while they moved her body, he got up to search for the prince and princess. Master Kitty came up to him and told him everything. That broke Henry down. He went down sobbing.

The next few days went by. No one spoke about the incident. The castle staff just did what they were tasked to do and that's all. Henry sent groups of men and volunteers to search for his children. Search for the avengers' base. He himself led the hunt sometimes, when he ordered Bobby to watch over the city while he was gone.

Henry ensured every dead victim of the attack a proper burial. They had to extend the areas of Alhora Cemetery for all the dead bodies to be buried.

Alhora is a massive land in the north just outside of Combination borders. Alhora Cemetery being the nearest, then the huge field, followed by Alhora Woods, which will lead to The Valley of Sorrows. Land continues northwest.

The two boys Henry found in the alley were now safe. They had told him their names a few days later after the incident. The older one is Jake, four years old. The brother is Nathan, one year younger. Henry adopted them as his own.

PART 5

THE SEED OF GRATULTYN

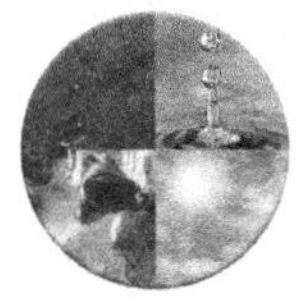

THE WHITE PRINCESS

Before you start reading the next chapter, finish what you're supposed to do first. Done? Carry on!

Silence. Silence. Silence. Scream. The piercing cries of Lady Matilda echoed throughout the quiet castle.

'Lady Matilda, I need you to breathe in and out, do not stop' a young lady said. She was wearing the servant uniform for female staff, a simple white dress and a white headscarf (optional). She has an additional nurse cap on top of her scarf. They were in the castle's medical chamber. Matilda was lying on the patient's bed gripping the lady's hand tightly. Matilda screamed again. Both hands gripping anything she can hold on to. Her legs are opened and bent.

'Push, milady' Annie said, standing on the other side of the bed. Matilda tried as best as she could. The pain was unimaginable. She was about to give birth.

The door to the medical chamber burst open and in came Lord Adam. Annie shifted her position so that the lord is standing by his wife's side. There were two other nurses. One was standing in front of Matilda's legs and the other was preparing towels, water and others.

'I am here, I am here' Lord Adam spoke, intending to motivate his wife. He held her hand and she felt more confident. Seconds went by and the voice of a crying baby filled the room. Adam was so excited. He went to his baby, looked at it with joy as the nurses took care of the blood. A baby girl.

'Milady?' Annie suddenly spoke. Adam turned in the direction. Matilda was lying peacefully, with her eyes closed. He felt a sense of fear as he guessed what had happened. The young nurse quickly checked her pulse on her neck. She then moved her hand away very slowly, refusing to believe what she had just found out. Adam instantly went to his wife's side, understanding why.

'Matilda!' Adam shouted, hugging his wife who complied very easily to every movement he caused on her because she was no longer conscious. She died shortly after giving birth.

Another farewell, the third well known person in just a year. It's been five months since Queen Dorothy's farewell. The season has changed from summer to autumn, and winter. Lord Adam was gifted with a beautiful baby the same day he lost the love of his life. Sadly, Adam was so devastated that he died that very night in his bed, just after Matilda's farewell. A fourth farewell was conducted in his honour. And the baby was left with her uncle, King Henry, as her guardian. She hasn't even gotten a name and she has become an orphan. King Henry adopted her, calling her as his own. She was given the name Flyra. Princess Flyra of Combination. Henry also has two other sons, Prince Jake and Prince Nathan, both are orphans as well. He found them in an alley during the battle in White Shore five months ago. White Shore is now an abandoned town, filled with rubble and ruined buildings. Lord Adam and Lady Matilda of White Shore had lived in Combination Castle for the past five months, helping Henry with his duties as much as they could.

Henry started cleaning up the two royals' chamber. A few servants helped him pack the items into separate boxes labelled, Valuables, Unwanted, and Sentimental. In one of the drawers at the bedside table, he found a small golden case with a note underneath it. It was Matilda's handwriting.

'To be given to my little angel' the note stated.

'Stop' Henry said immediately. The servants stopped packing immediately and stood straight.

'We'll leave this room as it is for now' Henry said again. The servants bowed their heads and left. Henry sat on the bed and opened the case. Inside was a single white substance surrounded by soft cotton. It's probably a nut, it's not purely white as it has a bit of brown. It has the shape of a water droplet. But Henry knew what it is the moment he touched it. It's very soft and fragile. If he applied more force, the nut would break into millions of pieces like how sugar cubes dissolve in water. Henry was shocked actually. He has the expression that what he just saw was impossible. The seed of Gratultyn is right in front of his eyes. How did Matilda come to find it? The seed of Gratultyn holds mysterious powers. A very rare seed that can be found only in Gratultyn. It came from a snow white flower in The Isle of Nature. Matilda must have had connections with the sages there. Henry knows a lot about this from the books he read in the castle library. Being a bookworm when he was young, Henry learnt a lot from spending most of his time in the library. The sages or high masters of Gratultyn have powers that even the most powerful masters in Southernere cannot match with, that's what Henry came about with. No one knows for sure if all the information in the books are true. But regarding the seed, Henry believes them now. Another thought disturbed him. Matilda wrote this note like she knew she was about to die. And if she did, she didn't even say goodbye or touching last words before she left. But Henry pushed the thought aside, getting emotional is not going to move himself or Combination forward. He learnt that five months ago. For a few weeks after the incident, he was too occupied with finding his children that he neglected his duty as a king. But he has changed and now he's better than ever. Every morning when he wakes up and sees the left side of the bed empty, he spends time reflecting on what happened the previous day and thinks positive thoughts for the day ahead. He will always try to see the bright side of things. Now he focused more on his duties. He still sends search groups out even though they explored a huge radius of land around Combination already. The north all the way to Cappidop Bay was fully explored. The south all the way to Marina Straits. And the east all the way to East Shore Bay. All that's left is the west. They had only reached The Waterfront lake. But had not gone any further. The search groups he sends now are one group per time. Reason is to save men for the duties needed in the city.

Princess Flyra was lying soundlessly in her crib. Her chamber was just beside Princess Erieka's. Since his children were kidnapped, Henry had left both chambers untouched. He rarely enters because everytime he does, it saddens him.

A young lady about twenty years old named Laura was given the task of being Flyra's personal handmaiden. She was sitting by her crib, accompanying her. Since the incident, no one is to leave the children in the castle at any point of time even if the king summons them, unless someone else can take over their places.

'Your majesty! An honour' Laura curtsied.

'You don't have to curtsey if you do not wish to seek anything from a royal' Henry said, partly mentoring her. The handmaiden smiled in embarrassment.

'Don't worry, I'm not mad. Annie hasn't taught you that I presume?'

'No your majesty'

Henry smiled in reply. He revealed the golden case he had brought from Matilda's chamber. Laura observed in curiosity. She dared not to ask anything, even though the questions in her mind were pestering her to ask. Henry took the seed out and held it very gently.

'Flyra?' Henry called looking down at her. Their eyes connected. Flyra was being a very good baby. Lying in her crib with her angelic blue eyes and very short brown hair. She was only a few days old but she already looks like she's going to be someone very bright in the future. Henry carefully helped the seed into Flyra's mouth. Knowing no harm will come to her even though she still has no teeth to bite. Because the seed will break apart and dissolve upon contact with her saliva. By the time she swallows it, the solution will be in her and there are expected to be changes, spiritually and physically. Henry and Laura stared at the princess who was still staring up at the ceiling soundlessly, her throat moving as she swallowed saliva. Nothing happened at first. Seconds later, Flyra's whole body glowed. For a moment a blinding white light shone the entire room. Henry and Laura had turned just in time before their eyes would be blinded for who knows how long. The light dimmed down. And Flyra was different. Her face which is her number one identity of her appearance was still the same. But her skin colour and hair colour was different. Her skin had turned from pinkish white to pale white. Her brown hair was now as white as snow. Only her eyes are still in the same colour. But above all that, she was still very pretty. A bright and beautiful princess she will be.

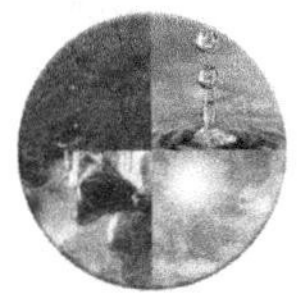

20 YEARS LATER

Swords were clashing. Arrows were shot from bows made out of the majestic woods of Silverside. The field of Combination Castle was bustling with many kinds of activities, mainly combat. Prince Jake and Prince Nathan, both grown and handsome young men, twenty-four and twenty-three respectively, were training their sword fighting skills. Bobby sat on a chair observing their methods with a to-do list on his lap. He was multitasking between mentoring the princes and answering the servants' questions about the jobs remaining that had to be completed by the end of the day. Princess Flyra was shooting arrows at a target board twenty metres away. And she was scoring bullseyes straight even though the wind was blowing in different directions. Her glamorous light blue dress and headscarf swaying in the wind. Laura was there assisting the princess with the arrows. Flyra had told her she was not needed but Laura had insisted. Captain, Bale and Oliver were there too, watching her and giving her support. They became best friends with the princess ever since she was able to walk. And they love telling her stories about the incidents that happened and mostly about their lost best friend, Prince Edward. That was how Flyra began to notice her father's expression saddened most of the time when he thought no one was looking. Now she knows what he had been through. And she was planning to do something about it.

Towards the northwest of the field, is the north pond. Dewi and Annie were there feeding the fishes swimming happily inside. They became best friends over the two decades. Lillain was part of the group as well but she was nowhere to be seen at the moment.

Away from the field, in the gazebo of the main gardens, King Henry was having a conversation with Master Jenny, the royal master of Combination and headmaster of SHAW Academy, over a cup of tea. They were discussing locations that had been searched for his lost children. Whether the location has magical force preventing them from finding what they intended to find. The entire map of Southernere was laid on a long table just beside the tea table. Combination somewhere in the middle, White Shore towards northeast. Towards north is Alhora, followed by The Valley of Sorrows. Barenge to the northwest of the city, further straight is Arstar, just beyond the Waterfront Lake. Directly towards the south of Arstar are two small towns, Waterfront and West Coast. They must be quite important in the alliances with Combination to be displayed on the map. Further south is the city of Trisnarim. Crossing the wide river above Trisnarim Bay, towards the east is Silverside. Further east will lead to the Marina Straits. Marina Island and Tiny Island are just south of Marina Straits. Dotted lines separate The Inlands and The Outlands. All the cities and kingdoms mentioned are part of The Inlands. The cartographer did not even care to add in towns and cities of The Outlands. They're not important to any Inlanders.

From the outside, anyone can see the castle's new look. It's new twenty years ago. They had started redesigning and reconstructing the castle three weeks after the incident and they had finished four months after. The reconstruction was not just for the damaged parts but they also renovated the entire castle. Even the basement and dungeons were renovated. The theme of the castle is now white and brown with a little bit of other colours here and there. Overall, the whole castle with its gardens, the field, and woods around it is still beautiful and magical.

'I doubt they have stopped coming' King Henry said.

'Your majesty, it has been peaceful for twenty years' Master Jenny said.

'That does not mean they won't attack anytime soon. Aside from finding my children, protecting the city is of utmost importance. This is the proud settlement of Combi. Set aside the rebellious Outlanders. We have a legacy to protect. I need more men trained, I think we're going to have an attack very soon, calculating the time. My daughter should be twenty-one years old now. Who knows what has she become'

Princess Flyra shot her last arrow from her quiver. Another bullseye. Laura rushed to take the arrows off the board. Ten boards have been used. Three arrows for each board. She scored bullseye for each shot. Flyra placed her bow and quiver on the foldable table set on the grass behind. Captain, Bale and Oliver cheered for her brilliance in archery.

'Talented as always Flyangel' Captain said. That's the nickname he gave her since she was young. One reason was because of the note from her mother, which Matilda referred to her as her angel. Secondly was because she is so beautiful.

'Thanks Cap' Flyra said, smiling gracefully. 'Do not forget our plan later'

Flyra winked.

'What plan?' Laura asked, she overheard the conversation as she was walking back towards them.

'Oh. Just a playdate with my best friends here' Flyra replied quickly.

'You have not been having playdates with anyone since you're fourteen'

'I did! With Annie, Dewi and Lillain only a week ago!'

'That was just a tea party your highness. A tea party that I was not told about' Laura ended her sentence with a sad tone. Flyra smiled, her usual sweet and affectionate smile. She reached for Laura's hands and held them gently.

'I told you I am sorry I forgot to tell you. It was Dewi's idea and it slipped off my mind to remember to invite you and any other handmaidens of your acquaintance.

I promise the next time there is a tea party or any other ceremony, I'll invite you alright?' Flyra said. Her words were spoken in a very polite manner. She is well known as the most soft-spoken princess in all of The Inlands. Laura smiled in reply. She cannot pretend to be sad any longer. The princess is just too nice for that.

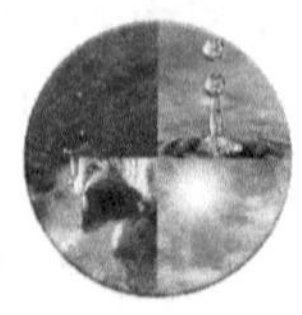

ALHORA

Before you start reading the next chapter, finish what you're supposed to do first. Done? Carry on!

The streetlights went on as the sun set. Most people were already at home spending time with their family. The skyline of the city was magnificent at night. Lights shone from the windows of the houses, shops that were still open and most beautiful of all, the castle.

Princess Flyra was wearing a shamrock green dress and a light green headscarf. An emerald green cloak with the hood on covered her entire body with another layer of clothing. The hood was pulled down such that her eyes were hidden. Clearly she does not intend to attract attention. Flyra made her way as quietly as possible towards the castle gates. With a few casts of magic, she had made the security guards fall asleep. She hoped that there would be no intruders for the next half hour because until then, the guards won't be conscious to realise. She walked past the sleeping guards and onto the main road, leading to the city square. Everyday between noon and evening, this place will be crowded with workers, shoppers, businessmen and many others, filling the square with many activities. Mainly trading and businesses. But now, the street was empty. A few shops still have their lights on. But from the shop windows, Flyra could see the shop owners cleaning up their store and preparing to close them. She walked to the middle of the square where a small marble pole with the replica crown of Combination on top stood in a circle basin of water. Water comes out from an opening in the top and flows down into the basin. A signage was fixed into the road and it states "The King's Crown". Flyra sat on the side of the basin. It's not meant to be seated but it's wide enough for anyone to sit. Then she waited. Soon all the shops were closed but Flyra was still waiting. She started to pace around the square. A few minutes later three animals ran up to her.

'Why are you late?' Flyra asked. She has an angry tone in her voice but even so, her words came out light.

'Sorry princess, we were trying not to cause any attention. The animals are having a party. Everyone's still awake. So we had to sneak out of the woods very carefully' Captain said.

'Have you been waiting long, Flyangel?' Bale asked.

'No worries, I enjoyed the silence' Flyra said, her smile came back to her flawless face.

'What was the plan again?'

'Head north. That's where the avengers went right? Everytime after an attack?' Flyra said.

'That's true, as far as our observation goes' Oliver replied.

'Then that's where we'll be heading. For sure their base is in the north'

'For the last time, are we sure about this? The king will be worried when he finds out you're missing. He has a lot going on in his mind since twenty years ago' Bale said.

'I left a note on my table. I am sure'

'Alright, let's head north' Captain said.

'And what is north of Combination? Did you bring a map Flyangel?' Oliver said.

Flyra took out a rolled paper from within her cloak and handed it to them. Her long sleeve green dress poking out of the cloak for the few moments Captain took to receive the paper, then hid them back within her cloak. Captain unrolled it.

'North of Combination is Alhora. The field is our next stop. Followed by the woods' Captain said.

They set off into the night, walking into a more quiet and creepy street. The kind where you thought someone was following you from behind but actually it was just your shadow. The streets became more narrow and the houses are no longer close to one another. They reached the furthest north of the city where there was less development. The Combination Border Woods was just straight ahead. And they went into the darkness. The moonlight was blocked by all the trees. Flyra's magic was the only source of light. She casted a floating ball of gaslight on her palm to see the path ahead. As soon as the city was out of sight, Flyra pulled back her hood. Her beautiful face slightly gave off radiance even in the dark.

The woods were very cold. It didn't snow as much as

how it did in the south, whenever winter comes. Rarely northern Southernere snows. It was a few weeks after winter first arrived and the snow had just started to fall in the south.

'Your birthday is next week!' Captain said excitedly, breaking the silence.

'Yes it is indeed!'

'How is your celebration going to be this time?' Oliver asked. Flyra let out a sweet and soft laugh.

'First we have to finish our mission. And that is to find the avengers' base and rescue Prince Edward and Princess Erieka' she said.

'But I'm not feeling very confident' Bale said. Captain glared at him like he just spoke the most ridiculous thing ever.

'We'll just follow Princess Flyangel wherever she leads us!' Captain said cheerfully. There was a pause.

'Why are you not confident Bale?' Flyra asked.

'King Henry searched them for twenty years but never found them. Not even the avengers' base. I am sure the base is a big building or even a city to hold all the avengers and soldiers of the army. And such big places could not be missed that easily' Bale explained. There was a longer pause.

'You're definitely right. There must be magic involved' Flyra said in agreement.

'If such magic exists, what if their base is in Combination all along?' Captain said.

'Then your observation of them heading north is false' Flyra reminded him. Captain went silent, embarrassed that he made himself sound like a fool.

'It's okay to make mistakes Cap, no one is perfect. But the most important part is to learn from those mistakes and avoid it as far as possible' Flyra said with her usual smile on her.

Less than an hour later they came upon a massive field. It is bigger than the castle grounds, SHAW Academy grounds and the city square combined. And even after placing all that, there are still a lot more spaces to be filled. All around the field were trees. Towards the south is the Combination Border Woods and towards the north is the Alhora Woods.

'The Alhora Field. It is so massive and magnificent that some even called it with a grander name, The Field of Alhora' Oliver said.

'Yes, a lot of books mentioned about this field' Flyra agreed.

'It's historic' Captain said. They all nodded in agreement.

The Field of Alhora is a historical place. A very important event in the CombiNation. It was where the first war between Majuza and Sofya took place. And subsequently, many other wars occurred here. The amount of blood dropped onto this field is uncountable even by magic. But the grass is still fresh and alive and very much green. Magic has always been the solution to clean the battlefield when peace came after every war.

'Should we set up camp here for the night?' Flyra asked.

'It's been a long walk from home. I'm exhausted, I definitely need some rest' Bale said. Oliver agreed to his suggestion and Flyra started working with her magic.

Magical sparks floated all around the casted areas as Flyra moved objects, changed their shapes or crafted something else. Sticks and broken twigs floated towards the field from the nearest trees and changed forms. The wood became like liquid (like it was melted) combined with other liquid woods and formed a rectangle. The liquid turned back to solid. It became a wooden door. Flyra continued working, it was a wonderful sight. The three animal friends sat on the grass watching the free show. Five minutes past and a few metres from the nearest tree of the border woods was a small wooden house of one room with a beautiful roof on top. Inside was even more amazing. Flyra had also formed four wooden beds, one for each of them. A pillow on each one, a leaf that has grown in size. A stone bowl was in the middle of the room. And Flyra casted the gaslight from her hand towards the bowl. The room lit dimly.

'Now that's amazing' Captain said. The three clapped.

'Thank you' Flyra said. 'Alright, rest well'

'Who'll keep a lookout? This house will surely attract attention' Oliver said.

'I'll do it!' both Captain and Bale said together. Then they both went into a short argument.

'No one has to keep watch' Flyra said. She twirled her hand. Snowflakes appeared around her hands twirling as well in a line towards the wooden floor. Snow piled up and formed a snowman. The differences between this and a typical snowman are that it has no carrot for a nose, and no buttons. Its eyes are just two holes carved in the face. It's completely made out of snow.

'Now Mister Snowman will keep watch' Flyra said, nodding at the snowman. It glided across the floor, leaving a trail of snow wherever it went. It was about to bump into the door when Flyra sent a force, opening the door. It continued straight out like there was no door in the first place. Flyra closed it back after the snowman left.

'Goodnight princess' the three of them said.

'Goodnight Cap, goodnight Bale, goodnight Oliver'

Flyra put the gaslight out and the room went into total darkness. A few seconds later, Flyra's face glowed. And she went to her bed to sleep.

The sun was up. The house was gone. The snowman was nowhere to be seen. Trails of snow were everywhere. If they want to track it, they have to figure out which trail to follow. Flyra had turned them back to sticks and pebbles. They continued their journey across the field to the other side. Ten minutes past. The Alhora Woods stand tall before them. The trees were much bigger. And in the dark, people may go crazy thinking they saw things they don't want to see here but actually it's not there. The woods tend to trick people's minds. But the creatures living inside are not to be messed around with. In the day, anyone will just have to watch out for these creatures. The tricking part doesn't really work in the day. Flyra went to the nearest tree and traced her fingers around the tree. The bark is dark brown in colour. It is very smooth and slippery-looking. Even from far it seems like the trees are wet.

'Alhora wood' Flyra mumbled.

'Let's move' she said, leading the way. The roots are so big and many. They spread out all around the ground. They hold the ground firm but it is an unstable place to walk on. Flyra looked behind her, the three friends were all huddled up. Their faces presented fear.

'What's wrong?' Flyra asked.

'We've only been in here a few steps and there's already the sense that something is watching' Oliver said.

Suddenly, there was a growl. They all turned towards the direction. It was coming from straight ahead into the woods. Then they saw it. A wild beast. Something like a tiger but it was all black. It's eyes green, it's paws bigger than any four legged animal, it's mouth has fangs poking out and it's speed was super fast. Captain and Bale were already screaming. The beast was charging fast. Flyra released a stream of water from her hands, spun it around and as the beast was a few steps away from jumping on them, she channelled the water to its paws, up its body and freezing it. From behind some trees, the snowman emerged, moving towards the beast now covered in ice.

'Where did he come from?' Captain said, referring to the snowman. The snowman blew ice cold wind out of its eyes at the beast and now the ice seemed a lot thicker.

'That's amazing!' Bale said. 'Your trick is amazing as well Flyangel'

'Thank you Bale. That won't be the only thing we're going to face. I'm sure there's more. Let's keep moving' Flyra said.

They walked past the new sculpture and the

snowman, smiling at it as it moved, not paying attention to any of them. Snow trails went far into the woods showing where the snowman must have been exploring the entire night.

THE VALLEY OF SORROWS

Before you start reading the next chapter, finish what you're supposed to do first. Done? Carry on!

King Henry had fallen sick after he found out Flyra was missing. And when he saw the note she had left, he obtained a high fever. The staff were in panic. Especially Laura. She is her personal handmaiden, she has to know her whereabouts at all times. And now thanks to the note, they know where she is, or where she is heading to, but it does not make the king feel better. He didn't know that Flyra knew about his children. He never shared anything about the incident with any of his adopted children.

'The king is too sick to carry out his duties at the moment. He left me in charge of Combination's affairs. But I am passing it to my brother, Prince Nathan, because I will be forming a team to follow me and bring Princess Flyra back here' Jake said to the council members in the meeting room. Ever since King Henry was no longer bothered by the incident, he had formed an official council, The Royal Council of Combination, which consists of important members of the royal family. The king and queen (only one of these two will attend the meeting every time), the royal advisor, the head of the king's guards, the royal butler, the royal master, two exemplary SHAW masters, a prince or princess appointed by the king or queen, and one nobleman. Jake had been appointed by the king to be part of the meeting since a few weeks ago. Now he's sitting in his father's place addressing the members. All around the round table, some are familiar faces and some are new. Beside Jake was Bobby, followed by Master Jenny, Master Kitty, Master William, and Lillain. King Henry added Lillain to the council to honour Master Jackenzie and because of Lillain herself being a loyal family friend despite her grandmother being otherwise.

'Yes your highness' Bobby said. 'The men and I will be ready at your service if we're needed'

'Great Bobby, thank you. But I need you to come with me. Assign one man from the king's guards to replace you while you're away, I trust your decision'

Bobby nodded in obedience.

'Master Kitty and Master Lillain, you'll be following me as well. Since both of you were very close to Prince Edward. While our purpose is to find Flyra, at the same time, we'll find our lost prince and princess'

Lillain is now known as a master of SHAW Academy. She started teaching there a few years ago. Mainly because she wants to continue her father's hard work.

'Yes your highness' Kitty and Lillain said together.

'Prince Jake, may I obtain permission for Dewi to

come along. She will be very helpful as well, especially in medical requirements if needed' Lillain said.

'Absolutely Master Lillain. Thank you for suggesting. The more people helping will be great. Now back with our home affairs, Master Jenny, you will resume your duty as the royal master to ensure Combination's safety, both citizens and artifacts, in magical matters. Bobby, your representative will be in charge of all soldiers in defense with combat and weapons matters. Master William, you will assist Master Jenny with any help she needs. Above all, council, ensure Combination's safety as much as possible'

Everyone acknowledged their respective duties and the meeting was dismissed. Afterwards, Jake told Nathan, the temporary replacement has been confirmed. And he got ready to head out, northwards, with Kitty, Bobby, Lillain, and Dewi.

Flyra and the three friends were coming towards the end of the Alhora Woods. The huge trees are slowly returning to normal size trees and a lighter wood colour. Surprisingly, they did not encounter any more wild creatures since the first one. The atmosphere was changing. The further they went, leaving Alhora behind, the more mysterious the atmosphere became. The air is filled with dark magic. The dark magic feels old like it has been there for many years.

'The Valley of Sorrows is ahead' Flyra said looking into the map. The others shuddered at the name.

'Don't worry guys, we just have to follow the narrow

stream to the end of the mountain range and we're closer to our destination' Flyra said.

'How do you know? What if we have reached our destination without we realising it?' Oliver said.

'I don't feel it. My instincts are telling me it's still far away. Anyway, I don't think it would be that easy to find the enemy base'

They understood. And the valley came closer as they continued their steps towards it. It was still midday but the sky was dark. Darker than how rainy day usually looks like. The clouds seemed very heavy like it was about to burst anytime soon and spray a huge amount of water everywhere. Then in the distance was a quick flash of lightning. Followed by a brontide.

'It's going to rain' Captain said with a little fear in his voice. He has always been afraid of heavy rain, lightning and thunder.

'I don't think so. I don't have the feeling' Flyra said, breathing in the air that was a mixture of dried leaves and magic. For a place with a sky that seems to send heavy rain all the time and an active narrow stream, the place was quite dry. Dead leaves fell from their trees and covered the brown grass.

'I don't think it ever rains here. Not since it was known as The Valley of Sorrows. The sky is just like that all the time I think' Flyra said.

'I agree, look at the colour of the trees and the grass!' Oliver observed his surroundings in disgust. 'No wonder only beasts live here' he said.

'There's more here?' Captain and Bale said together, tensed.

'It sure is. But think positive guys, we have not met any creature aside from the bear earlier, whatever that thing was' Flyra said.

'I don't think that was a bear Flyangel. A bear would be fatter' Bale said.

'Yes, whatever that thing was' Flyra repeated her phrase in agreement.

There was another flash of lightning and thunder. Then they heard a different sound. A sound belonging to a creature of their worst nightmare. It was a rumble. Another rumble. Then came a longer rumble. Downhill from where they stood, the stream cut its way through the mountains, curved here and there and turned a corner and out of sight. The mountains were very high. Huge openings in some parts of the rocks meaning there are caves inside. And the sound must be coming from one of those caves. All the caves must be connected somehow because the rumbling sound came out of all the openings, echoing throughout the valley.

'Please don't say that creature is what I think it is' Oliver said fearfully. Nobody answered him because immediately after he said it, a jet of fire as big as a common house in Combination, shot out of one of the caves.

'A dragon' Captain said, dragging the last word to a soft whisper. Everyone was in shock, staring at the cave, expecting the dragon to come out but also hoping otherwise.

'Follow me, let's try to get past that cave without causing any attention' Flyra said, leading the way down the hill. They were by the side of the stream. The cave was not far ahead. A few metres of climbing and they'll be directly in front of it. No matter what, they will have to climb it if they don't want to get wet. The path ahead was a dead end with just the stream touching both ends of rocks. To follow the stream exactly where it is all the way, they'll have to get into the water in some areas. Which of course Oliver rejected that idea. He was seriously afraid of water. Specifically bodies of water that no one knows how deep it goes. So they climbed the small rocky hill up to the mouth of the cave. The rumbling sound was no more. But instead a low hum came out of the cave. Flyra understood. The dragon was sleeping. It probably has a sore throat and occasionally releases fire to ease the pain like it just did just now.

'Move around that boulder there' Flyra whispered, pointing to the boulder she was referring to. A huge rock by the side of the cave entrance. A small path goes around it to the other side. Down below, the stream follows the direction of the path. Earlier on, the stream doesn't look very deep. But up here, it looks like it leads down without knowing how much further is the end point. The water wasn't that welcoming anyway. It does not have that fresh water look. So it did not tempt anyone to enter. They had to walk carefully with their backs touching the boulder. Actually, only Flyra had to. The others are small enough to just walk normally. The path was a little wide for them and a little less than just nice for Flyra. The path ended sooner than they expected. Up a small step, was a wide clearing filled with small pebbles. The top of trees from the side of the stream below pokes out above the edge of the big ridge. A few caves went deep inside the mountain on their right. More steps to climb out to the next ridge. A smaller one, where the path continues. Upon seeing what was in the centre of the clearing, Flyra immediately bent down, pulled everyone gently back and hid behind the boulder. She peaked once in a while to check. There was a creature lying in the middle. Its body moved up and down in a constant rhythm, meaning it was breathing and alive. Flyra can't really make out what creature it is. Its back was facing her. A big animal like a bull, smooth brown back, short fur, a long tail with a bushy end. That was it. Flyra could not see the head.

'What is that?' Oliver said in curiosity and fear.

The creature moved its body a few centimetres, finding comfort. It tilted its head and Flyra could make it out a little. It has a pair of long sharp horns sticking out above its ears. The exact same ears of a bull. Not very hairy. Its features are exactly like a bull. Only its horns were exaggerated. And definitely its size as well. This is probably the same size as two bulls combined.

'It's a bull' Bale observed.

'That's bigger than a bull alright' Captain said. 'The bulls we saw in the Southern Meadows are no match for this one'

'Southern Meadows? You went out of the city before?' Flyra said. Southern Meadows is south of Combination. Way out of the city. From there, continue on towards the west a few kilometres is Silverside. Many farmers live there. And most of their harvests are sold in the city square.

'It was just an adventure. We followed this delivery

carriage because they have all this food we can't resist' Captain said.

'You mean you can't resist' Oliver snapped. And if Flyra had not stopped them, they would have started a fight and for sure the bull and the dragon would wake.

'Get it together. All of you are older than me, you are supposed to guide me' Flyra said.

'Forty-two years of an animal's age in Southernere is like twenty-one years of a man's age' Captain said. 'We're just older than you by one year'

'Wait a minute. You're just eleven year old twenty years ago? You're only eleven when you're friends with Prince Edward?'

'Kind of' Bale replied.

'But physically you're…'

'Twenty-two' Oliver finished her sentence. 'That is why we played with Edward like he was our friend. We were kids'

'Wow' Flyra was genuinely surprised. She never acted that surprised when they told her stories of the past. She wasn't even sure why she was surprised by this. Probably the aura of the valley, changing a person's character a bit without them realising. There are stories of it, people who survived journeys through the valley, telling people how crazy the place is. But they're just stories. The avengers probably pass this valley all the time when they travel between their base and The Inlands. They're all still the same. No fear or horror on their face that proves they have encountered terror in the valley. But again, they always travel by air. Or maybe this place is tamed by the avengers. Obeying their orders. That should explain the dark magic in the atmosphere.

Flyra peaked again. The bull was gone. It has been so quiet. How could the bull have moved without making so much noise? Flyra hid again, heart beating fast. She was thinking of possible incoming attacks and ways to defend and survive.

'Everyone, hold my hand. I will try to make us all invisible' Flyra said.

'Something tells me you had never done this before' Oliver said.

'I just learnt from Master Kitty. Even he has difficulty with this magic at times. We have no other options. I have to try'

They all stood together holding her hands. She concentrated hard. Eyes staring straight into them. They looked at each other awkwardly. Flyra's stare was funny. Sparkles appeared on the surface of their skin, wrapping them all over before disappearing again.

'Was that it?' Captain said. 'Did it work?'

'If we let go of your hands the magic will stop right?' Bale asked.

'I think not. I pass the invisibility to you. For the next few moments that power is part of you. Then it will run out. Let go' Flyra said, removing her grip from their hands or paws. Immediately, they disappeared from her sight. It was the same for each of them.

'Hey all of you vanish!' Captain said excitedly.

'Shhhh' Oliver scolded. 'Yes each of us are invisible as what Flyangel said. The bull is still somewhere around. Noise will only attract it'

'If we can't see each other, how do we know how to follow Flyangel?' Captain said.

'I didn't think about that' Flyra said. She concentrated again. Harder this time, sensing where everyone was standing, channelling her magic into them as well. And everyone became visible again.

'Wait, now we are visible' Bale said.

'No, we are only visible to each other. I controlled it as such, everything else can't see us' Flyra replied.

'Cool' Captain said, holding back from exclaiming again.

'Follow me' Flyra said. She walked slowly and very carefully into the clearing where the bull used to rest earlier. All around her there were only rocks, mountains and scenery. No other signs of life except for the trees. She made her way up the rocky steps that leads to the path above. That was when the ground shook so badly. From one of the cave entrances, a huge dragon came stomping out. It was really a massive dragon. The beast they had heard its roar and saw its fire earlier. Only one weird thing is, the dragon is wingless. That means the dragon is a crawling fire-breathing flesh killer. They froze in their tracks and stared at it as it scanned its surroundings. Then it fixed its glowing red eyes on them.

'Um, isn't that creepy?' Captain murmured.

The dragon roared.

'Run!' Flyra exclaimed. She climbed the last few steps and ran along the pathway. The rest followed. The dragon stomped towards them. Clearly its vision can see through invisibility. Either that or Flyra's magic in invisibility was failing her. They were in the middle of the pathway leading to a slope going downwards this time. Cave openings around them seemed so widely open, like they were luring them to enter. The dragon's claws suddenly appeared towards one side of the path. It climbed up and soon it was standing tall, blocking their way.

'How did it get here so fast?!' Oliver hissed in panic. Flyra looked in between its two legs. She could see the path ahead, but there was no space for them to pass through. The dragon's legs and feet are so fat that in order to get past it, they have to climb over the claws and feet or anything as long as it's a climb or a jump. The dragon opened its mouth. Its teeth are pointy but not so sharp. Red light was coming out of its mouth.

'It's gonna blow!' Captain shouted. He turned to run back the way they came from. The others followed his actions except for Flyra who stared at its mouth curiously. Long blast of very hot fire shot out of the dragon's mouth at them. It was too late to run. But they were not hurt. They looked around and realised that they were wrapped in a translucent sphere the colour of blue with a whitish glow. The fire curved its way around the sphere and did not pass through. Flyra's dress was glowing. The green colour was so amazing. And her eyes were pure white.

'Flyangel?' Captain called in fear and confusion. Flyra wasn't responding. She was like, in a trance.

'Princess Flyangel?' Captain called again. The glow of the dress and the sphere were getting more intense. It seemed like they're about to explode with brightness and blind everything that watched.

'Flyra?!' Captain called once more in panic. He wasn't sure which to fear more, the dragon or the glow.

Flyra blinked upon hearing her name, though her eyes were still white in the trance. Then the most powerful magic the three animals have ever felt occurred. A blast of frost exerted from the sphere a few times, spreading like the ripples of water, freezing everything in its path. The ground shook, and even from inside the safety of the sphere, they all felt the pressure and the cold. Then it became extremely quiet. The sphere vanished. Flyra dropped on her knees. She was no longer glowing and her eyes were back to normal. But the surrounding changed. Well everything was still the same, in the same place but they were all frozen. Only the rock they were standing on was not covered in ice. A grey circle stood alone underneath them, protected by the sphere just now. The dragon was a frozen statue. It's jaws were wide open. Part of the fire it exerted earlier was also frozen. It came out of the dragon's mouth only halfway. Aside from that, ice could be seen everywhere, spreading far away in a huge radius. Maybe it even went further than the valley.

'How can a fire be frozen?' Oliver asked in disbelief. The other two were standing by Flyra's side, checking on her. She was still closing her eyes but she was breathing just fine.

'You pushed your power's limit?' Captain asked. Although they were all standing and Flyra was kneeling but their height was still a little shorter than Flyra's head. Only Oliver was a little bit taller because he's a cat.

Finally Flyra opened her eyes and breathed in the

air which temperature has dropped probably about half a hundred degrees from twenty.

'I did not intend for that to happen' Flyra said. When she breathed out, they could see the water vapour. They were starting to feel the cold. A few more minutes and it'll be unbearable.

'Oliver, you're a Sprite right? You can radiate heat?' Flyra said.

'Sorry princess, but heat is only Helaze's specialty'

'But I've read somewhere that Sprite being nature's friend can do the same'

'Well, not for me' Oliver said simply.

'Then we'll have to find shelter quickly, while I figure out how to increase the temperature'

Flyra stood up and made her way to the nearest cave. Ice was still visible even after a few metres into the cave.

'How deep is this cave?' Captain broke the silence. His voice echoed.

'I just hope that the ice does not cover the entire cave or we'll be frozen by the end of it' Bale said.

Flyra was leading up front, at the same time, feeling deep inside herself, searching for an ability to radiate heat or removing the huge damage she had caused on the sacred land.

'What I've learnt the past years I'm alive and being a SHAW myself is, you have to let the magic flow like water. Don't think too much, or else you'll end up producing powers you didn't mean to like what had happened all those time' Oliver said. The memory of the beast they first encountered in Alhora was still fresh in his mind.

'Thank you Oliver' Flyra said.

The ground was no longer covered in ice. It was all rocks now. The cave was pitch dark except for the light glowing from Flyra's outfit, and radiating from her pale skin.

'Let me shine some light in here' Flyra said. She raised her hand, palm wide open. A ball of light came out of her palm, grew bigger as it floated near the cave's ceiling. Bright light illuminated the entire space they were in. The cave was a room. More like what used to be a room. A room for one person. A bed with worn out red sheet, a round dark wooden table, a mirror and a dark chest. What was more interesting was the wall. It was covered in drawings, every bit of it. One side there were lines in a few rows like dominoes, each with a straight line struck diagonally through it. Like someone counted the number of days he or she spent in this cave. Other than that it was all images. Detailed images of certain events. Flyra recognised one of them. The first war. Two armies facing each other, a single leader leading at the front of each. One wore red and the other wore light blue. Majuza and Sofya themselves. Their bad relationship went to its climax with the first war ever to occur in Southernere. That was the start of the separation in the family. When two forces were formed. The Inlanders and the Outlanders (which they prefer to be known as The Avengers).

'This is the first war' Flyra said, staring deeply into the image.

'The war that started the everlasting feud?' Captain said. There was silence for a while as Flyra continued staring at the image.

'Yes' she said. Flyra turned her gaze to the other paintings. There was one image that caught Flyra's attention immediately. A lady in light blue (it's obvious that she is Sofya) was pointing a sword at Majuza's back. It was either Majuza did not realise or she did not care. She was busy cuddling a baby in a green blanket in her arms. Flyra can't help but feel curious and shocked looking at it.

'I never understood why the avengers are so determined to fight for someone so evil even if she was their great mother. But this picture just contradicts my belief. Majuza is the prey in this. And she's holding a baby!' Flyra was close to tears. She doesn't even know why. She just felt betrayed. But she regained herself. She cannot let a picture simply change what she stood for her entire life. Flyra approached the wall and touched the painting. Feeling the story within. A moment later, she found herself in the same space but from a different time. The air was warm. The furniture was clean and tidy. There were no paintings on the wall. Her friends were nowhere to be seen. But instead, two women standing in the middle of the room. One in light blue dress and white headscarf was pointing a sword at the woman in front whose back was facing her. Her expression was full of hatred. The woman in front was wearing a black dress with red lace and a red headscarf. The woman in black was cuddling a baby in her arms, her expression full of worry. The baby was sleeping soundlessly. Flyra couldn't believe that it actually works. She was reliving the story in the painting. She was in the same room as The Sofya and Majuza.

AN UNTOLD STORY

Before you start reading the next chapter, finish what you're supposed to do first. Done? Carry on!

The two sisters could not see her. It was obvious because she was only reliving a past and not in it. Flyra watched as the story unfolded.

'First you took someone I love from me and now you even dare to have a baby with him' Sofya said angrily. She has a soft-spoken voice, which made her sound like a child trying to show her temper. Majuza was close to tears. Hugging her child with full of love.

'Look at me when I'm talking to you. Mommy and daddy taught us well enough how to respect those older than us'

Majuza turned, her tears were at the verge of rolling down her cheeks.

'Don't act like you're the nice one here. You know your mistake' Sofya said.

'I did nothing wrong Sofya. Nicholas loves me as I

do love him. His heart is true with me. You're not even with him' Majuza cried.

'Who said I'm not with him?! You took him away from me, you scandalous freak!'

'I am not!' Majuza exclaimed. She was getting angrier rather than sad. The baby in her arms was starting to wake.

'He was never with you! No one even gets the idea that you're together. You may like him, but none of you inform publicly that it's official' Majuza explained.

'Do we have to tell everyone?!'

'No! You don't even tell me! What are sisters for if we keep things from each other?!'

'Everyone has secrets Majuza! Even some only the person herself knows that secret! You keep secrets from me yourself!'

'Then if that relationship you so call had with Nicholas was a secret, I have no way of knowing. And you can't blame me for marrying him in secret. He came to me. We both love each other. It wasn't my fault!'

Sofya breathed in deep, controlling her anger. She breathed out and smiled dryly.

'Of course it's not your fault. That's why I killed Nicholas…'

'What?! You said you got him captured!' Majuza shouted. The baby in her arms was fully awake now and crying very loudly.

'Yes I got him captured and killed him'

Majuza gave an expression of utter disbelief.

'And as I was saying Majuza, I'm going to let you off from such a scandalous crime because as you acknowledged it, it wasn't your fault. But I have one condition for you. You are to abandon that baby of yours. Either you…'

'I'm not giving James away to anyone! You're mad! You would kill someone you love?!' Majuza fought back. 'What would mommy and daddy say if…'

'Well they're not here aren't they Majuza?! They died a long time ago when you're too busy caring for your own emotions in this wretched place!'

'This was daddy's favourite place in all the worlds!'

'The point is, where were you when our parents were in their old age. Requiring our company? You were busy here entertaining your sad life!'

'Shut up!' Majuza shouted, exerting a wave of red mist that moved as quickly as a forcefield, damaging everything around her except Sofya who was protected by her personal shield.

'Get out!' Majuza yelled.

'You can't push me away. You know you are no match for my forces. Your magic is strong but you are still no match for me, the masters and the army. You are alone Majuza. You always stand alone. Maybe not alone, you have those ugly creatures standing with you. Listen carefully to what I wanted to say earlier. If you treasure your life, your power, your whatever home you make of this place, then abide by the rules I set. You committed a crime with Nicholas against me. You can live if you send that child of yours away. I don't care whatever you do, give her away and don't see her again. You have a week to do so. Disobeying my orders and you shall face the consequences' Sofya said. She had lowered her sword.

Majuza remained silent for the whole time, she couldn't bother to entertain her sister.

'What kind of judge are you? Sentenced someone to death for loving someone else. Is that what mommy and daddy taught you?'

The cave was filled with the sound of James crying.

'Don't question my judgement!' Sofya exclaimed. 'You have one week'

The vision disappeared into clouded figures and Flyra was back where she was before.

'Princess!' Captain exclaimed. Flyra could tell that he had called her a few times.

'Yes Captain' Flyra replied immediately, snapping out of the trance.

'Are you having the same effects again?' Captain said.

'This is different, Captain, I intended so. I looked into the past based on this painting'

'That is a rare ability Flyangel' Oliver said. 'To be able to see the truth about everything is real power'

'What did you see?' Bale said.

Flyra told them the whole story from the moment she realised she was back in time.

'So Majuza was not as evil as we think she is' Bale said.

'We cannot jump to conclusions. There are so many questions in my mind right now. The story was hanging' Flyra said.

'Then let's see the other paintings. Perhaps they will explain' Oliver said.

'We can't waste time on paintings that are only clues

of something much much bigger. That must wait. For now we know Majuza's avengers are against us, are our enemies. They will stop at nothing to destroy Sofya's nation. Our mission is to find father's children that they kidnapped years ago. Now they're definitely older than I am, lesser chance for any of us to recognise them, let alone myself who has never met them before. We must continue our journey right away'

Flyra turned around and walked briskly to exit the cave. She was very curious of the story she had just witnessed and is desiring to know more but she cannot let that distract her. Staying longer will only tempt her.

MASTER NVAGO

Before you start reading the next chapter, finish what you're supposed to do first. Done? Carry on!

The team of five had just made their way past the Alhora field when suddenly, the sky turned dark as quick as a flash and rain poured down heavily. Bobby took out five umbrellas he had packed before their journey. But Master Kitty simply rejected it and cast a spell that covered them from the rain.

'You could have told me that we won't be requiring umbrellas' Bobby said.

'You know I am a SHAW, for many years now and you're still not used to it' Kitty replied. Bobby grinned.

'There's something you all should know' Lillain said suddenly. The others turned to look at her like she was about to confess a big crime.

'I don't think this is natural rain' Lillain said.

'I know' Kitty replied.

'And that's not important for us to know?' Prince Jake said.

'It's because we're closer to The Outlands, encountering

avengers with their dark magic now is not a surprise' Kitty explained. 'However, I must say, the magic in the rain is not dark. It has greater power. Far greater than light magic'

'Yes, that's what I wanted to say' Lillain said. 'You don't think this has got something to do with Flyra is it?'

The others looked at her curiously.

'I mean, think about it, she's a child of the seed of Gratultyn'

There was a pause as they absorbed what Lillain had just mentioned. A highly amazed expression formed on Kitty's face.

'She must be an hour further than us' Kitty said.

'How do you know?' Jake asked.

'Have you forgotten my apprentice? I am a wielder of the wind and the atmosphere. I can feel the distance. Flyra has a strong magic and knowing her specialty, she's more of an Ice person than water. So if she were to exert such strong power, it would be ice. We are facing rain and not snow. So in conclusion, we are not close to her as we might think. She's about an hour away' Kitty said.

'You got all that from the air?' Jake said.

'Yes my prince. Let's continue. Flyra's not going to wait for us' Kitty said. 'Oh and before that, beyond this field, starting from the woods ahead, just keep in mind that you are on foreign grounds. Lots of creatures lurk around, literally waiting for a prey'

He stepped first making his way into the woods. That was when they saw the frozen beast. Still frozen in its place.

'The ice is so strong that even the warm temperature cannot melt it' Kitty said.

'Flyra?' Jake guessed.

'Most probably' Kitty said. He concluded based on the direction the beast was facing.

'Be alert at all times' Kitty warned and made his way forward as the rest followed.

Meanwhile, the team of four had just proceeded down a small hill that was part of a huge mountain at the other end of the valley. Princess Flyra had managed to cast a shield on all of them, strong enough to block the bite of the cold air. The view of the snowy woods not far ahead was a relief. Flyra remained positive but the three friends had started to doubt they were getting out of there alive.

'What forest is that?' Captain asked. Flyra unrolled the map and searched.

'There isn't a name for it. But we're on the right path. Further up is Cappidop Bay. What we're looking for should be very close' Flyra said. Captain shuddered partly from the cold but mostly because he was very nervous. He doesn't know what to expect from meeting with the avengers, meeting Prince Edward for the first time in twenty years. Edward should be twenty-eight years old now.

'Wait, who's that?' Oliver exclaimed staring at something or someone peeking from behind the trees. It was a person, face hidden underneath a long wizard cloak. The man turned around as if on cue and started walking briskly away.

'Wait!' Flyra called, running after him. It was difficult for her to run properly with her dress lagging behind. The man did not even turn, he continued with his quick pace.

'Flyangel wait! We don't know who he is' Captain said, concerned. Flyra did not reply. She was catching up with the man who was also unable to run with his cloak dragging along the grass and roots heavily.

'Sir, please wait!' Flyra called again. The man did not stop a single second. He also neither decreased or increased his speed.

Suddenly, the man disappeared with ripples of forcefield, camouflaged to its surroundings, spreading vertically around the area he was before. Flyra stopped in her tracks. The others did too.

'Where did he go?' Captain said, surprised. Flyra made her way towards the ripple, now gone. She reached her right palm into the air in front, at her shoulder level. The same, but only a single ripple appeared as her hand rested on something that should be the camouflaged forcefield. She dragged her hand across the air. Ripples appeared like she had just dragged her hand across a calm water. Flyra gasped as she realised what she was seeing. It was no wonder why no one could find the avengers' base. They are hidden by magical barriers. Flyra walked forward and disappeared the same way as the man before. The three friends shouted her name in panic as they watched her entering the unknown.

The surroundings were the same. Except there was no snow. The trees are its natural colour, green and very pleasant to the eyes. But there was a small town now right in front of Flyra. It was like some giant had just sucked all the snow out and smacked buildings randomly among the trees. It was a quiet peaceful town. Few villagers, living in small houses walked about the dirt paths, making businesses at the small market in the centre. No fancy buildings. Just houses, huts, few small town buildings like a stable, and the market. A sign fixed to the ground at the outskirts of town. It says 'Trading Village'. The man from before was nowhere to be seen. A few seconds later Captain, Bale and Oliver came through the barrier.

'Whoa!' they said together.

'We're making progress' Flyra told them. 'I'm sure gather has not discovered this place yet'

'If we can enter, what makes you think he has not discovered it yet?' Oliver said.

'I just feel it. Like this is a new discovery. Come'

Flyra went past the sign. She approached a lady in a maiden dress and a white scarf only covering part of her head with a basket filled with fresh bread, probably she had just returned from a bakery.

'Excuse me miss?' Flyra called.

'Yes can I help you? Oh you're such a beautiful lady!' the lady said quickly.

'Uh, thank you miss' Flyra smiled shyly. 'Have you seen a man in a cloak passing by?'

'No I haven't but I know of the man you're speaking of'

'Who is he?'

'Master Nvago. He is the keeper of this town'

'Where can I find him?'

'Oh he'll come to you' the lady smiled very kindly to the extent that some might see it as a little bit creepy. 'Have a nice day!'

And she walked away, leaving Flyra very confused.

'Something's strange about her' Flyra said.

'That's because she's not a real person' a voice of an old wise man came from behind. All of them turned around to see the man from before. He had pulled the hood of his brown cloak back. He is an old man with fewer wrinkles than other people his age. His hair is grey. He has a long beard of the same colour. He has a very kind smile, the one that will calm anyone who sees him.

'Everyone in this town is just a trick of the mind. Everyone except me. I am Master Nvago, protector of trading villages and portals, keeper of travellers, portals, and businesses'

'Nice to meet you sir. why were you hiding from us?' Flyra said.

'I wasn't hiding, I led you here'

'I don't understand, why?'

'To help you with what you're looking for of course!' Master Nvago laughed.

'Just now you mentioned your name and your titles. Portals? You control portals?'

'Not control my child. I just maintain the peace. If you ever heard of Gratultyn, the core for all magic, Responsibilities were given to the sages and high masters of the realm. I am only a master and I am in charge of the least difficult tasks among all The Fifteen. But we're not here to talk about me or any of The Fifteen. I can show you the way to what you seek. Follow me'

The old master turned and walked peacefully ahead. He led them to a small house made of wood. From the outside it seemed like there was only one room. But as they stepped inside, the house seemed like a cottage where people go to, for their vacation. There were at least three bedrooms, a kitchen, two bathrooms, and a living room where the fireplace is, although there was no chimney from the outside.

'Make yourselves comfortable, I'll come back with tea' Nvago said and proceeded to the kitchen.

The four were still amazed by the magic. They admired the decorations around as they went into the living room. There were mostly potted plants. Master Nvago must have a green thumb. A moment later, which was quite fast to prepare tea for four or five if including the person himself, Nvago came into the living room carrying a tray with five cups and a teapot.

'I'm sorry this is going to sound impolite but do you have milk?' Oliver asked.

'Yes, very impolite of you Oliver' Nvago replied, placing the tray carefully on the coffee table. No one was sure whether the master was really hurt or he was just joking because he spoke monotonously.

'Wait, how do you know my name?'

'I'm the keeper of travellers. You are a traveller. You all are. That gives me advantage on you'

Nvago smiled like that was not creepy at all.

'Princess Flyra, Captain, Bale, and Oliver'

'You said you could help us find…'

'Prince Edward and Princess Erieka? Yes I still can, not I could' Nvago said, cutting Flyra's sentence.

'However, I must warn you. The persons you're looking for are not who they were before' he said.

'What do you mean?'

'That I can't tell you. Every power has its limits. I can only tell you when I see it with my own eyes. But for now, all I can say is, don't expect to find Prince Edward and Princess Erieka as the cute innocent children you know they were'

'I have never met them'

'Yes but you heard of them from these three' Nvago said, referring to the animals. 'Marcala abducted them. Thinking logically, how do you think Marcala would raise them assuming she did not kill them'

'She did not. Because if she wanted to kill them, she would have done it back at the castle. Why go through the trouble of bringing them back to the avengers' base if she wanted to kill them all along'

'Smart girl' Nvago said, smiling calmly.

'Now as you see earlier, the forcefield barrier?'

Flyra nodded.

'That's a dimensional spell. Sofya first used it for… for something. That's not important now'

Flyra frowned for a short while. She dislikes it when someone increases her curiosity but ends up crushing her hopes.

'It blocks whatever the caster wants to be hidden from the view of others outside of it. In this case, I casted it so that random mischief won't find its way into the town'

'The town looks so real, even after you said it wasn't, it still does!' Flyra said, partly amazed.

'It's all fake. I made it as such, so that people who came in, mostly people who lost their way tend to find the gateway of the dimensional wall, I made it so that people who come in will see it as a normal town. I'm protecting a portal here from any mischief that is possible to occur'

'There's a portal? To where?' Captain asked excitedly.

'That's classified information. You are not in need of it at the moment'

The clock on the wall by the fireplace chimed.

'Oh it's time for me to move!' Nvago said all of a sudden.

'Move where?' Flyra asked.

'The portal is shifting to another place. I must clean the town up and make a new one wherever the portal is going to'

'The portal moves?' Oliver exclaimed.

'All of you are asking me questions that are not of your concern at the moment. Back to your objective! What else do you need to know?'

'How can we find them? You haven't told us anything' Flyra said.

'Oh I did tell you princess. I explained about the dimensional spell. Why do you think your uncle could not find the base?'

'My uncle?'

'King Henry. Thought you knew?'

There was an awkward pause.

'I guessed… but I didn't expect it to be true'

'That means Prince Edward and Princess Erieka are not my siblings'

'There you go princess' Nvago said, nodding like a teacher proud of his student.

'And I'm not a real princess'

'There's no such thing as a real princess. By blood you are still royalty. Princess is just a small title'

'Alright' Flyra said, accepting the information she had just absorbed. 'My uncle could not find the base because it's hidden behind a dimensional barrier'

'There you go again' Nvago smiled.

'And how am I supposed to find the barrier. I found this one with your help'

'No it wasn't. I was simply a hint'

Nvago acted out Flyra's action when she swiped her hand across the barrier earlier. Flyra shook her head slowly, trying her best to understand but she couldn't.

'Your own self Flyra. You have the power in you' Nvago said. 'Trust yourself. Let your power within you guide you. And don't stress too much. Magic needs a calm host to shine. That is also why your uncle could not find the base. A calm host would. If it makes you feel better, you are a Winterain, commands not only water but ice as well, that's more than common for a typical Winterain. And you're a child of the seed of Gratultyn. You may not realise it now but I assure you. No one messes with a child of the seed. Not even a high master'

'Thank you Master Nvago' Flyra said. She felt humbled to be praised with all those titles.

'Now run along, I've got tasks to do' Nvago said and he disappeared. No magic sparks or anything just completely vanish.

'Where did he go?' Captain asked.

'Come on! He's shown us the way, let's go' Flyra said and she walked quickly out of the house.

FIRE AND AMULET

Before you start reading the next chapter, finish what you're supposed to do first. Done? Carry on!

The atmosphere was still silent in Combination even though it's almost peak period, the time when everyone finished their jobs and started to head home. As King Henry was still bedridden, Prince Nathan took over the king's duties. Hopefully for the day only, assuming his brother returned by the end of the day with Princess Flyra. There was a sudden explosion in the city square. The few people who were walking the streets were thrown everywhere. Children were separated from their mothers as the next explosion occurred in the shops and markets. Those still standing started screaming and running in panic. Those who live close by made it back to their homes only to be caught in an explosion later on. One by one, buildings and streets burst into flames from the square all the way to the edge of the business district. Black birds flew down from the sky to random streets in the area and transformed into avengers. The moment the innocent citizens saw them, they got more panic. The avengers started chasing people and killing them. Slowly the business district was becoming a place of massacre. They only left the children untouched, unless they died from the fire or other means. All of them regrouped at the end of a junction leading up to the castle. By this time, the soldiers had reached the downtown area and started trying to control the situation. Hundreds of them were made out of the elite soldiers. But most of them cannot stop the person leading the avengers uphill towards the castle. And it isn't Marcala, or better known here as Widow. The person is a beautiful young lady in red. From her scarf to her boots hidden underneath her dress were all red. Her scarf was not worn very properly, a lot of her perfect brown hair was showing. Her neck was partially visible and a glowing red amulet was hanging from it. Every step she took nearer to the castle, the amulet emphasised its glow. The soldiers charged with their weapons and some with magic but all were countered and killed by this lady. And close by her side, acting like her bodyguard is Marcala. The attack was so overwhelming. Even before this group reached the castle, an explosion occurred there, at the dome of the main ballroom. The roof that was made, mostly out of glass, shattered and the pieces fell onto the grand marble floor. There were servants working inside and they were badly injured, but most of them died. A few more black birds flew in from the broken roof and transformed into avengers. Morgan and Alphaga were among them. Morgan brushed dust off his clothes dramatically.

'What was our task again? Kill them all?' Alphaga grinned wickedly.

'No idiot, we are to take the castle and hold it until the successor arrives' Morgan said responsibly.

'Which equally means kill anyone standing in our way!' Alphaga deduced excitedly.

'Spread out, make sure every corner is secured' Morgan commanded. The avengers moved in a hurry to perform their task. Just outside the ballroom, a fight started. Morgan and Alphaga walked to the doors and opened it. The sound of swords clashing and powers thrown became clear. Quite a number of the king's guards accompanied Prince Nathan as they defended the castle. Further down the hallway, near the castle's main entrance, were the SHAW masters and a few servants battling the avengers who came in through the front.

'This will be fun!' Alphaga grinned.

'No Alphaga, there's a much simpler way' Morgan said.

He held up his hand, a wave of forcefield exited and the whole fight froze. Everyone could not move. Only their eyes could.

'Listen to me, we will stop this fighting and you shall surrender the castle. If you don't, and when we succeed, the entire city will be destroyed. Your choice acting king' Morgan said, staring at Nathan.

'What are you doing Morgan?!' Alphaga scolded, feeling very annoyed because he is craving for a fight.

'Making everyone's life simpler, now shut up!' Morgan said. He moved his hand, palm facing the direction of the prince. Nathan could move again.

'Now answer me young prince'

'We shall surrender the castle' Nathan said.

'Clever boy' Morgan said and waved his hand, everyone could move again. 'Now, follow me'

The avengers took charge. They took the weapons away from the king's guards and group by group they locked them up in the dungeons.

Morgan, Alphaga, Nathan and a few of the avengers, who were holding on tight to Nathan so that he could not escape, made their way to the entrance hall. The royal master Jenny was still duelling with an avenger. Master William and Master Asher were there as well fighting another.

'Stop!' Morgan shouted. His voice exited his mouth like a wave of radiation, full of heat and pain. That caused everyone to instantly stop what they were doing.

'Your prince has surrendered. You should do the same. If you refuse, death awaits you' Morgan said.

'Nathan?' Jenny called in disbelief. Nathan felt very pressured. He was too occupied to pay attention. He cared for his family and the whole city. He made the decision to save them. Jenny refused to agree. She summoned a fireball in her hands.

'There's no way you're making me' Jenny said.

The fire in her hands behaved oddly all of a sudden. Before Jenny could do anything, the fire spread all over her, burning her inside and out as she screamed in pain.

'We don't have to' a lady's voice, cold and evil, spoke from behind. The lady in red was standing at the doors. Marcala was beside her grinning. The fire died out and a burnt black body fell onto the ground. Nathan stared at it with eyes wide open.

'Now who wants to join her?' the lady in red said. 'Who's the leader?'

'The king… is… is sick, successor, the person…' Morgan stuttered. Clearly this lady frightens him.

'I asked who's the leader Morgan, straight to the point!' she exclaimed. A wave of heat swept past them.

'Prince Nathan' Morgan shoved Nathan forward.

'Well, lock the others. I shall have a chat with this one' the successor said. She casted a spell. Red light shone the outline of Nathan as his legs left the floor. He floated around as he was magically dragged by the lady to follow her. The successor found a room of her liking, the king's room. King Henry was lying on the bed asleep.

'Morgan! Remove this old person from here and lock him up!' the successor called. Henry sat up immediately, awoken by the mad shouting. He stared at the successor in shock and confusion. Then he saw Nathan beside her, floating in red light, unable to move except for his eyes. Then Morgan walked in with a few of his soldiers and brought Henry away. As soon as they were out, the successor slammed the door shut with one magic force and threw Nathan onto the bed. She spread his arms and legs apart and created four long ropes securing each limb to one corner of the king-sized bed.

'Now handsome, since you acted in your father's place, you're going to tell me, where are the others I heard so much about? I know there's more of you than a useless sick old king and an amateur clueless young prince. Or I'll make you. And I am always fun when I make someone talk. I'll take away his dignity' the lady grinned naughtily and full of evil.

'You don't want to lose your virginity don't you?' the successor grinned. Nathan stared at her with eyes wide open in disbelief.

'That's unholy and inhuman! Never have I heard even an avenger is up for that!' Nathan snapped.

'Well you should be blushing, I'm praising you, you foolish prince. You think a person will want to do it with her enemy? You're crazy that is! Except if the enemy is a gorgeous man then I'll reconsider. Now answer me! Or I'll make you'

She started removing her scarf.

'Just kill me, you're insane!' Nathan shouted.

'Oh, I wouldn't waste such a good body so soon!'

She removed her scarf revealing a clear view of her perfect long wavy brown hair and her neck with the red amulet, glowing very brightly.

'Wait! They're finding my sister, Princess Flyra. She went to find our long lost siblings' Nathan revealed. The successor was a little surprised to hear the last part. She quickly regained herself.

'Lies! For twenty years no one came looking! Are you telling me suddenly after so long, everyone starts caring?!' she shouted.

'The king has been searching for the past twenty years. He never stopped' Nathan said, desperately hoping to be released from this torture. The successor walked to one side of the bed and bent down closer, placing her hands on it. One of Nathan's tied arms was in between her two hands.

'Do you know who I am?' she asked. Nathan thought for a while, he had only heard about Master Widow, also known as Marcala, Morgan and Alphaga. He shook his head.

'Well handsome, I am Erieka. Princess Erieka of Combination. And your father failed to find me for the past twenty years. Instead, he had new children to replace me' the successor said, revealing a big identity of herself. Nathan froze, aghast.

'The fact that you want to do this to me is just sick' Nathan muttered. 'Let me go'

'I will' Erieka said seductively, caressing his foot.

'Thanks for telling me where they are' Erieka winked.

'You're insane' Nathan said, rolling his eyes.

'Guards! Take him away!' Erieka shouted suddenly, startling Nathan. She swiped her hand briefly in the air. The ropes that tied Nathan to the bed vanish. The guards (Morgan's soldiers who were now under Erieka's command) came in and brought him to the dungeons. She rejoined Morgan in the meeting room with Alphaga and a few other avengers inside. They were arguing on which part of the city should be controlled by who. The moment Erieka entered, the room went silent. Everyone sat straight.

'First things first. I know where the missing people went' Erieka began.

'Successor, I would love to volunteer on this remarkable journey and bring back their heads for you' Alphaga said confidently.

'We're going to leave them be' Erieka said. The grin on Alphaga's face disappeared.

'Where's Marcala?'

'She said she's taking care of something' Morgan reported.

Marcala was strolling down the hallway right outside the royal chambers. And she stopped in the middle and waited. Suddenly, red mist swirled beside her and Erieka appeared in its place.

'What are you doing Marcala? Shouldn't you be in the meeting room?' Erieka said.

'Quiet' Marcala said. Erieka showed an expression like she was offended.

'Ouch' Erieka said. She looked back and forth at Marcala then at whatever she was staring at. Her eyes led her to the floor in front.

'Taking care of something is staring at the floor?' Erieka said dryly.

'Quiet'

Erieka rolled her eyes and disappeared as red mist swirled around, like it was devouring her. As if on cue, green sparks sparkled in front of Marcala at where she was staring at. A familiar white mouse appeared in its place, dazed and confused.

'Welcome back Mousy' Marcala said, smiling in satisfaction. She let her regain focus.

'You!' Mousy exclaimed all of a sudden. Marcala held up her hand. A translucent purplish-black magical shield wrapped all over Mousy except for her head. It prevented her from moving.

'Release me!' Mousy yelled.

'How long have you been gone?' Marcala asked.

'Release me!' Mousy yelled, struggling to break the magic.

'You can't fight dark magic with your common magic. So answer my question'

'Twenty years!' Mousy shouted angrily. Marcala's face lit up.

'So the other dimension exists?' Marcala asked, accelerating excitement in her tone.

'I've answered your question. Now release me!'

'You're making this hard on yourself Mousy. Enjoy the dungeons' Marcala snapped, feeling very irritated. She swiped her hand and Mousy disappeared in a cloud of blue mist. Marcala rejoined the meeting with the avengers.

'Attention, The Avenger enters' someone called out as everyone stopped discussing and sat straight.

'Yes yes carry on' Marcala dismissed, a little bit annoyed. 'You have a new leader now and that's the successor and not me'

'So, we were saying Marcala, I shall leave the business district to you' Erieka said. A map of the whole city was laid on the table.

'That's nice. Thank you' Marcala replied. 'The other districts?'

'I'll take the encampment district' Morgan said. 'The soldiers shall be disciplined with our ways'

Marcala nodded in satisfaction at every word. The encampment district was the only district drawn in red on the map. It lies just a few centimetres to the right of the royal grounds.

'Alphaga will take the merchants' district' Erieka said, pointing at an area below the business district.

'You'll be pleased with what I will do to everyone there' Alphaga grinned, his bunny ears stood tall with excitement.

'Pertum and his brothers will take the forest district' Erieka said.

'Which one? There are a lot, successor' one of the brothers asked.

'All of them. Four of you will sort it out yourselves. Don't interrupt me again' Erieka said, giving him a cold stare at the last part. 'Alright, and Lydia and Tora will take all of the village districts, one to five. I'm sure you'll handle the commoners well. Let them know and remember who's in charge now'

'Yes successor' Lydia replied obediently.

'I will be controlling the royal grounds. I am a princess here anyway' Erieka said. Everyone except Marcala smiled awkwardly at the last comment.

'Don't worry, successor, sounds better for me. I should get a new name' Erieka said happily. She paused as she thought for a while. Everyone except Marcala stared at her uncomfortably, like she was wasting their time from chasing their dreams.

'I know! Empress Erieka! Ooh, I love that! Call me, Empress Erieka!' Erieka exclaimed excitedly. 'Let everyone know. Empress Erieka is now the ruler of Combination'

'I'm sorry to interrupt your beautiful dream successor

but don't forget our actual reason for overtaking the city' Marcala said.

'Yes, to avenge great mother Majuza of course! How could I forget? Other matters are just extras. But don't spoil my mood from having fun alright!' Erieka said.

'I hope you don't forget who was truly evil. Who was the oppressed. And which side are you on' Marcala reminded.

'Yes master' Erieka said obediently, her excitement died down.

'Now, who will follow you to take all the other cities? I don't want you to leave Barenge out of the list. They may not be associated with Combination anymore but they are the same, they are not on our side. Our mission is to avenge Majuza and get everyone on our side. Let everyone know, the Outlanders they hate so much are now in power' Marcala said.

'Yes Marcala. Lydia and I will lead the avengers and soldiers. First to Barenge. They're the nearest'

'And don't be a fool. Be cautious. Barenge has very strong defense. Their musketeers are trained to shoot to kill'

'Definitely. It'll be fun to see Jonathan's face when he watches us tear his army down' Erieka said.

'One more thing, use your amulet well. That thing has more power than what you learnt about it from me. Don't do something I did not teach you. You'll misuse it'

Erieka frowned, partly confused and partly annoyed that Marcala did not teach her everything about the amulet.

'And Erieka, you don't want to meet your father

first?' Marcala asked. The question made the meeting room become more silent than before.

'Why would I want to meet the person that gave up looking for me?'

'He never gave up on you. Or your brother'

'Then he failed, for twenty years! Don't get me mad about this again!' Erieka shouted, tears appearing in her eyes. The room was not just silent anymore. It was heating up. 'I'm not weak like my brother. I know depression and shutting out won't get me anywhere! And you shouldn't even ask me that! How dare you! How dare you?! You took me away and now you want me to reunite with my father?! And what? I'm going to betray you and help my father now?'

'I know you won't Erieka. I know you understand why you're doing this. I know you understand which side is right'

'I am supposed to be against you. I finally saw my father and I'm rude to him' Erieka said, her anger was turning to sadness. Her tears rolled down her cheeks. 'I even killed his men'

'Get it together Erieka. I don't encourage the killing' Marcala said, glaring at Alphaga at the mention of the word killing. 'But we have to do whatever is necessary to spread our message. Even if it means to kill. But remember, remember what you have learnt all those twenty years. Majuza deserves to be heard. Her side of the story. And the Inlanders won't listen except when danger comes to them. And even after, they still won't. But we must do whatever it is to spread our story and avenge Majuza'

Erieka nodded obediently.

'Alright. I can meet my father anytime. I'll do it after Barenge' Erieka said, wiping her tears away. She left the room with Lydia following behind. The room went silent for a few more seconds.

'That was intense alright' Morgan said finally.

'And embarrassing as well' Alphaga said.

'At least we know for sure she won't betray us now' Marcala said.

'I still don't understand the power of the amulet' Alphaga said.

'I don't know everything about it. But I do know the amulet holds very great power. And as long as it is worn or used by the successor, the power is multiplied' Marcala said.

The Prince Returns

Before you start reading the next chapter, finish what you're supposed to do first. Done? Carry on!

The smell of the ocean was getting stronger. Flyra knew Cappidop Bay was not far ahead. They had travelled for more than an hour, but Flyra was getting nowhere with her search for the dimensional barrier.

'I understand why would anyone not give up by now' Bale said.

'Bale, don't give up yet. We still have a few kilometres more from the ocean' Flyra said, her voice was full of hope.

That was when a group of Morgan's men, his swordsmen, walking in between trees and joking around. And some of them caught sight of the four.

'They saw us' one of them said, drawing his sword.

'Run!' Flyra managed as she turned immediately to run without caring where she's headed. The other three listened and did the same. But all of them got separated from one another. One good thing was that the soldiers had to split up to catch everyone. Two were chasing Flyra. One chased Captain. And another chased Bale. There was no one left to chase Oliver. He stopped and turned to see his friends running as fast as they could. The soldiers, quite stupid, were running with their swords in hand. Oliver had enough time to get to Bale and stop the soldier chasing him. Oliver succeeded and regrouped with Bale.

'Where's Cap and Flyangel?' Bale asked, relieved that he was no longer being chased.

'I saw Cap running east from your direction. I don't know about Flyangel' Oliver said.

Flyra was sure she outran them. She saw no movements from the corner of her eyes. So she stopped running and caught her breath. But she was wrong. Suddenly one of the soldiers came charging with a sword in hand. The other was close behind. Flyra was quite frustrated, her magic was failing her. First, she couldn't find the barrier, now her senses failed to warn her she cannot stop running yet. Fortunately her reflexes are still good. The sword came slashing at her neck, which she ducked just in time. She did not rise back up, guessing the soldier was going to make another strike backwards. She guessed right. If she had risen, she would have lost her head already. Flyra pushed the soldier with both her hands. He was flung backwards with a magical force. Flyra breathed in calmly. She felt content that she had not lost any of her magic which she thought she did. The other soldier came with a sword ready to strike. Flyra conjured ice from her palms. The ice piled up around the soldier, building its way up, guided by Flyra's hands. Soon the soldier was no longer in sight. A long groan came from behind. Flyra turned quickly. The first soldier was charging at her again with the sword. He was so close, she wouldn't have enough time to pile up more ice. Visible water vapour came out of her mouth as she breathed out. The weather was not that cold. The soldier knew she was using magic again. He attacked anyway. He swung the sword forward. Flyra raised her hands to block. To his surprise, her hands were covered in thick ice, very pure blue ice. The sword bounced off her icy hands, unable to hurt.

'What magic?' the soldier stumbled backwards and said in fear.

'One you should not mess around with' Flyra said confidently and sent a wave of ice magic towards him. Soon an ice sculpture stood in its place. Everything was covered in ice, from the tip of the sword to the grass around him. She breathed out again, the ice on her hand melted away super quickly. She suddenly remembered she needed a guide to help her find the avengers' base. She melted the head portion of the ice. The soldier gasped for air.

'Please! It's very cold!' he pleaded.

'Tell me, where is the base?' Flyra said firmly. She was still working on her firm voice. It came out okay or because the soldier was already frightened that he was going to die from the cold, because he immediately answered her.

'You already past the dimensional barrier. That's why you can see us and we can see you' the soldier said, struggling to withstand the cold.

'Thank you' Flyra said. She did him a favour. She melted away the ice all the way except for the feet.

'I can't let you run freely while I need to complete my mission' she said. 'And I certainly cannot leave that with you'

She held up her palm and the sword in the soldier's hand unstuck from him and moved in the air towards her.

'But this will be useful to me' Flyra said, smiling as she inspected the sword.

'Take care of it for me' the soldier said.

'Don't worry about it. You won't have to see it again. I give you back will only help me destroy myself' Flyra said and again she smiled, like she was saying thanks for the sword. She walked away. Satisfied with herself. With knowledge that the base is not far around, she hurried in the direction she remembered where the soldiers came from, hoping that they came from the base. So she travelled west. Now Cappidop Bay is to her right. And soon, she saw smoke rising above the trees. She got excited and ran towards the direction. In a small clearing stood a small house. The smoke was coming from the chimney of this house. Her face lit up even more.

'A building! Wherever you are Captain, Bale and Oliver, I hope you are safe' she said softly and excitedly. But she did not immediately go to the front door. What if it's dangerous, she thought to herself. She inspected the surroundings. She sensed no danger. So she proceeded to the front door. The house was actually beautiful. The fact that it most probably belongs to the avengers is scary. There was a small garden around the front side of the house. A path at the back leads to a small shed. She peered through the window but could not make out clearly what's inside with the curtains blocking her view. But someone must definitely be inside because of the smoke coming out of the chimney. She knocked on the door. Few seconds passed. She knocked again. Still no answer. She knocked again. After a few restless minutes, she turned the knob. It wasn't locked. She went inside. The house was filled with the smell of fresh bread still baking in the oven which Flyra noticed in the kitchen to her right. There were no walls to separate the kitchen and the living room. Also the dining room, which consisted of only a small table and two chairs. There were three doors in front, one with a small window on it beside the kitchen cabinets. That probably leads to the back. One of the other two was opened. A bed is inside the room, which means it was a bedroom. There's no one at home at the moment. Suddenly the other door opened and a very handsome man stepped out half naked. Only a white towel was wrapped around his lower body. Flyra can't help but stare at him. His face, his chest. They are so perfect. He was not too thin and not too muscular. And his face was just like a world-class model. Even his brown hair, which was not combed yet, looks amazing. He saw her and his eyes went huge for a second as he stepped back into the bathroom.

'I'm sorry' Flyra said, immediately looking away.

'What are you doing in here?' the man said.

'I came looking for someone' Flyra replied, keeping her eyes away from looking and clearing her mind. She glimpsed the man's figure walking back to his bedroom and heard him closing the door. She looked once again, now the bedroom door was closed. She smiled, thinking how silly that had been. One minute passed, and the man finally came out of his room. He was wearing a grey long sleeve shirt and a black vest over it. Now that she saw his face even more clearly, he looks more handsome than before. His hair was combed back neatly. His beard was shaved. And he reminded her a lot of King Henry. And she couldn't speak.

'Good afternoon milady' the man said, bowing like a perfect gentleman. 'What brings a royal princess to this… house?'

Flyra froze. Not that she was in fear or anything. She was just lost for words. Looking at him, she just couldn't speak. And he seems to know about her. He smiled looking at how uneasy Flyra seemed. His smile was also perfect. The more reason for Flyra to be distracted.

'Don't worry I don't know you' the man reassured. He thought Flyra was too creeped out to speak. 'I just know you're royalty because only royals dress like that, unless you're a rich merchant. And you're young, so that means you must be a princess'

The man is not just handsome, but smart too. Find more reasons to add to his model-worthy points. Flyra summoned her power to focus. She eventually snapped out of it after the man was the one getting uncomfortable.

'You're beautiful. I mean you're smart' Flyra said quickly, feeling embarrassed by herself. The man chuckled.

'You're beautiful as well. I mean of course you are. I mean you're royalty!' the man said, feeling more embarrassed than Flyra. He made Flyra less uneasy, and she laughed a bit at his actions.

'I'm Princess Flyra'

'I'm Ned' he stuck out his hand. Flyra shook it.

'You have a beautiful bracelet!' Flyra said, admiring the plain silver bracelet on Ned's left wrist.

'Trust me, it's not as beautiful as it seems' Ned said. Flyra tried to process what he meant but she couldn't understand.

'You said you're looking for someone?' Ned asked.

'Yes! But wait. May I know who you are?' Flyra replied.

'I already told you my name'

'I meant as in in relation to the avengers. You are in their dimension. I need to find their base'

'You are not one of Marcala's associates?'

'What? Why would I be the avenger's associate? I'm a princess!'

It was Ned's turn to process what Flyra had just said. He was very confused.

'You mean you found this dimension without Marcala's guidance?'

'Yes. Well with my magic. I guess'

Ned's face lit up.

'Wait, are you working for Marcala?' Flyra said, getting suspicious.

'Never' Ned said with a certain anger in his voice. It sounded like he wanted to take revenge.

'Then why do you have a house here? And how do you know so much about Marcala's deals with her associates?'

'I am a prisoner here. I have no magic to allow me to leave this dimension. I am trapped' Ned said. He maintained his cool face but his voice sounded like he was about to cry.

'I thought the dimension is just a barrier?'

'It's a barrier but its gateways to the other side are only small and limited and it changes from time to time' Ned explained. 'There's no way out without magic or permission from Marcala'

Suddenly the oven bell rang.

'That's my bread' Ned said, smiling once again as he put on his oven gloves and took out the tray of scrumptious freshly baked bread. He cut the bread in two and offered one of the halves to Flyra.

'Thank you' Flyra accepted it.

'Marcala has random associates from cities and kingdoms that I do not know of. Hopefully those from The Outlands. I hate the idea of having another betrayer or spy among the Inlanders especially if they're royalty, who are supposed to lead and show good examples to the people' Ned said while savouring his bread.

'Another betrayer?'

'Haven't you heard that Marcala used to be the royal master of Combination?'

'You know a lot about this matter Ned' Flyra was

complimenting. She was impressed. A handsome, smart, and knowledgeable person.

'I will lead you to the base' Ned said kindly.

'Really? Thank you!' Flyra was so grateful.

Just as the evening sun had started going down, the two of them left the house. Ned led the way southwest of Cappidop Bay and it was not long before they came across a big long wall that goes around like a circle, enclosing the big castle and small buildings inside it.

'That is Morgan's Kingdom' Ned said, staring at the buildings behind the walls. 'And that is the avengers' base' he said, pointing at the huge dark brown castle.

'I never imagined it as a kingdom' Flyra said, feeling very nervous.

They were hiding behind some bushes and when a few soldiers passed by, that was when they realised that that was a bad hiding spot. Ned quickly and gently pulled Flyra back and lay down still.

'Thank you' Flyra said, she realised she should have waited to thank him. Her face was so close to Ned's. His arms around her, helping her get down, was warm and cozy. Ned managed a smile. For a few seconds their eyes met and stayed connected. Flyra had never felt more attracted to someone before. Flyra pulled away and Ned regained focus. He peeked over the bush, the soldiers were gone. They got up to a crouching position.

'Who are you looking for in there?' Ned asked the same question he did not get an answer earlier.

'Prince Edward and Princess Erieka' Flyra replied. Ned's face became shocked.

'What's wrong?' Flyra said, noticing he was just frozen in his shock expression.

'You're Princess Flyra of?'

'Combination'

Ned was lost for words.

'I… I am Prince Edward' Ned admitted. Now Flyra was frozen in shock.

'You… you lied to me?'

'I didn't. Ned is also me. Ned is me when I am wearing this' Ned held up his left hand with the silver bracelet. 'Because of this, I am weak. I am not the Edward I used to be. I can't spoil my name with my new self. So I created a new name'

Flyra was close to tears. Ned/Edward thought that he had made a terrible mistake of not telling the whole truth. But Flyra placed both of her hands on Edward's cheeks. Her gentle touch sent a static charge through his body. He had never felt more comfortable and attracted to someone before.

'I found you' Flyra cried tears of happiness. 'Your father misses you so much. He has been searching for you for twenty years. And I want to help him. And now he can finally meet his son' Flyra cried, feeling very happy. Edward can't help but let out tears as well. For ten years since he was abducted, before he gave up and accepted his fate, he too searched for ways to leave this place. And now someone's here to rescue him.

'Where's your sister?'

There was a short pause.

'I'm afraid she's lost forever. They had taught her and brainwashed her from the moment she was able to speak' Edward said, feeling very disappointed with himself. 'I failed to help her'

'You didn't. You were just a child. And you were powerless' Flyra reassured. She stepped in and hugged him.

'Flyra, are we siblings?' Edward asked, the awkward feeling was coming.

'No we're not' Flyra laughed.

'Oh great. That would have been weird' Edward said. The awkward feeling disappeared again.

'What would have been weird?'

'Nothing' Edward said quickly. He thought of how he was very attracted to Flyra from the moment he first saw her.

Flyra finally pulled away. They wiped their tears. Flyra cried the most. She straightened her scarf and dress.

'Alright, now let me lead you out of here' Flyra said, smiling happily. She extended her hand for Edward. He took it and she led him away from the base.

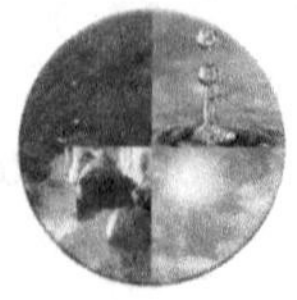

THE AVENGERS' BASE

Before you start reading the next chapter, finish what you're supposed to do first. Done? Carry on!

The team of five went through the obstacles with very little difficulty. They only needed to endure the cold of the frozen valley. Other than that, Princess Flyra had done a good job to clear their path ahead. The wingless dragon and his fire were still frozen. There's no telling how many hundred years or more it will stay frozen. Flyra hadn't just caused ice everywhere, she had changed the weather condition. They stepped into the snowy forest that was headed towards Cappidop Bay. Master Kitty immediately sensed something.

'There was a strong magic here' he said.

'Yes, we already know that Flyra did all this' Prince Jake said.

'No, someone else's' Kitty added. 'Someone with very high knowledge. His magic is almost invisible to sense'

'What gave it away?'

'Flyra. She kind of messed with the magic. Flyra has unimaginable powers which I can't explain much due to my lack of knowledge. But I know, even Marcala is no match for her. Even if she uses Majuza's amulet'

'So the magic that is almost invisible is Marcala's?' Bobby asked.

'Probably'

'That is not convincing' Jake said.

'But I said there was strong magic. Now it's gone. Don't ask me about that because I also don't know why. Let's just continue'

Kitty continued up ahead. He passed by what used to be the doorway to the trading village. Now it's obviously gone because like Master Nvago had said, the portal's going to change its location.

They continued walking for the next half hour until there was no more snow. They came across a few dead bodies lying on the grass belonging to Morgan's army. There were few splotches of blood on the grass and tree barks. The soldiers' swords were covered in blood as well and were lying in random places. Lillain almost vomited upon seeing them.

'What happened here?' she blurted out.

'This is not so bad. They suffered only a few cuts. Perhaps our friends passed by here, or some wild animal attacked' Dewi said. She came closer to inspect the wounds. 'I take that back, this is no wild animal attack'

Kitty winced at the word wild animal. He has never met one. He just couldn't imagine how any animal in Southernere can be so far from culture and magic that they became wild. Usually wild animals are Outlanders. Or those under the control of the avengers.

'And these are still fresh' Dewi continued. She

immediately looked around. Everyone understood the hint. Jake and Bobby drew their swords. Kitty stood in a ready position to pounce. Lillain summoned the tree roots to obey her commands. The roots grew up above the ground until they're the same height as them (except for Kitty, he's the shortest) and waited.

'Wait! It's just us!' Captain's high voice spoke as he came out from behind a large tree. Bale and Oliver followed.

'You guys?' Lillain said. 'What are you doing here?'

She sent the roots back into the ground. The others lower their weapons.

'You know them?' Jake said.

'Yes, they're my friends. Prince Edward used to play a lot with them'

'I remember, you guys also hang around with Flyra right?' Jake said.

'Yes' Captain replied.

'What are you doing here?' Lillain asked.

'We were with Flyangel and then…'

'Fly what?'

'Flyangel. Oh I mean Flyra, Princess Flyra'

'Nice name you got for her' Jake smiled.

'Then we got separated'

'How?' Lillain said.

'There were those men' Bale said, pointing to the dead bodies. 'There were four. They saw us and Princess Flyra asked us to run. We were separated since then. Two of them were chasing us, the other two chased Flyangel. But actually Oliver was not being chased. He helped me. Then more came. Then…'

'Very long story chipmunk. But we got the reason' Kitty said, a little bit annoyed. But he thanked them.

'Do you remember which direction she went? Please think carefully' Jake asked.

They thought for a while. Then Oliver spoke.

'We were facing Cappidop Bay. We know it because the smell of the ocean was getting stronger. She ran towards the left'

'She went west' Jake concluded.

The three of them joined the team and together all eight of them proceeded forward, turning a bit to the left every few minutes.

The more Prince Edward looked at her, the more he became mesmerised by her beauty. Princess Flyra is very beautiful regardless from any angle. She's the kind of person which, whatever face she does, happy, funny, sad, or even mad, she still looks pretty. She was sitting on the dining chair waiting for Edward as he was packing some items he wants to bring back to Combination.

'Is your sister really cannot be saved?' Flyra asked. She was still uncomfortable with the decision. She came here intending to bring back both. But she managed only one. She could see Edward in his room, inserting some items into his backpack. He stopped and looked up as she asked that question.

'Twenty years. She has been fed false knowledge for twenty years. I can't imagine she would even listen to reason' Edward said.

'You are not like that. What makes you so sure she's not like you?'

'I was brought here when I was eight. I was already able to think for myself back then. She was brought as a baby. Knows nothing except what has been taught since then'

Flyra kept quiet. She knows from the tone of Edward's voice, he was too upset to talk about it. Edward came out with his backpack on his shoulders. He made eye contact with her. She felt static charges on her skin even though he did not even touch her.

'How can I save her when I have given up on myself?' Edward said. Flyra's mind went blank. She suddenly has no idea what to say. Edward went to the kitchen to pack some food. Flyra scolded herself for not trying.

'Edward' Flyra called, ignoring her blanking brain. 'Let's go save your sister'

Edward kept the last packaging he intended to bring and turned to face Flyra.

'I am not the kid I used to be Flyra. I can't'

'You can't or you won't?'

'It doesn't matter! And I'm powerless!'

'Who says you need power to survive?!' Flyra snapped. This time her voice came out like a roar. And she was shocked about it herself.

'I'm sorry' she said. 'Edward, you don't need power. You don't need magic. You need you. You need to find yourself. You lost that, not your powers. Erieka lost that too. She lost that to the false knowledge given to her. And besides, you have me. Until we can find a way to get that bracelet removed, I shall be the power for both of us'

Edward felt enlightened by Flyra's words. There's no better way to deliver that message than how Flyra had done.

'Alright, let's go save your sister' Flyra said. The both of them headed out of the house. Edward carried the backpack and a sword. Flyra had changed into a more warrior type outfit earlier in the bathroom. Edward had given her a black pants, a long black sleeve shirt, and a dark green vest over it. Another layer of clothing covering it, a crystal-like blue medieval jacket or a coat. And she has a brown bow and quiver full of arrows on her back. She has the same light green headscarf, which she wore simply this time, and tucked into her shirt.

'How come you get all these items? I thought you were a prisoner here?' Flyra said.

They were walking back towards Morgan's Kingdom.

'Marcala doesn't care about me anymore. She doesn't care whatever I do because she knows there's no way I can leave this place. And because I'm powerless. So I obtained them from the castle. Just to collect or spend my time everyday sword fighting and stuff. About the ladies' clothing. Whenever Marcala has her associates come visit, my house is a guest house for them. That's why there are lots of ladies' and men's clothing hanging in the wardrobe' Edward replied.

'I see'

Flyra suddenly stopped in her tracks.

'What's wrong?' Edward asked.

'I sense someone's coming'

Flyra turned around to look. The sky was getting darker as the sun was setting. Soon the forest will be pitch dark. It will be harder to see.

'Flyra!' Lillain's voice, excited and relieved, came from the right. Flyra turned just as Lillain's arms surrounded her in a hug. Prince Jake, Master Kitty, Bobby, Dewi, and the three animals were behind.

'Flyra, we've been worried about you!' Lillain said.

Flyra was too surprised to speak what was in her mind.

'Why did you leave without telling? Father's worried sick!' Jake said.

'You… you guys followed me?' Flyra finally managed to say.

'Yes Princess Flyra, we can't leave you going off alone' Bobby said.

'I left a note, remember? And I've got my friends following me'

'Your father has fallen ill upon seeing that note'

'I didn't mean for that to happen' Flyra said, shocked.

'Hi Flyangel' Captain said suddenly.

'It's good to see you again' Flyra replied.

Before anyone could notice the stranger with Flyra, he has already stepped forward to reunite with his loved ones. He grew up and his face changed. But the others are quite similar only a bit older. So he easily recognised them.

'Bobby' Edward said. The others turned to look at the stranger. Flyra was smiling. She was so excited to reveal the stranger's identity but she kept it to herself. It will be even more exciting if the person himself revealed who he is. Bobby looked at Edward in confusion. He has no idea who this person is but the person seems to know about him. And Edward was smiling, longingly. Which might be creepy in some ways.

'I'm Edward'

Bobby's eyes widened in joy. He embraced him. The rest were happy to hear the good news as well. Flyra had found the lost prince. Master Kitty, Lillain, Dewi, and the three animals especially were most elated. After Bobby, the rest took turns hugging Edward. And lastly was Jake.

'Hi Prince Edward. I'm Jake, your brother' Jake said, extending his hand. Edward pulled him into a friendly hug.

'Jake, there's something you should know' Flyra said. 'We all aren't siblings'

Jake was confused.

'You and Nathan are. Edward and Erieka are. I'm alone. King Henry isn't our actual father. My mother was Lady Matilda of White Shore. Which makes King Henry my uncle. Half uncle. Your parents died in the attack in White Shore twenty years ago. We are just King Henry's adopted children' Flyra explained the truth. Only Jake was very shocked. And Edward was a little, now he knows his adopted siblings' origins.

'Which means, I am not of royal blood' Jake said.

'I'm sorry Jake. I had to tell the truth sooner than later'

'We were not supposed to let you three find out about this' Bobby said suddenly. 'Your father, King Henry never wanted you three to find out about the truth. He wants you to have a happy life' he said, referring to Flyra, Jake, and Nathan.

'That means I don't have to be king!' Jake suddenly exclaimed excitedly. The rest looked at him in confusion.

'I knew that I was never meant to rule. I knew

there must be a reason why King Henry looks so much different than me and my brother. Same as you…' Jake said, he pointed at Flyra when he said "you". 'Look so much different than any of us'

The happy reunion conversations continued until Kitty voiced out.

'I'm sorry to interrupt but we are missing the princess' he said.

'We were on our way to the castle to rescue her' Flyra replied.

'Castle?' Lillain said.

'The avengers' base' Edward said.

'Alright, count us in. I am so ready to give Widow a piece of my mind' Kitty said.

'She doesn't go by that name anymore' Edward said. His tone was filled with anger and resentment. Kitty understood why. Young Edward had had bad memories with her. Edward prefers to call her by Marcala, the already known evil. Rather than Widow, the hypocrite and a murderer of her own son, Master Jackenzie, Edward's favourite master.

'I'm sorry Edward, I know how much you've been through' Kitty said.

'That's okay. Let's go'

Edward led the way.

They arrived a few minutes later. The sky was already dark. The lights from the streets and buildings lit the surroundings. The castle was quite dark. Only a few rooms were lit.

'We should expect a huge fight' Kitty said.

'I don't think so' Jake observed the kingdom as best

he could from behind the walls. 'The castle is empty. Except probably the servants and some soldiers. I don't think the powerful avengers are around'

'How are you so sure? Don't let the lights fool you' Kitty replied.

'If I may say your highness, we need to take out those guards first' Bobby said, pointing to a group of guards patrolling the grounds, heading towards their direction.

'Allow me' Lillain said, stepping out of the bushes and shrubs to get a closer aim. The guards came closer and she swiped her hand up. The ground around the soldiers' feet break apart. Sand spouted upwards replacing the sinking grass. They started screaming for help but the sand was quicker. Soon only their heads were above ground, gasping for air over the struggle to get out. The sand was devouring them so quickly. And then, they were gone. The sand went back in and the grass came back out. Everything was back to the way it was.

'You could have shown them mercy at least' Flyra said.

'That's not what I saw happened to the dragon, or the bear' Lillain replied immediately. Flyra kept quiet. Lillain was right.

'But thank you by the way. You helped clear the path for us, even though you had no idea' Lillain said. Flyra held her hand in hers appreciatively.

'Alright, now let's get the guards at the gates and get inside the castle' Jake said.

There were only a few guards patrolling the gates, both on ground and in the two watchtowers on either side.

'They are really not good at defense' Lillain said.

'Either that or the avengers are not even home. And they brought an army with them to fight whatever business they're having' Bobby said.

'I am so ready to have a chat with my grandmother' Lillain said fiercely. 'More than a chat'

'Who's your grandmother?' Jake asked.

'Marcala'

Both Jake and Flyra were shocked.

'That's not something important or I should be proud of to go tell anyone' Lillain said. 'She killed my father, her own son. This is a long awaited moment for me'

'Lillain, you have been at peace for twenty years now. Don't let this sudden memory pull the dangerous desire out again. Darkness is not something to dwell about' Kitty advised. Lillain nodded her head in embarrassment, realising her mistake.

'Apologies master, let's go save Princess Erieka' Lillain said.

First, they took care of the guards in the watchtowers. There were about three soldiers watching out in each watchtower. Kitty controlled the wind around the watchtowers. He sent the wind blowing into the watchtowers from all directions, disabling them from moving. Flyra took her cue and added cold into the air. And soon, the wind was blowing frosts at the soldiers. The frosts turned to ice as they went in contact with the soldiers. Soon all of them were fully covered in ice.

'That's not mercy princess' Lillain whispered playfully. 'But it was impressive'

Flyra managed a warm smile. Then they took care of the six guards below. Lillain did her trick. Instantly, the surface area where all six soldiers were standing became soft and they sank underneath very quickly that their screams were only heard for a short while. They came out of cover (the bushes and trees) and headed to the closed gates. Kitty force-pushed the gates open. A street led all the way up to the castle, about four hundred metres ahead. Buildings on either side are utility buildings. There were a lot of work objects, bales of hay, carriages, barrels, and a lot of others to prove that there are no houses here. Except maybe the one long building behind a stable. It has windows but no other designs and decorations. Maybe those are the bunks for the soldiers and some avengers. The rest should be staying in the castle. The street was nearly empty, except a few old folks sweeping the grounds. They don't seem to notice the gates opening aggressively. Either that or they were just ignoring because the team was about to be ambushed. Flyra ran straight to the nearest old lady without thinking further.

'Flyra!' a few of them shouted at the same time. It was too late. But it wasn't totally unfortunate. The old lady just gave Flyra a creepy grin. Then she transformed into a beautiful young avenger. Soldiers came out of the buildings on both sides and stood in one line. They all were equipped with a bow and arrow. And they all aimed at Flyra. The ones closest to the gates, aimed their arrow at the team. The other two old folks apparently are real old people. Because as soon as the soldiers went out, they scurried away with their brooms fearfully. Should have ran to the other two instead, Flyra thought.

'Don't try anything funny princess. You're surrounded and alone' the avenger grinned.

'She's not alone' Kitty replied.

The avenger glanced behind Flyra and rolled her eyes.

'You are there and she's here. Our arrows can get her before you do' the avenger said.

'Try me?' Kitty said. For a few seconds, both of them started a staring contest. While that happened, no one realised Captain, Bale, and Oliver were sneaking up behind the soldiers. Oliver was alone on the left. Captain and Bale on the right. Captain and Bale started the distraction. Both of them suddenly jumped on one of the soldiers, pushing him to the ground. The heavy armour he was wearing helped. Then they started jumping up and down on the soldier's helmet. If he was still conscious after he fell, he was definitely not now. Some of the soldiers really got distracted and pointed their arrow at them instead.

'I'm a Sprite, and Sprites can radiate heat' Oliver told himself, standing and unseen behind one soldier. He summoned all his power intending to radiate heat from himself. At first it didn't seem to work. The avenger force-pushed Flyra backwards. Flyra fell and the avenger made sure she stays that way with her force.

'What nonsense is this?!' she exclaimed. It was clear that she was extremely annoyed. Captain and Bale had to stop whatever they were doing or Flyra would suffer. Oliver was starting to doubt himself when the soldiers in front of him started fidgeting. The fidgets turned to aggressive movements. They dropped their weapons and removed their helmets. Their faces were covered in sweat. It was working!

'What now?!' the avenger shouted, getting more angry. Soldiers on the opposite side started doing the same. Everyone else started to feel the heat. The team, quite a distance away could feel the heat already and they're not wearing any armour. The soldiers one by one died of heat exhaustion before the avenger could realise its source. Oliver stepped out of the porch happily, feeling very proud of himself.

'You!' the avenger yelled with a voice full of vengeance. While she was distracted, Flyra took the chance to attack her. From the lying position, she pushed her left palm forward. A wave of forcefield flung the avenger backwards. Flyra got up and quickly drew her bow. The avenger was quick too. But not as quick as Flyra. When the avenger was standing up, Flyra's arrow was already aimed right at her chest.

'You don't try anything funny' Flyra said, getting back at her. The avenger reluctantly raised both of her hands up in the air as a sign of surrender. Flyra was surprised. She didn't expect their fight to end that simple.

'You are alone. Marcala and the others are not here' Flyra said, realisation dawned on her. The avenger did not respond. She just kept showing a hatred face. The team went in and Bobby took initiative to apprehend the avenger. He let Dewi check on her for any sharp object or weapon in her possession.

'Where are the rest of you? Morgan's mighty army?' Jake asked demandingly.

'Answer the prince' Bobby said, tightening his grip on her arms.

'I do not need to answer you' the avenger replied stubbornly.

'You better' Lillain said and held her palm up in a "C" shape at the avenger's throat, force choking her.

'Lillain stop' Kitty reprimanded.

Lillain resisted the command. She told herself to force choke her with a stronger force. Suddenly a warm hand touched her sleeve. It was Edward's. He gave her a caring look. Her anger cooled down. She let go of the avenger's throat. The avenger gasped for air as she touched her throat with both hands.

'You are the real monsters!' the avenger shouted. Her voice came out hoarse this time.

'I'm sorry' Lillain said. She walked away briskly, disappointed with herself.

'I'll go after her' Dewi said. She walked away.

'You are all too late. Your princess went with them. She is one of us forever' the avenger said, smirking.

'What are you talking about?' Jake asked.

'Haven't you heard? Oh I know! You've been away from home for a long time' the avenger continued mocking them. 'Your Combination is going down. By this time I think even Barenge is defeated. Your princess, our successor, Erieka if you have no idea who I'm speaking of, she's in charge of the attack. All our victories are thanks to her. So dream on if you're planning to save her'

Edward physically went to her and grabbed her neck.

'Edward!' Kitty exclaimed alarmingly. Jake and Bobby helped to push Edward back gently. Bobby prised Edward's hands away from the avenger's neck.

'What's your name avenger?' Kitty asked, focusing straight to the point. He doesn't want anyone else to lose their anger and control and cause more damage.

'Myra' the avenger replied rudely.

'Alright Myra, you're going to send a message for us' Kitty said.

'You can't make me'

'Oh we can't! But we can use magic to make you' Kitty replied with sass. Myra was silent for a moment, realising she was losing.

'Let me go!' she screamed.

'Edward, would you like to do the honours of what message to be sent?' Kitty asked.

'My pleasure' Edward said, smiling at Myra. Bobby and Jake restrained her more firmly as Kitty touched her leg with one paw. And the other paw, Edward held it. As Edward began to speak his message, Kitty led the message flow through him and into Myra's mind by magic. If he could reach Myra's head, that would have been better for him. The message won't have to go through the joints in the legs, then the body, before reaching the head. But he's just a cat. He can't reach that high and it will waste more time for Bobby and Jake to lay her down on the ground plus restraining her.

'Marcala, Morgan, Alphaga, all avengers. Edward is speaking. And for your annoyance, I have been reunited with my family. My real family. And we have taken over your kingdom. Morgan's Kingdom. You have taken Combination. But just remember, that we have friends there which you no longer have here. And I promise, we won't rest until Combination is safe once again from your hands. We still have friends and allies from other cities which you don't have the strength to conquer yet. You have provoked the peace, and thus declared war. To Erieka, my sister, I know you can make the right choices. It's never too late to turn back' Edward delivered his message. Kitty passed the message through and let go of both, hand and leg after the magic was done.

'You got the message in me. No way I'm delivering them' Myra said.

'Oh you'll see' Kitty said, mockingly. He stared into Myra's eyes. When she realised what he was trying to do, she wanted to turn away or look up but she couldn't resist.

'You shall deliver Edward's message to Combination. You shall deliver the message to the avengers' Kitty said every word carefully.

'I shall deliver Edward's message to Combination. I shall deliver the message to the avengers' Myra repeated the sentences almost like a robot.

'Now go' Kitty said. He released his stare. Bobby and Jake released their grips. Myra transformed into a black bird and soared into the night sky.

'That works?' Jake asked, amazed.

'It does. It was easy because she was already staring at every one of us' Kitty said.

'Let's take shelter in the castle and turn this place light and bright' Jake suggested.

'That is definitely a must. Since Edward has officially declared a war with them. We need a base' Kitty said.

'They declared it first by their actions' Edward said, defending himself.

'I know, I'm just joking with you my prince' Kitty smiled.

Seeing him happy reminded Edward of old times. Then he remembered Master Mousy.

'Where's Mousy?' he asked.

'Marcala did something to her. A curse or something' Kitty replied.

'We'll get everyone back' Edward said, reassuringly.

'There's the optimistic prince I remember' Kitty said, smiling more warmly. He missed the old times. He missed teaching and playing with his student. Now he was all grown up. He had missed him growing up. He had missed countless lessons he could have taught him more tricks. Thinking further, what about King Henry. His own father. He had missed his own son growing into a handsome man. His teenage life. His problems. But what's important now is what is ahead. Kitty can spend time with him now to make up for the past. But first, everyone needed to rest.

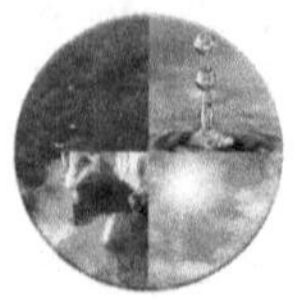

FALLING OF BARENGE

Before you start reading the next chapter, finish what you're supposed to do first. Done? Carry on!

A few hours ago, when the sun was about to go downwards. Barenge was under attack by Erieka and Lydia leading their men past the broken walls. Erieka has her headscarf back on properly. Both of them with a group of ten avengers sent powers like fireballs and electricity that finally got the wall down. The musketeers on the battlements of the wall worked very hard to defend. They shot their arrows from bows and crossbows, and threw magical powders that explode upon contact. But the battlements were then destroyed. Squads of musketeers came rushing out of the barracks. They aimed their crossbows and bows at The Outlands soldiers now making their way into the city through the broken wall. Most were killed. But there were too many soldiers. The first few rows went down when the soldiers killed them with their swords. The crossbows and bows were only strong enough to prevent two or three strikes. But then, the sword managed to cut through and killed them. Barenge's elite soldiers and knights came marching out of the barracks. Two-third of the knights were cavalry. About minutes passed and Barenge was doing well for a huge army with magic that was storming into their city. They still managed to hold them at the wall. No one can get past the cavalries yet. And they're just behind the musketeers. King Jonathan and his elite musketeers joined the battle with the royal master by his side. He and the royal master got magic on their side. But the ten avengers with Erieka and Lydia were a magical combination they cannot match.

At the Unity Square in front of the castle steps, Queen Alice and Princess Darleen, assisted by some of Barenge's soldiers, were leading the ladies, children and senior citizens away from the chaos. The Unity Square was not far from the broken wall. At least seven buildings away. The sound of the battle was a nightmare, especially to the children.

Back at the wall, four of the avengers had started to go in. They transformed into black birds and flew swiftly away from the fight. They landed in the Unity Square and back to their human forms. The people started screaming as the avengers conjured fire and other magic. The fireballs and other attacks sent by the avengers were deflected by the warriors' shield or sword. Queen Alice was led away by some of the elite musketeers up the steps and into the castle. The rest stayed behind with Princess Darleen to fight. She received a sword from one of the warriors.

'On me!' Darleen shouted. The warriors and elite musketeers got ready for charge. Ten warriors, five elite musketeers, and a brave princess, the four avengers did not stand a chance. The avengers were separated. The good thing is, they're all standing alone. The bad thing is, there's more than one area of target.

'Now!' Darleen exclaimed and she was the first to run to the nearest avenger. The avenger threw fireballs at her but Darleen successfully deflected it with her sword. The fireballs went in other directions like into a tree and burnt it. Two avengers went down not long later. Darleen went to assist the warriors dealing with the other two. From Bowman Road on the castle's right, which led to the back areas of the city, came two groups of masters. The first group of ten masters immediately killed the two avengers and proceeded ahead to join the battle. The second group of three masters-in-training went to help the princess as she checked on buildings and houses that still have citizens inside.

Inside the castle, Queen Alice was writing a few letters to warn the other cities of The Inlands. She folded them and attached each letter to a raven's foot. Every castle has a post chamber where the ravens who delivered messages rest before they were tasked to send another letter.

'Please be safe' Alice told all the ravens. They flew out the chamber's opening. It was specifically designed for that reason. She then headed to the castle's armoury and took a crossbow off one of the hooks. She was ready to fight.

At the wall, things were starting to get really bad. Erieka herself was marching in with Lydia right by her side. She was unarmed. But that was just a lie. Her powers plus the amulet can bring a city down in less than a day. And that's what she intended to do. The cavalries and the knights were dying. Now it was the elite soldiers' turn to defend all they can. They are already about four buildings away from the wall. Three more to go before the Unity Square. King Jonathan and the elite musketeers were retreating just as the ten masters joined in. The six avengers behind grinned happily as they saw them. Finally someone worth fighting with. The Outlands soldiers continued forward as the last of the Knights went down. Barenge's elite soldiers took their cue. Those of the soldiers who are SHAWs managed to survive longer. Other than that, mostly Erieka's magic killed them. She was already using her amulet. Every step she took towards the castle, the amulet glowed brighter. And with every glow, a magical force was released, throwing Barenge's troops backwards and rallying The Outlands soldiers. The avengers and masters took their fight to another street on the right. The streets are now empty, thanks to Darleen and the citizens who took initiative to help. The citizens are all gathered at the back areas of the city. So the masters went all out in their defenses and attacks. They didn't care about the buildings and objects destroyed in the battle. At first the six avengers were winning against ten masters. It wasn't a fair match for the avengers but they're still winning. One master died after a fireball burnt him. Then the three masters-in-training came and helped. Princess Darleen and the elite musketeers and warriors arrived as well. The musketeers shot their arrows, careful not to shoot the masters duelling the avengers. Princess Darleen and the warriors bravely went closer and attacked with their swords. The avengers defended with magic. But the sword strikes were faster than their magical reflexes and a few avengers went down. Three avengers left. Suddenly Erieka stepped onto the street. Lydia followed behind. She released a magical force. Her amulet glowed brightly as it happened. The dead avengers rose. The dead master rose as well. But now, the master was fighting for the enemy.

'We need to get that amulet' Darleen told her warriors. The battle continued. This time, the masters and Barenge's troops could not make a difference in the enemy's. The avengers stood stronger than before. The dead were even stronger. It was like they got back alive and wanted revenge so they did better.

Back at the other street, Barenge's army was retreating back more and more. They were a few metres away from the Unity Square.

'Fall back! Regroup at the circle' King Jonathan ordered. He and his men retreated and regrouped in front of the castle steps. The Outlands soldiers advanced.

'For Barenge! For Inland!' Jonathan rallied his men and they charged back again at the soldiers.

Queen Alice arrived at the masters' battle. She went inside a two-storey building. It was a bakery with a house on top. The house door was already open. She went in, checked for enemies hiding, and went to the window. She could see the battle going on below. She inserted an arrow and aimed the crossbow at Erieka. She fired the arrow. The arrow flew swiftly towards Erieka's chest. A translucent shield suddenly appeared around her and deflected the arrow. The arrow went in forcefully into a master's chest instead. The shield then went back to being invisible. Alice stared at what just happened in shock. Erieka was already finding where the arrow came from. Alice hid quickly behind the wall before she could be seen. But it was too late.

'Queen Alice! How nice of you to join us!' Erieka's voice was projected loud and clear. The fight paused for a second as everyone got distracted. Darleen looked at the buildings around. Her mother is in one of these buildings. She needs to find her before Erieka does.

'Distract the avenger with the amulet. Get that amulet if possible' Darleen instructed the warriors. She went into the nearest building. A bakery store, but different from Alice's. She ran up the stairs to the second floor. Of course, Alice wasn't there. She went to the window and observed closely all the windows on the opposite side. A fireball came crashing into the window where she was standing. If Darleen had stood openly, she could have died. The heat burnt the right side of her arms and face. She uttered a yelp as she staggered backwards. She rushed back downstairs. As she exited the bakery, she saw another arrow shot into the chest of an avenger. She traced it back to where it possibly came from. She entered another bakery. This time, she found her mother on the second level, ready to shoot another arrow. The arrow was released and hit another avenger. Two avengers went down. And the same two stood back up joining the army of the dead.

'Mother' Darleen called, walking quickly towards her. Alice went back to hiding behind the wall.

'Sweetheart!' Alice exclaimed in shock. 'What happened to you?!'

She looked at Darleen's burnt half, trying not to touch them.

'You weren't careful!' Alice scolded softly. Tears were forming in her eyes.

'Mother, it's okay'

'We won't be able to win. They are too strong. With the amulet on their side, none of us can defeat them' Alice said.

'Mother. We have to survive. I need you to leave Barenge, get help. You have many friends from the other cities'

'We don't deserve help. Combination was attacked and we did nothing. We only cared to strengthen our forces and that was worthless'

'Mother, the other cities, Trisnarim, they're far from here. They might have not yet received messages of The Outlands attacking. We need to warn them'

'I already did. I wrote letters to Trisnarim, Silverside and Arstar. The ravens should reach all cities by midnight'

Darleen hugged her mother on her left side. Carefully not to make contact with her right. She could still feel her right side burning very painfully.

'I need you to leave Barenge' Alice said, pulling away. A tear rolled down her left cheek.

'What?!'

'Listen, you must do as I say. Leave Barenge. Find Princess Flyra. Find her, there are rumours that she wasn't in Combination when they attacked. She's known as a child of the seed of Gratultyn. She's the key to defeating the amulet. There's no time to waste. Please, leave us' Alice said, tears continuously rolled down her cheeks.

'I won't leave you! I will lose all my family!' Darleen was also starting to cry.

'Your dad was wrong to break the alliance. Don't forget Darleen, King Henry, his children are your family as well. All Inlanders, we are brothers and sisters. Children of Sofya. For the good of Inland. You must find Flyra. Tell her what is happening. Help her to win this war'

Darleen wept. She hugged her mother fully this time. The burns felt like needles were poked into every corner as she went into contact. But she didn't care. This was most probably the last time she'll be seeing her mother. Her father. There was no time left to meet him. But she has a duty. Duty to her bigger family. To her nation. For Inland. She pulled away quickly. Staying longer will make her hate leaving even more. She took one last look at her mother as she was aiming her crossbow at another target. The fight was still going on below. But when Darleen exited the bakery. It was obvious the avengers were winning. Only a few masters and musketeers left. All the warriors were dead. But there were no more dead people standing up. Maybe Erieka did not need them anymore since the masters were dying. Darleen turned away from the fight. She ran to the other street which was where the battle started earlier. The fight with the king was nowhere in sight. But the sound was probably somewhere at the castle steps or even inside. She ran to the broken wall. She looked around carefully just in case any Outlanders stayed behind to kill anyone escaping. No one. She ran out. The city's main entrance was not far away. But she's not going to follow that road. The road will make her more visible to the enemy. She ran straight to the nearest forest, a hundred metres away from the wall. Thinking where to go was not important now. Getting out of here alive and far away as possible is the main priority.

THE KING'S DEATH

Before you start reading the next chapter, finish what you're supposed to do first. Done? Carry on!

Erieka returned to Combination alone. The battle in Barenge was a success. Lydia, a few other avengers and the soldiers stayed to rule the new city under their control. King Jonathan and Queen Alice were killed. The king died in battle and the queen was executed in the aftermath. The citizens were forced to go back to their homes and help the avengers get whatever they want whenever they want them to. Some who are loyal to the king and Inland were tortured and others were killed. Only the children were spared.

Marcala was already standing at the top of the castle steps, waiting for her.

'Barenge?'

'Victory' Erieka replied, feeling very satisfied. She walked past her into the castle. The main entrance doors were wide open.

'Erieka' Marcala called before she could get out of sight. She turned to face her. 'Your father is waiting'

'No he's not'

'Go and meet him' Marcala said firmly. Erieka knows the limit. When Marcala has started using that tone of voice, there's no more fooling around. She obeyed and proceeded to the dungeons. The cells were always empty, except only a few criminals. Now all ten cells were full of people. And the arrangements were messy. No one can tell at a single glance where the king was. It's all mixed up. Everyone braced themselves, they didn't know what to expect from the successor. She finally spotted him in the same cell as Master Mousy and many other king's guards. He was lying on the very small bench. There's only one bench for each cell. And it is not comfortable at all. She approached the cell, third from the right. Between each cell is a small walkway. Metal bars covered three sides of the square. The fourth side is a wall with no window or opening since they were underground.

'Hello' Erieka began awkwardly. 'Henry'

'What do you want?' Mousy asked sternly.

'Shut up rat' Erieka said.

'I'm a mouse!' Mousy conjured sand to pile on her palm and she swirled it on the spot.

'Your magic can't reach me from in there, let alone hurt me' Erieka mocked her.

'Her magic can't but a sword can' one of the king's guards said. He drew his sword and jabbed it through the bars. A translucent shield appeared as he made contact with the sword. A forcefield repelled the sword, throwing it and the user backwards. The guard crashed onto his buddies and they all fell down. Erieka laughed, feeling very amused.

'The cell is not just sealed with anti-magic, idiot. We are not stupid to leave you in a cell with weapons without sealing it with anti-metal as well' Erieka said happily. 'Henry!' Erieka called again.

King Henry suddenly sat up. He was asleep earlier. His eyes proved that he was really tired.

'What do you want with him? He's still sick and needs rest!' one of the castle servants who was also in the same cell spoke.

'You are in no place to speak to me!' Erieka yelled. A lot of people flinched as Erieka's powerful voice sent a wave of fear throughout the dungeons.

'That's alright. I'm alright' King Henry reassured the servant. 'What do you want from me?'

'Just to talk' Erieka said. She was still feeling a bit awkward that her father was just in front of her. A father she always imagined meeting one day. Everyone looked at her like she had just said the most ridiculous thing in the world.

'Talk?' Henry asked, just in case he heard wrongly.

'Yes, talk' Erieka said. 'We have met before. In a different situation'

'I'm sorry, but I don't know you'

To be honest, Erieka actually felt hurt.

'You lost a daughter twenty years ago' Erieka said, her tone rising but she was still holding back.

'Yes I do. And all because of you and your people' Henry said. He was holding back tears.

'I was only one twenty years ago! I have nothing to do with this! You did a poor job of taking care of your children! You failed!'

'That's enough!' Prince Nathan said. He was in another cell, second from the left.

'You didn't tell him?' Erieka turned to look at him.

'Shouldn't you do it yourself. Why must I say something that is such a big disappointment?' Nathan said.

'You watch your mouth!' Erieka exclaimed.

'Who are you?' Mousy asked. Erieka turned her attention back to her father's cell.

'I am Princess Erieka, true heir to the throne' Erieka said. Everyone in the room that had not learnt that yet was shocked. Henry's legs felt like jelly. He couldn't move a limb. Mousy was equally the same. She staggered backwards for a second before regaining her strength and remained standing.

'I have proof' Erieka said. She lifted up just a little bit of her scarf to show Henry her neck. The amulet hung from her neck, glowing normally. 'You know who could break the seal and release the power within. A Helaze of royal blood. Who else fits that description? No one but me'

Henry couldn't hold back his tears anymore. His long lost daughter was right in front of him. Only now, she's not who he imagined would grow up to be like. She was on the enemy's side. In fact their leader. Majuza's successor who could break the amulet's seal and then use the power within.

'My sweet Erieka. What happened to you?' Henry cried.

'Your failure happened! But don't worry father.

Brother is still on your side. But he's weak. So I'm still a far better child'

'Erieka, the avengers are evil people' Mousy said. Now that she knows who this rude lady is, she softened her tone.

'Suddenly a nice mouse? The avengers may do evil things but Sofya's children are blinded from the truth. Sofya is the true evil' Erieka said.

'Okay if you want me to believe that, what proof do you have? What proof do all avengers have?' Mousy said.

'I don't need proof for the truth. The truth shall be revealed when the time is right'

Erieka left. Immediately afterwards, King Henry started to feel pain in the chest. He was very heartbroken. He placed his hands on his chest while breathing hard.

'Your majesty?' Mousy said. 'Help! Erieka come back! Your father needs medical assistance immediately!'

'Use your magic' one servant said.

'I am not that skilful. And there's no magic which can mess with a heart. His having a heart attack'

'Help!'

A few servants started calling for help to help their king. The soldiers started too.

'Shut up all of you!' an Outland soldier stood at the stairway. He came from upstairs and the commotion actually worked. Everyone became silent.

'Help! The king needs help!' Mousy shouted. The soldier came running to the cell.

'I'll inform Marcala' the soldier ran out again.

'No no wait!' Mousy called but he was too fast.

King Henry was already lying on the ground. His

hands over his chest. He was in deep pain. Mousy placed her palm facing his chest and tried using magic. Nothing happened except Henry kept on wincing from the pain.

'We need help!' Mousy yelled, getting frustrated. Marcala came and the dungeon became more silent than before. If more quiet than silence is possible, this is how it was like. She went to King Henry's cell.

'Please, Widow, help him' Mousy pleaded.

'Has Erieka came to meet him?' Marcala asked.

'Yes, now he needs help!'

'Then let him die. He's no longer needed'

'No! Help him!' Mousy yelled. She got up to the bars and banged on it. The translucent shield appeared everytime she hit it.

'Why would I do something that doesn't benefit me or the avengers? This insolent behaviour is not helping you'

Marcala walked away.

'Come back! Help him!'

'With the king dead, we can officially crown a new queen. Long live Queen Erieka' Marcala turned to face her and said, amused. She then continued up the stairs. Mousy gave up. She was already exhausted from all the shouting. She went back to the king's aid. Henry was not moving anymore. His eyes were closed. And his chest was not moving up or down. Mousy removed his hands gently away from the chest and placed her ear over it. There was no heartbeat.

'He's gone' she said, tears forming up. All the king's guards, from the other cells as well, went down on their knees if space was possible, and bowed their heads at the king in respect. Mousy wiped a tear and snuffled.

'Farewell Henry, son of Harry, father of Edward and Erieka, King of Combination. May you have found peace in your life before' Mousy said. And she started crying softly afterwards.

OFFICIAL DECLARATION OF WAR

Before you start reading the next chapter, finish what you're supposed to do first. Done? Carry on!

A black bird landed at the top of the castle steps and transformed into a lady, Myra. The Outlands soldiers guarding the castle doors straight away opened them for her. She did not say anything or even look at them. Her eyes were fixed forward like she has a motive and intends to do it anyway possible. She stepped inside and paused for a while. She tilted her head up a little and her eyes moved like she was sensing. Sensing for someone's position.

'Avenger, is everything alright?' one of the soldiers asked. Myra did not answer, she continued walking and turned right towards the east wing at the end of the hallway.

Marcala and Erieka were sitting in the lounge with Alphaga hopping about the room. They were having some sort of an interaction time. Erieka talked about how fun it was in Barenge. How she threw a fireball at Queen Alice at the execution post. Alphaga was too bored hearing someone else bragged especially when he couldn't. Then Morgan came in with Pertum behind him carrying a tray of metal jug and five cups.

'I brought coffee instead' Morgan said.

'You mean I brought' Pertum replied. Morgan gave him a look of "don't test me".

'Why do you need to carry that? Use your magic you silly little man' Marcala said.

'Once in a while, it's good to not use magic' Pertum said. 'It's like taking a break'

'Talk about good, boring!' Alphaga scoffed. He dragged the "boring". 'Too much good and you'll turn out like these Inlanders. They think they're so right. They can't even accept the truth!'

A pause.

'Coffee?' Morgan broke the silence. He passed around cups and asked Pertum to pour the coffee.

Suddenly the room door opened and Myra came in.

'Myra!' Marcala said. Everyone was surprised.

'Shouldn't you be back at the base?' Marcala asked with suspicion.

'Marcala, Morgan, Alphaga, all avengers. Edward is speaking. And for your annoyance, I have been reunited with my family. My real family. And we have taken over your kingdom. Morgan's Kingdom. You have taken Combination. But just remember, that we have friends there which you no longer have here. And I promise, we won't rest until Combination is safe once again from your hands. We still have friends and allies from other cities which you don't have the strength to conquer yet.

You have provoked the peace, and thus declaring war. To Erieka, my sister, I know you can make the right choices. It's never too late to turn back' Myra said with intonation exactly like how Edward did.

'How is he able to do this? His magic is disabled for twenty years now' Alphaga said in disbelief.

'He got help. He mentioned he's been reunited with his family. Use your brain Alphaga. The main matter is they threatened us. Now this is officially war' Marcala said.

'Great!' Alphaga exclaimed excitedly. He was already imagining all the creative ways he's going to kill the enemy.

'Duty Alphaga. Not fun. Duty' Marcala said.

'So when do we meet and where?' Erieka asked like an attentive student.

'First, we reply to their message' Marcala replied. She glanced at Myra with distaste. 'Such low skill magic'

She swiped her hand in Myra's direction and instantly, she fell out of her trance.

'Marcala! Successor! I... I'm sorry' Myra said nervously.

'Off you go' Marcala dismissed her. 'I'll write a letter. Just prepare for war. They have no idea what's coming to them'

Marcala walked away confidently towards the post chamber. She took a piece of paper, dipped the quill in ink and started writing. Then she attached the rolled letter to a raven's foot and sent it to Morgan's Kingdom.

The letter arrived less than half an hour later. The

castle in Morgan's Kingdom was already secured. The only other people there left were the old folks who were the servants of Morgan. The raven found Edward in the living room with the fireplace. He was catching up with Bobby, Lillain and Dewi. The others were probably washing up or cleaning. The raven landed on the tea table in front of the couch.

'What does it say?' Lillain asked when Edward detached the letter and unrolled it. Edward read it out loud.

'Dearest Edward. We accept your threats and we will be ready when you are. Meet us on the battlefield. The field of the first war. Three days from now. Prepare your best, because we will, and we're ready to enjoy your suffering when you face ours. Love Master Widow'

Edward crushed the paper and threw it into the fire. The fire erupted.

'You okay?' Lillain asked. She went to sit beside him. Edward nodded his head, he was controlling his anger.

'Edward, did you see that?' Dewi said. Her expression showed she was very amazed.

'I saw your highness' Bobby said. 'Your powers. You may not be able to use powers to your maximum or whenever you want to because of that cursed bracelet. But I think you can still use them in some ways. You were angry, that caused the fire to react that way'

'I can't give in to anger. Everyone who does will end up with dark magic' Edward said.

'Maybe anger is not the only way my prince' Bobby said. Edward smiled.

'What's funny?'

'No, it's just, for twenty years I've forgotten the ways of royalty. I'm not a prince, no one calls me your highness here' Edward said.

Princess Flyra, Prince Jake, Master Kitty, Captain, Bale, and Oliver came to join them. They told them about the letter.

'The Alhora field' Kitty said after hearing the description of the location.

'And we got three days to be ready' Lillain said.

'We'll do all we can. For the good of Inland' Flyra said.

Lastly, Edward said, 'Together'.

PART 6

THE BATTLE OF ALHORA

THE PREPARATIONS

Before you start reading the next chapter, finish what you're supposed to do first. Done? Carry on!

With the war coming, Southernere was not getting anymore peaceful. Not even the furthest of the lands. All three remaining independent cities had received the warning letter sent by Queen Alice. Not long later, word of the avengers going to war with the few people on Edward's team, spread very quickly. Both avengers and the team made full use of the two full days they have to train and seek people to join them. The avengers however did an extra job. They made the lives of Combination citizens worse than any nightmare.

In one day, the avengers had managed to influence the people of Waterfront town to join their army. Many freelance soldiers from anywhere agreed to join as well. It was obvious to them which was the winning side. Marcala and Alphaga did not only seek help from people. Beasts and animals that have always hated Sofya's family were being seeked as well. By the morning of the second day, Combination was overrun with many different soldiers and creatures. No citizen dared to leave their homes. They could only hope that one day, they could be free from this misery.

Up north, the team was focusing more towards training. Their group was not big enough to cover all of Southernere and seek people to join them before the avengers do. But two missions were agreed to be completed before the second day. First mission, Prince Edward was to head out and find Master Nvago so that he can help remove the cursed bracelet from his wrist. Bobby followed him. The second mission was, Princess Flyra was to head to all three cities that were still standing strong, Arstar, Silverside, and Trisnarim, with Master Kitty and Prince Jake following. They were to seek help from them to join the war. Arstar was chosen as the first destination because the city was the farthest from Combination for the avengers to reach. Going to Silverside and Trisnarim first would be suicide. Silverside is just miles southwest of Combination. Trisnarim is even further down and must cross water to reach. Lillain, Dewi, and the three animals stayed behind to protect their new base. And they were hopeful too, just in case anyone came to help and join the war. Master Kitty had removed the dimensional shield that hid the base from the land. This way, anyone in need of help can approach, that is if they know that the avengers were no longer staying here.

A raven arrived in the afternoon of the first day

with a letter from Combination. It delivered news of King Henry's death.

'This is very terrible news' Dewi said. The other four were already in tears. Dewi was the least among them who knows about King Henry. But she loves him very much. She sees him as a father figure. A kind man who provided her a home in the castle twenty years ago. Even though she was a stranger from an unknown land at that time.

'They are doing this on purpose' Lillain scowled. 'They know for sure when Edward, Flyra, Jake, everyone here receives this message, it'll bring everyone down. That's what they want'

'We can't let a few words bring us down!' Dewi said.

'Then hide the letter!' Lillain suggested desperately. She stuck her hand out, gesturing for Dewi to give her the letter. 'We must not let them know'

Dewi stared at her in disbelief. Lillain's sudden desperation and wild suggestion was unbelievable.

'We can't do that!' Captain argued.

'Yes we can. They'll eventually find out when we win back Combination' Lillain said.

Again more unbelievable words that came out of Lillain's mouth.

'Lillain, listen to yourself. This isn't you!' Dewi said.

'Then what is?!' Lillain snapped. Her voice was projected so loud and powerful that it reached every room in the castle. Dewi instantly took one step back, feeling that she would fall if she didn't. Upon seeing that, Lillain seemed to snap out of a trance.

'I'm sorry. I... I lose control again' Lillain cried.

'You don't have to apologise Lillain' Dewi said. Interlocking her fingers with Lillain's. 'I'm your friend. And I am not being a good friend if I don't care about you and let you fall into the darkness'

'Thank you Dewi' Lillain said, she let go of Dewi's hands to wipe her tears.

'Now, we can't hide the news from our friends. We have to tell them'

Lillain nodded her head obediently.

'Okay, now I have to go and pray. I'll be right back' Dewi said and walked away.

'I don't understand her' Captain said. 'I've noticed, there are days that she prays, whatever she calls it, and there are days that she didn't. Why's that?'

'That's something you won't understand unless you're a woman and have periods' Lillain said. 'She can't pray when she's having them'

'Okay, understood' Captain replied immediately.

'I really hope our friends are doing well with their mission' Lillain said.

Just then, there were a few loud bangs on the castle doors. They all looked at each other with worry. Lillain went to check. The three animals following behind. She opened the door and saw Princess Darleen standing there, a little bit of dirt here and there on her dress. Her headscarf was loose, revealing parts of her brown hair. By her facial expression, even a child could tell that she was extremely tired and she had faced many problems on her way here.

'Princess Darleen!' Lillain exclaimed, very surprised.

'Lillain, Help me' Darleen managed to say weakly

before she collapsed. Lillain caught her before she hit the ground and brought her to the living room. Dewi walked into the room.

'Princess Darleen?' Dewi said. 'What happened?'

'She just came. I don't know' Lillain replied.

They did not have to wait long. Darleen became conscious again seconds later. She sat up on the couch.

'What happened? We thought you were dead. We heard the avengers attacked Barenge' Lillain said.

'I escaped. I left' Darleen said, and her voice broke. She was about to cry. 'I left my parents to die. Mother asked me to leave, find Princess Flyra. And I know from how the attack was going, Barenge would fall. And it did'

'It's alright Darleen, it's alright. You're safe here' Dewi said. She sat beside her and comforted her.

'We will take back our home'

'Darleen, Queen Alice asked you to find Flyra?' Lillain asked.

'Yes, she said there was news that Flyra was missing. Flyra is very important. She's the key to defeating the amulet the new avenger is wearing. To defeat the avengers' Darleen explained.

Lillain exchanged sad looks with Dewi when Darleen mentioned, "the new avenger".

'Darleen, there's something you need to know about the new avenger. She's your niece, Princess Erieka' Lillain said.

Darleen was speechless. She was very shocked.

'She was raised by Marcala for twenty years. She is now on Marcala's side. Fortunately Edward did not fall for her teachings. Edward is on ours'

'My niece is evil?' Darleen murmured. She could not believe what she had just heard, nor could she accept it. 'She burnt me'

They noticed her burnt half. Her once beautiful face, half of it was now burnt. That will leave a permanent mark.

'You need to wash up' Dewi said, helping her up. 'Let me help'

Dewi brought her away to one of the rooms.

'Everything is just getting worse!' Oliver grumbled.

'We need hope Oliver. Let's stay positive. Negativity won't help. It might lead me back to the darkness again' Lillain said.

Prince Edward and Bobby were reaching the frozen valley of sorrows. The air was already very cold. But the trading village was nowhere to be seen.

'Princess Flyra already reminded us that the village has shifted its place. We are wasting time my prince' Bobby said.

'Bobby, just checking is worth the risk of wasting time. Now we know for sure. May you suggest where we look next?' Edward replied.

'Definitely not here your highness, the air is getting colder. It's more unbearable than the last time we were here. Head back west, then we turn southwards'

'Lead the way'

They retraced their steps until Edward's old small house was in sight. Then they headed south. About some time later, Edward could sense dark magic not far ahead.

'I think we should change direction' Edward said.

Bobby did not intend to argue but he was curious. So he looked at Edward questioningly.

'I am sensing dark magic in the air' Edward said.

'Alright, let's head west now' Bobby said. As they changed their route, they saw something up ahead that was not naturally there. A mountain of it, as tall as the trees. Dead bodies were piled up in a small clearing of the forest. The stench of the corpses was overwhelming.

'Oh my' Bobby murmured.

'I think I know where we are' Edward said, pinching his nose. 'We're close to Barenge. That means, we're in The Inlands. Those inhuman treatments were the works of the avengers. Those are most likely the people of Barenge'

Bobby could no longer stand it, he started covering his mouth and nose as well.

'Let's quickly move away, we do not want any avenger to suddenly spot us here' Edward suggested. They took the longer way around the mountain of corpses.

Soon, they were far away from the stench's reach.

'Your highness, do we even know what we're looking for?' Bobby asked. The thought of a shifting trading village with fake people was starting to sound crazy.

'We just need to find signs or sense magic, light magic. Flyra mentioned that the master who guards the village is one of The Fifteen. Whatever that is. I asked her but she doesn't even know what is, The Fifteen. But it definitely has something to do with light magic' Edward said.

'Southernere is a huge island, your highness…'

'Bobby, as long as we're out here, and I am not yet officially crowned prince, just call me Edward'

'Right, your high… I mean Edward' Bobby said uncomfortably. Edward patted his shoulder and continued walking.

'We don't have magic with us to travel fast or quickly sense the magic. But we'll do our best. I just got the feeling we're close' Edward said.

Further north, Princess Flyra, Prince Jake, and Master Kitty were travelling fast, a few kilometres away from the imaginary border line that separates The Inlands and The Outlands. Master Kitty had transformed into a white bird. He transformed Flyra and Jake as well because Flyra didn't know how to and Jake has no magic. They took a few minutes to adjust to the wings and flying before flying away from Morgan's Kingdom. They were a few miles away from Arstar. They just have to fly over the extended side of the Waterfront Lake.

By the end of the early afternoon of the first day, they arrived in Arstar. They landed in front of the long steps to The Grand Palace. The royal grounds of Arstar were much bigger than the royal grounds of Combination. In fact, it was the biggest royal ground among all the big cities of Inland. Everything was grand. The city was so big that they have more than enough citizens to employ for jobs. Because of that, the palace has so many servants that every corner of it was constantly clean, even the outside. A roundabout goes from the entrance gates and around the grand fountain in the centre. Long steps led all the way up to the huge double doors. The building was rectangular. It's structure did not seem to come from this era. Almost all the structures in Arstar seemed to come from somewhere or sometime else. Tall windows arranged in symmetrical on the sides of the palace. Trees decorated the garden and grassy areas around the grounds. The palace was built on a hill, that was why the long steps. Hence, the garden was built to fit around it. The garden was unique because unlike all the other gardens from other castles and palaces, The Grand Palace's garden was sloping, taking the shape of the hill.

Princess Flyra, Prince Jake, and Master Kitty were greeted the moment they transformed back to themselves. Like there were many servants, there were also many soldiers deployed to guard the palace. Arstar's special unit is called the guards. They were dressed very smartly just like the servants. That made Flyra ponder, how is their armour or war uniform like. The guards greeted them in a very courteous manner.

'Welcome to Arstar your highnesses. I believe you are the famous Princess Flyra, child of the seed of Gratultyn' the guard said.

'Wow, thank you. I didn't even know I am that famous here' Flyra replied, blushing at the unexpected compliment. The guard smiled.

'Dear fine soldier, can you lead us to your king. We have very important and urgent matters to discuss' Jake said.

'Yes your highness, right this way' the guard said. He led them up the steps and into the palace's throne hall.

There was a short wait outside the hall as the servant announced their arrival to the king. King David of Arstar lived alone. There was a queen twenty years ago. But she died two years after the incident. She wasn't even fifty or having any disease. She just died peacefully, as her time had come. The moment the three of them entered, King David got up from his throne and went to hug Kitty. He kneeled down just so that Kitty could reach his shoulder.

'Master Kitty!' David said cheerfully as he approached him.

'It's been a while Dave' Kitty replied.

They hugged. The two young royals looked at them curiously.

'Are we missing something? You didn't tell us you and King David are… this close' Jake said.

'Yes, we are about the same age, we went to SHAW Academy together back when we were young. We're old friends, me, him, Jackenzie and Mousy' Kitty said.

'We had lots of fun back in those good old days' David laughed. He was certainly a very cheerful person.

'But I have to apologise David, the time now is not a happy one. We came with a specific reason' Kitty said.

'Yes, I do know. Queen Alice sent a letter informing about the avengers taking over Combination and Barenge'

'She did?' Jake said instantly.

'Yes, and I know what you came to ask. I'll join you in this war. For the good of Inland. And for my dear friends' David said. His words came out of his mouth all right and satisfyingly. Everything he said was nothing but pleasure to the ears. First his cheerful character. Then his understanding in the conversation and answer even though no one had properly asked a question. And his replies were just non-arguable. The three of them were so happy that Arstar was joining them. Arstar's army is well known for their resilience. They went through the same tough training repeatedly to train them to get used to the pain. Barenge's army is well known for their discipline. But if the avengers were to attack Arstar as well, Arstar would have survived longer than Barenge.

King David served his guests one long table of buffet. He then prepared his army of hundred guards, five hundred soldiers and fifty elite soldiers which was three quarter of Arstar's forces. And they set off for Morgan's Kingdom. Kitty had shared with him the location. David left his royal advisor in charge of the city. He also prepared food and bottles of plain water for Prince Jake, Princess Flyra, and Master Kitty for their journey south towards Trisnarim. They parted ways at dusk.

Trisnarim is situated at the end of the western lands, in front of the Southern Ocean. About the Southern Ocean, since Southernere is the only island aside from The Marina in the entire world, when travellers travel all the way down, they'll end up back in the north which is still the Southern Ocean. No one knows why south is chosen to be its name instead of north which if named north will also bring questions. It's just known as the Southern Ocean since the time of Combi.

Trisnarim is a city built at the corner of the land. Overlooking the beautiful ocean. The wide river and the Southern Ocean by its side. In fact, one-third of the city was built on or in the water. It's castle is a majestic one. Built with diamonds and trisnal stone. An almost common resource in the waters of Trisnarim but impossible to find in other parts of the ocean. That was also how Trisnarim got its name. Trisna from trisnal, and rim because Trisnarim is at the southeastern corner of the eastern lands. Diamonds are naturally transparent. Trisnal is a bit lighter than ocean blue, which makes it tough to look for. Back to the castle, one quarter of it is made out of diamonds, another quarter is made out of trisnal stone, and the remaining half is made out of ice. Real ice that glowed blue light especially at night due to the trisnal stone within. Having being in the south and further away from the sun's direct contact, Trisnarim has a very cold climate. The temperature prevents the ice from melting. Two factors that made Trisnarim Palace look even more magnificent are that it's on water and the lights that shine into the diamonds projected rays of colourful lights. Walkways of glass serve as roads for walking into the ocean districts and back. Glass tunnels with stone stairs led down into the water to the buildings underneath. If Arstar looks like it is from another era, Trisnarim looks definitely like it is from the future.

Before reaching Trisnarim, the three will have to pass by Waterfront and West Coast towns. Which they avoided because words that King David also received were that one of the two towns has joined the avengers for the upcoming war.

Three white birds landed on the ice floor, a big

empty space in between the front of the castle and the entrance gates that were made out of trisnal. It was an hour after midnight. The three birds transformed into Flyra, Jake, and Kitty. Unlike Arstar, there were no servants or soldiers around.

Up the small ice steps stood the huge ice doors glowing pinkish-blue light.

'I'm speechless' Flyra gasped, staring in awe at her surroundings. 'This is my kind of place'

'Where are the servants or guards?' Jake said. They only saw the few citizens that were still walking about the streets at this late hour. Unlike Combination and the other cities, there were no soldiers having night shift in Trisnarim.

'I actually don't know. I've never visited Trisnarim before. Trisnarim is a very difficult city to get to by land' Kitty replied. 'When royals visited Trisnarim, like your fa… King Henry did, they travelled by sea'

'Alright we're meeting the royals, that means that way' Flyra said, getting straight to the point. She pointed at the ice doors.

'The royals are a queen and a princess. Let's see who they are' Kitty said.

They walked up the ice steps and the double ice doors opened automatically. Immediately, snowflakes swirled around a fixed position in the centre of the doorway. The snowflakes joined together and formed a figure of a beautiful snowy blue lady. From her headscarf to her long dress, everything was snowy blue.

'Welcome to Trisnarim Palace' the lady spoke in a very formal way. 'Please state the intentions of your visit'

The three of them were very surprised to say anything just yet. From the automatic door to the snowflake host, Trisnarim was full of magical surprises aside from its magical beauty. That was probably another reason why there were no soldiers around. This is certainly a type of magic that Kitty himself never heard about before.

'We would like to meet your queen' Jake answered after a few seconds.

'State your name' the snow lady said.

'Jake'

'With title' Kitty reminded him immediately. Just as fast, Jake corrected his answer.

'Prince Jake of Combination'

'Greetings your highness, please wait, a host will attend to you shortly. Have a nice day!' the lady said. And she vanished as snowflakes that formed her earlier broke apart and disappeared into thin air.

'Just wow' Flyra said, she was extremely amazed. 'I can't wait to meet the queen'

They waited for a few more seconds. That was more than enough time for them to admire the interior of the entrance hallway. The walls on both sides are mostly made out of trisnal with a few diamonds scattered to reflect the light. Ice sculptures are the art of statues here instead of marble. Four entrances to other hallways divided equally on each side. A very young lady, probably even still a girl, came from one of the hallways towards them.

'Good morning your highnesses. Welcome to Trisnarim. I'll be assisting you for your visit. Feel free to ask me questions anytime. Right this way to the meeting room. The queen is waiting for you' the girl said.

'Thank you. How can I address you?' Flyra replied.

'Hostess Jenny your highness' Jenny answered.

'Thank you Jenny. I have a question. How do we not feel cold even though we're only wearing one or two layers of clothing?' Flyra said.

'That's because the queen casted a magical shield against the temperature for warm-blooded beings like us. The cold will never bother you as long as the magic is there' Jenny explained.

'Interesting!' Flyra exclaimed, becoming more impressed.

'How old are you Jenny?' Jake asked.

'I'm seventeen years old, your highness' Jenny replied.

'That explains. You look very young' Jake complimented.

'Thank you your highness' Jenny said, blushing.

They entered a room mostly made out of marble stone. Most of the furniture like the meeting table and chairs were made out of wood. A few ice sculptures decorated the empty spaces. A tall lady wearing all white. If Flyra was to wear that, she would have completed the whole set. The lady's skin was less white than Flyra's. She has reddish white skin, while Flyra has pale white. A diamond crown fitted perfectly on her headscarf. Her headscarf and dress were very long. The length of her scarf extended below her waist. This was definitely the queen.

'Good morning your highnesses of Combination. I

can't tell for sure if you are telling the truth or otherwise because the only royal I know still alive and ruling Combination is King Henry. Who I have also not met for twenty years. Not since Queen Dorothy's farewell. Such a tragedy, what happened. But I heard about the child of the seed of Gratultyn and I'm sure you are her' the queen said. Her voice came out cold. But she wasn't being mean or evil, it's just probably her magic. She spoke with interest as she mentioned about the child of the seed. 'So I believe you for your claims. Your highnesses of Combination. Please be seated. Queen Lady Lith of Trisnarim'

She finally invited them to sit and said her name.

'I am sorry for what happened. I received news that Combination and Barenge had already been taken over by the avengers. And I know why you came'

The three of them were so happy. Another good news? Just like King David, Queen Lady Lith is going to say she's joining even before they asked.

'But I'm sorry, I have to tell you, I can't join you in the war' Lady Lith said.

The three of them dropped their jaws. Not literally. To the queen's view, they just widened their eyes in disbelief. Their hopes were disappointed.

'Most importantly because I have to protect my city first. The avengers are coming. Even the natural power the city has is not enough to counter their attacks. But, I won't let you leave empty handed' Lady Lith continued. All three perked up, can't wait to hear what is the good news.

'I shall allow my daughter, Princess Nathaliya, and

her royal troopers to join you. If she agrees to help. Apart from that, I shall give fifty men from one of my elite units to you. Your choice between Guardians of the sea or the honour guards. Guardians of the sea are specialised in water combat. They can fight on both land and water. Our honour guards are specialised in sword fighting and their blades are made out of trisnal stone. Iron may kill faster, but trisnal stone deflects magic'

'Your city is most certainly a wonder, your majesty' Flyra said. 'There's a lot to learn'

'There's more than that' Lady Lith said, smiling sweetly.

'I'll let you discuss first. I'll come back later with my daughter' Lady Lith said. She got up and walked out of the room. There were only the three of them with the hostess, Jenny, and two other men, most probably, are part of the royal troopers (protecting royal persons and property).

Flyra, Jake, and Kitty discussed the choices they were given. Soon, Queen Lady Lith came back. She was followed by a beautiful lady that looks like a younger version of her but a bit shorter. Princess Nathaliya. She was wearing everything white just like her mother. A tiara rested on her headscarf.

'I bring good news and bad news, your highnesses' Lady Lith said, sitting down on her chair. Princess Nathaliya sat on the chair to her right.

'Bad news, Silverside has fallen'

There was a second of silence as everyone reacted to the news, shocked and worried.

'That is certainly not good' Kitty agreed.

'The more reason I have to stay and protect my city. Trisnarim is closer to Silverside than Arstar is. We will be the next target' Lady Lith said. 'With all the iron and wood they can take from Silverside, the soldiers will be stronger than before'

'I think that means our journey ends here. We'll have to head back to Morgan's Kingdom now' Jake said.

'I seek upon the blessings of Lady Feramein, protector of Isle of Nature and Southernere, keeper of seasons and elements, to guide my acquaintances, highnesses of Combination, for their journey back' Lady Lith said, closing her eyes and concentrating hard.

This was the second time Flyra heard someone mentioned protector and keeper. The first time was with the mysterious Master Nvago who claimed himself as a protector.

'I'm sorry, your majesty. But I heard someone mentioned about protectors and keepers before. He claimed to be a protector himself...' Flyra said.

'You met a protector before?' Lady Lith interrupted. She was clearly very interested.

'Yes, he said his name is Master Nvago'

'Master Nvago is here?' Lady Lith spoke with enthusiasm. 'Of course he is, he's a protector of trading villages and portals for Southernere'

'What are those? And those other protectors you seemed to speak to just now?'

'They are members of The Fifteen. The fifteen great masters of Gratultyn with responsibilities across the realms'

'How do you know about all this?' Kitty said. 'This

information cannot be found in any of the books I've read regarding Gratultyn'

'That's because no explorer or traveller has ever been to the actual place. They may have found the portals, travelled to the realm of passageways, but to get to Gratultyn is more complex than that. They could only write what they assume or heard about Gratultyn without actually having proof. The only proof we have that the place exists is the Gratultyn magic people wield. But we have something different. We have a classified high valued item in our possession. It speaks to us once in a while, messages from Lady Feramein herself, which the item belongs to. That was how we learnt about Silverside's fall. If you ask me how the item got here, I don't know the answer. It has been there since before my grandfather even learnt about it. That was how we learnt, well myself, my daughter, and people we trust, about The Fifteen and Gratultyn'

'So where is Lady Feramein? She's a protector of this land right?' Jake asked.

'She is a protector of Southernere but she can't interfere with dealings occuring. She has to let it continue naturally. She can't pick sides. Both Inlanders and Outlanders are inhabitants of this land. Changing things or altering nature is against the law of magic. I just simply seek her support for you to return home safely. Morgan's Kingdom? Shouldn't you change the name to something… better?'

'We'll think about it' Jake replied.

There was a short pause. Everyone digested the information they received.

'The good news is, my daughter has agreed to join you in the war' Lady Lith said, referring to her daughter beside her. Princess Nathaliya nodded her head with respect.

'She's a very quiet person. The only words I hear coming from her everytime are about duties and responsibilities. She can't take jokes' Lady Lith said.

'Thank you, your highness. We are very grateful for your support, and yours, your majesty' Flyra said, to the princess and to the queen. 'We have decided to go with Guardians of the sea for the fifty men'

'Excellent your highness. I'll get them ready in twenty minutes. You'll have three tankers with five soldiers handling each. You'll find out soon what's a tanker. You'll also have one Guardian, the name of all our finest ships. Boarding it will be its crew members, twenty archers, and fifteen Ocean Masters. I believe you know, what are the Ocean Masters. They are all Winterains but more advanced. They master everything related to water, snow, ice, water, mist, and even air. That's our specialty. All together, you have fifty men. The Guardian will bring you up the wide river to the Waterfront Lake. From there, the rest of the journey by foot. I believe by the evening of tomorrow, you will reach your base' Lady Lith said.

'Thank you very much your majesty' Jake said. They all thanked each other, for the queen's assistance and for the three's visit.

'I hope the best for your defense against the avengers when they come' Flyra said.

'We'll seek blessings from Lady Feramein. Thank

you. I hope for you the best in the war. May Lady Feramein offer her blessings to you as well' Lady Lith said. All the time she has been speaking in a very formal way. She suddenly changed her tone to be more friendly and informal and said, 'May we meet again someday'

They all stood up. Princess Nathaliya hugged her mother.

'I love you' she said softly. Her voice was the only sound in the room at that moment. So everyone was able to hear it. That was also the first time they heard Nathaliya's voice.

'I love you too' Lady Lith replied. 'Stay strong, be safe. I'll want to see you again after this is over'

Lady Lith wasn't asking. The tone in her voice showed that she must see Nathaliya again after the war. She would be very depressed if she found out her daughter died. Nathaliya just managed a weak smile. She couldn't promise anything. So she hugged her mother tighter. This might be the last time she saw her.

Two hours passed since the three arrived. Now they were ready to set off. Queen Lady Lith had prepared what was promised. The Guardian was a magnificent ship. From the street level they could see its vast architecture. It is far greater than all the other ships at the docks below. Units that made up the Guardians of the sea were all lined up in a very orderly manner. First were the tankers, followed by rows of Ocean Masters and archers. The Guardian's crew was already on board the ship. Lady Lith introduced them to the tankers. The tanker is not a person. It's an object. Five soldiers are tasked to handle each of the three tankers given. It is like a huge barrel that can fit six people inside, with a few more spaces afterwards. A small hole is near the edge at the top for refilling of water. A small round piston is attached to the centre of its top. Another hole at the bottom of its side with a rubber hose attached for water to flow out. A valve is in between the hose and the hole to control the flow of water. This is a weapon. The piston at the top will provide additional pressure to the water when it flows out at the bottom. Lastly, a device to project greater surface area of the water is attached to the end of the hose. Lady Lith calls it the sprinkler. Water will shoot out of it very strongly. It will injure anyone close to it if they resist the current. If not, they'll be flung backwards.

The Ocean Masters and archers are both wearing the same uniform. Mostly white in colour. The ladies have additional clothing on them, white headscarves. The archers' bows are all shiny-looking. The wood that was used to craft the bows are from Silverside's majestic woods.

'I apologise to have you summoned at this early hour. I thank you for your devotion to your duties. We know the avengers are a huge threat to our city, our land. They are taking over the cities one by one. All fifty of you here are sent to follow our highnesses of Combination as they go to war two days from now. Serve well. For the good of Inland' Lady Lith spoke to all her subjects.

'Yes ma'am!' they cheered in response. Flyra, Jake and Kitty looked astonishingly at the loyal soldiers.

Five minutes later, they were already on board

the Guardian and heading up the wide river towards Waterfront Lake.

Earlier in the day, Prince Edward and Bobby were already lost. They know Barenge was behind. They had managed to go a longer route around to avoid the fallen city. But the surroundings changed drastically all of a sudden. The trees turned from green to red. Everything was red. Not autumn red but real red colour. The grass was a lighter shade of red. Other substances like rocks seemed red as well because almost everything else around was red.

'Where are we Bobby? I don't recall having red trees near Barenge' Edward said.

'I have no idea Edward' Bobby replied.

They kept walking until they were sure that they were still at the same spot. It did not feel like they were going around in circles. It was like they had been walking on the spot.

'Prince Edward' a voice belonging to an old man spoke from behind. They turned quickly to see Master Nvago standing calmly in front of them. But Edward and Bobby had no idea yet that he was the master they're looking for.

'How do you know my name?' Edward asked.

'You're a prince. Everyone knows you' Nvago replied.

'The last time anyone saw me was when I was a small boy'

'I see you've lost some of your amazing intellect, your highness' Nvago said, smiling like an old mentor who cares for his student. Edward kept quiet. He understood what he meant. Edward used to be a bright person. He could guess, predict or even read people's emotions.

'I'm not the same boy everyone knows me for'

'Oh I know that. Everyone changes through time. But that your highness is a trait. A trait stays with a person for as long as he lives. You buried that trait deep within you for a very long time. Now it is time to bring it back out. You'll be smarter with it. Just saying. I'm helping you. You're looking for me right?' Nvago said. He winked at the last sentence. Edward's and Bobby's face lit up.

'Master Nvago?' Edward said.

'You would have known if you had brought back that intellect of yours out' Nvago said.

'How do you know so much about me?'

'Let's just say, the protector of this land knows whoever's on it and whatever they're doing. And I'm friends with her'

'Whatever they're doing?'

'Not that detailed obviously' Nvago said. 'Hurry up your highness. You have to find that intellect, you'll suffer without it. It's a part of you'

'I came to seek your help to remove this'

Edward showed him the cursed bracelet on his left wrist. Nvago observed the bracelet. Edward and Bobby could not understand what he was thinking because he showed no reaction.

'Marcala put them on you?' Nvago asked suddenly.

'Yes. It's been on me for twenty years. Perhaps after this is removed, I can finally find back what you asked me to find' Edward said, getting impatient.

'Calm down my prince. What I asked you to find is nothing related to magic. Impatience is one of the reasons you're unable to focus. And without concentration, that is how you are blinded from seeking the truth. In this case truth about yourself'

'I'm sorry'

'Let me see that' Nvago gestured for the bracelet. Edward brought his left hand closer to him and he examined the bracelet. Nvago swiped his hand a few centimetres above the bracelet. The two ends that connected the bracelet into one circle became loose and the bracelet fell onto the ground. Edward made a short gasp as he felt his blood moving around his body at fast speed. He could feel it again, the power. He gazed at a nearby tree. An idea struck him and he intended to try out his powers. He swiped his hand upwards in the direction of the tree. Water exited in between his fingers and it moved in a wavy formation towards the tree. The amount of water that came out could fill a tanker. The water swirled around the tree continuously. Edward swiped his hand back down and the water splashed onto the tree. Edward felt like he had just regained his full freedom. He had also caused a sensation. Because both Master Nvago and Bobby seemed to be in a better mood. Nvago was smiling wider now.

'I would like to officially welcome you back, your highness. But I'll save it until you find that intellect. Above all the power you have, that is your greatest strength' Nvago said, smiling.

Edward glanced excitedly at Bobby. He could not wait to return to Morgan's Kingdom and share with everyone what happened. And more importantly, he could not wait to win the war and meet his father again. He missed him very much.

'Don't forget the bracelet' Nvago said.

'Why would I take it? It is the reason I was lost for twenty years' Edward replied.

'Perhaps you could make use of it in the future'

Edward never thought of it before. That bracelet is not any good being lost. He picked it up.

'Remember, only the person who placed it or anyone who is knowledgeable over it can remove it from someone's wrist. If you placed it on Marcala, she's able to remove it. Her knowledge is very great. Don't play with it'

'I don't have a bag or anything to keep it right now'

'It only works on people with magic' Nvago said, giving a hint. He was purposefully making Edward think. Nvago believed that Edward has one of the greatest minds of all time. If he lets his intellect find its way back out to shine.

'I can place it on Bobby!' Edward exclaimed, elated that he wasn't entirely dumb or useless in magical terms anymore. He was smart but he was dumb and useless in magic the past twenty years.

'Very good, your highness. Let it flow. Let it out. Don't keep your intellect locked up' Nvago marveled. Bobby obediently lent his hand. Edward placed the bracelet on. Bobby turned it around his wrist and pulled the connections apart. The bracelet came out easily. The curse doesn't work on him.

'You should come with us. We will need all the help we can get' Edward said.

'I can't interfere with affairs that are not mine. I am one of The Fifteen and bound to the laws of Gratultyn and magic. I will need permission from the protector of Southernere if I want to proceed' Nvago said.

There was silence. Edward and Bobby prepared to leave. They faced Master Nvago to thank him and say goodbye.

'One more thing your highness. Princess Flyra is no ordinary person. She's a child of the seed of Gratultyn. If it comes to a bad situation, she'll have a second chance'

Nvago's words almost sounded like a riddle. Both of them didn't understand.

'What do you mean?' Edward asked.

'Just know that you'll need her to win the battle. The rest you'll understand when the time is right. I have opened a gateway for you to leave this place, just right ahead. Be careful, you'll be close to Barenge when you return. Now go! Be safe' Nvago disappeared right in front of their eyes.

Edward and Bobby followed his instructions to walk straight ahead. The next minute they were back in a familiar surrounding. The trees and grass were green. Everything was pleasant. Except for the sound of screams. Most probably the citizens of Barenge were screaming for mercy as the Outland soldiers tortured them.

'Let's get out of here'

'Agreed' Bobby said. Bobby took a step forward and Edward held him back.

'Now we can do this' Edward said, attempting to

try something. He closed his eyes, concentrating hard. He transformed into a blue bird.

'Your highness! I thought only Master Kitty could do that? How did you learn to do it?' Bobby asked, surprised.

'Thanks to Marcala, she transformed me years ago, I guess the skill just automatically saved within me. And besides, I saw a lot of times the avengers doing so' Edward replied. His voice came out like a mixture of bird tweets and human voice. Edward touched Bobby and he transformed into a brown bird. The bracelet that was on Bobby's wrist fell off.

'Forgot about that' Edward said. 'That item is magic, I don't think I can affect it anyway so as to shrink it or something'

'I guess putting it around my neck won't hurt' Bobby said.

'Bobby, I don't think that's a good idea. You'll hurt your neck'

Edward transformed back into himself. He transformed Bobby too.

'We have to walk. We have one more full day to travel back. The time we took to come here is not even that long. Better be safe than late' Edward said. And they set off by foot.

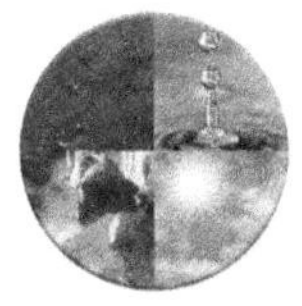

THE WAR PART 1

Before you start reading the next chapter, finish what you're supposed to do first. Done? Carry on!

Prince Edward and Bobby arrived at Morgan's Kingdom an hour after the sun had set. It was a very happy reunion between him and Princess Darleen. She couldn't stop hugging him, crying as she did. Her dear nephew had grown to be a very handsome man. And Edward also noticed the burnt half of his aunt. There was a long moment of Edward showing concern. Then Dewi delivered the terrible news of King Henry's death. Edward became speechless. He was so ready to meet his father. To tell him how much he missed him. And now he will never get the chance to do so. He's officially an orphan. He had been an orphan his whole teenage life. Twenty years he lived without his parents. His mother died when he was eight. He was separated from his father then. And when he could have gotten the chance to finally meet him, it was never meant to be. Edward shut himself off from everyone afterwards. He sat in one of the bedrooms which he had claimed.

The others let him be to give some space. They will have another hard time explaining to Princess Flyra and the rest when they return.

At around three in the morning, King David and his army arrived. There was a brief moment of panic between Lillain, Dewi and the three animals. Until Bobby found out and told them who David is. King David and few of his elite guards claimed rooms in the castle. The rest of the men stayed in the barracks or other buildings with bedrooms. Morgan's Kingdom was now like a real kingdom. Except there were no citizens around to complete the description. About three in the afternoon of the following day, Princess Flyra, Prince Jake, and Master Kitty arrived with the small army Queen Lady Lith provided from Trisnarim. Princess Nathaliya, without any introduction, was escorted into the castle by her royal troopers to claim an empty bedroom. Flyra explained to her friends that Nathaliya is not much of a talker. They met Princess Darleen who was very honoured to meet Flyra. Then they were told the news of King Henry's death. They were devastated. Between Edward's reaction and Flyra and Jake's reaction, no one could tell which was more sad. Both have very strong reasons to be extremely sad. Henry was Edward's biological father and he had not met him for twenty years. On the other hand, Henry was not Jake, Flyra, and Nathan's biological father, but he had been their father for the past twenty years, since they were very young or for Flyra's case, since she was born. Edward was feeling much better, not that he could already speak with people, but he had started leaving his room to walk about the kingdom. And when he saw Flyra, he just felt like he wanted to hug her. He tried pushing the thought away but he cannot deny. He loves her. More than a friendly relationship. He felt like he should be more open with her. Express his sad feelings to her. Share the feelings together. Because Flyra was also very sad over King Henry's passing. He did not know yet but Flyra felt the same way too. The moment Edward walked down the stairs to the castle's entrance, she felt her heart skip a beat. But they walked away, assuming the other party needed some space. But they questioned the same thing in their mind, "He/She didn't care to talk to me?". But they didn't let the thought bother them. There's a lot more important things to do. Like training. They have less than twenty-four hours before the war tomorrow. King David's army made use of the small training area behind the barracks. Princess Nathaliya went out alone and only informed her royal troopers of her whereabouts. She went to train in the forest outside of Morgan's Kingdom. The fifty men of Trisnarim trained anywhere else available. Master Kitty and those other SHAWs who have nothing to do trained on their powers and magic skills. King David, Princess Flyra, Prince Jake and Dewi went over a map of Alhora. They made last minute confirmations on the strategies and tactics. Prince Edward practiced his magic. He had been practicing for the past many hours since he calmed down from the bad news. He sat in his room. All four elements were placed in front of him. The fire burning in the fireplace, the stones on the tea table, the four glasses of water, and the surrounding air.

One by one, Edward recapped his elemental skills. Then he combined the skills together. In one movement, he raised the fire into a fireball above the fireplace. The water floated out of all four glasses, forming a large ball of water above the glasses. The stones floated just a few centimetres above the tea table. And the air blew wind around all three elements at constant speed. There was suddenly a knock on the door. Edward lost his focus and all elements dropped. The fireball dropped back into the fireplace. The stones dropped onto the table, bouncing further away from each other. The water fell, some went into the glasses, some wetted the table.

'Come in' Edward said hastily, relaxing his muscles. Using magic also involves the usage of muscles. Bobby came in.

'Edward, I think it's time we start back our sword fighting lesson' Bobby said. Edward looked at him like that was not a good idea at the moment.

'Magic is not the only thing that will help you on the battlefield. You need a real weapon as well' Bobby said, emphasising on the weapon part and showing his sword as he said it. It took Edward a few seconds to think it through and he agreed. So then Edward and Bobby trained sword fighting at an unoccupied space behind the castle.

The third day came so soon. They were ready to proceed to Alhora. But most of them were still nervous. They only have about eight hundred men against who knows how many avengers and Outland soldiers they will face. By eleven, they had arrived at Alhora field.

The whole land of Alhora was covered in snow due to Flyra's powers exerted before. They positioned themselves in orderly manner. Arstar cavalries, about two hundred men and horses, lined up at the front. Soldiers including guards and Trisnarim archers stood behind the cavalries. Mixed among them were the Ocean Masters. The tankers at one side at the front. King David and Princess Nathaliya stood with them. Master Kitty and Lillain stood together at another spot at the front. Prince Edward, Princess Flyra, Prince Jake, and Bobby stood together in the centre at the front, leading the whole army. Oliver stood to the other side of the front with other forest animals who came along from Arstar. Dewi and Princess Darleen set up a tent at the back, they will be in charge of medical issues. Captain and Bale will be assisting them. Everyone was facing the south, in the direction of Combination. That's where the enemy will be coming from. True enough, seconds after they positioned themselves, the enemy arrived. All wearing black. The avengers leading. About a hundred of them, looking too over confident. Behind them, a large army of Outland soldiers, about four hundred of them marching forward. And to the good guys' horror,an army of beasts joined the ranks of the enemy. Where in Southernere did they come from? There were many of the bear-like beast Flyra faced before. And many other creatures that were very scary-looking. At first it seemed like that was it. An army of about six hundred. The good guys could win this. But then, another group of the same forces arrived. Avengers, more of them, or they're probably just SHAWs but manipulated to join the avengers. More Outland soldiers and beasts as well. Then another army of about less than two hundred joined in between the first group and second group of avengers, Outland soldiers, and beasts. From their cheap armour and uniformed colour light blue, the good guys could tell which town they came from. It was the traitor town, Waterfront. They are lined up around the edges of Combination Border Woods facing Alhora Woods. Altogether, their numbers reached about two thousand. Up at the front of the third group, on the right side, Pertum and Lydia were leading. The front of the second group, on the left side, Alphaga was leading. At the front of the first group, in the centre, Erieka and Marcala were leading. Morgan stood a few steps behind, leading his soldiers. There was a few minutes of silence as both sides stared at each other, waiting.

'How are we going to stop them? There's so many!' Flyra said. She sounded like she was losing hope.

'Stay positive princess. We can do this' Edward replied. That was actually the first time they spoke to each other since they gave each other space back in Morgan's Kingdom. Nathaliya came up to them from the left.

'Your highnesses, we have the upper hand in terms of combat forces. The enemy has only people. The tankers will do well. I will command the archers the best I can. We'll support you as you make your way forward with the cavalries' she said.

'Thank you your highness' Edward replied. Nathaliya went back to stand with David. He looked at them from afar. They made eye contact, and he gave a reassuring look. They're all in this together. Towards the right, Kitty gave the same look. He and Lillain were ready to lead the SHAWs and their side of forces. Towards the far right, Oliver and the forest friends were also ready to charge. Edward looked across the field towards the enemy. He caught sight of Erieka and Marcala. They were staring at him. They're about more than a hundred metre apart but they could see each other very clearly. Erieka was grinning. She showed a hand signal, striking her thumb across her neck, trying to tell Edward that he's so dead.

'There's no way to bring her back now' Edward said. Silence for a while. The rest were not sure how to reply.

'I'm sorry Edward' Flyra said.

'It's okay. I moved on. We are doing this today to win back our land, our home. For the good of Inland' Edward said. Those who heard him repeated the slogan. Jake took the initiative to repeat the slogan loudly. He shouted it with confidence. The entire army of good guys shouted back.

Across the field, the evil guys are getting annoyed by the cheer and the waste of time.

'Enough of that. Let's show them a proper introduction' Marcala said very loudly. Those further away and cannot hear her clearly got the message from their mates passing it down.

'Attack!' Marcala shouted at the top of her lungs. The entire force of the second group charged forward. The Waterfront soldiers joined in as well. The first and third group stayed behind. Now a force of about five hundred and fifty men were charging at the good guys. The avengers were in the lead. The Outland soldiers behind. The beasts were faster, so they made their way up to the front. The Waterfront soldiers joined the charging Outland soldiers.

'They made their move! Arrow team!' Flyra shouted in the direction of Nathaliya. They were briefed well about their plans. Nathaliya was ready to react even before Flyra reminded her.

'Archers, Fire!' Nathaliya shouted. Nathaliya also released her arrow she had drawn as she shouted. The arrows whizzed up through the air and arching back down towards the charging beasts. Most of the beasts fell down injured. Some of the arrows managed to kill a few. Others killed two or three avengers behind.

'Cavalries, charge!' Jake shouted. Jake and Bobby were riding a horse. They led the cavalries forward. The horses galloped past Edward and Flyra. While that happened, Flyra pushed the wind, blowing snow towards the charging enemy. The cold made the beasts' speed slower.

'Archers, nock!' Nathaliya shouted on her cue, nocking her arrow at the same time. The cavalries clashed with the beasts. Swords slashing and sharp teeth gnashing. The battle between the beasts and the cavalries was intense. The cavalries were winning, due to the archers' arrows and Flyra's power.

'Fire!' Nathaliya shouted again. The archers released their arrow. It wheezed up and arched down towards the avengers and soldiers who were almost reaching the beasts. All twenty-one arrows hit a target who then dropped dead.

Flyra glanced in Kitty's direction. And he was also

ready. It was his cue to lead some of the SHAWs and Ocean Masters. About twenty men including Kitty ran forward. Lillain stayed behind with the remaining ten. Kitty was very fast. It wasn't just because he was a cat. He made use of his Ardni specialty to push the air around him and make him run faster. He was the first to reach the battle. The avengers arrived a second later. They threw their powers at the cavalries. Most of them were fireballs. Some got hit, they fell off their horse. Some horses continued fighting while others retreated into the forest. There are horses that got hit by the fire as well. Kitty defended most of the cavalries and attacked as well. He used a lot of air power. One avenger sent a fireball at him. He summoned the wind strong enough to alter the course. The fire charged back at the person who summoned it. It was too fast for the avenger to react, the fire burnt him to death. Other avengers sent multiple fireballs which Kitty stopped them with his air power. Some vanished, some melted a small spot in the snow, some burnt the avengers. The Ocean Masters were even more impressive with their calm movements of their hands and controlling every source of water around or even within them. The Outland and Waterfront soldiers came into battle. Right now, the evil guys outnumbered them. The good guys only have this one group of cavalries. The evil guys have three groups of the three forces. Although the ratio is so far apart, the good guys refused to lose hope. They need that especially at this time.

The SHAWs and Ocean Masters were working very hard with their magic. So were the avengers. Some avengers melted the snow around them with fire. They placed wood and threw fire into it. The fire kept the area snow-free. The avengers also made use of the existing fire to throw fireballs or other fire attacks at their enemy. A fireball came charging at an Ocean Master. The master, as all Ocean Masters do every time, moved their hands very calmly and smoothly, he moved his hand upward. The snow in front of him shot up. The fire crashed into it, vanishing as steam rose into the air. The snow cooled down the heat and the master sent it back down to rest. Angry, the avenger used water as well. He melted the snow in front of him and sent the freezing water at rapid speed towards the master. The master held up his palm. The water stopped charging. It flowed around in the air, forming a ball. The master used his other hand to melt the snow around him and raise the water forming separate balls of water. The avenger took the time to send another fireball. With his eyes, the master sent the snow up again to wipe out the fire. He turned the snow to water and added to his collection of water balls. He immediately sent all of them towards the avenger. The avenger took some fire from the burning wood in a hurry and tried to wipe the water balls out. But his fire was not strong enough. It died the moment it went into contact with the first water ball. The other water balls crashed into him. They did not just simply wet him and disappear. The master controlled them to trap him in a large ball of water when all the water balls combined. He moved the large water ball to nearby areas, catching other avengers in it. He managed to trap about five, and three soldiers. All of them struggled to get out. None of them were able to breathe. Then, there were no more movements. He dropped the water ball which melted the snow around as it spread. The eight of them were dead. Another Ocean Master was battling three soldiers. The soldiers were striking hard with their swords. The master countered every strike with magic. She had no weapon, just her powers. The first soldier slashed with his sword. The master froze her hand deep in ice and parried the strike. The second soldier at the same time was slashing his sword at the master's side. After the block, she defrosted her hand and pushed the second soldier with a powerful forcefield. She exerted the force very quickly that the soldier was flung backwards violently. He lost grip of the sword in his hand which the master took it, and just in time, she parried the third soldier's strike with it. She continued the sword fight with the two remaining soldiers, releasing forcefield or water magic occasionally.

'They're using the snow to their advantage, melt them all. Heat up the ground and temperature' Marcala said, observing the battle. Erieka nodded obediently. She breathed in calmly. Her pupils turned crimson. The amulet hidden under her headscarf glowed very brightly that the light could be seen partially from outside. She wasn't moving anything but the power she was exerting was very great. From far, Flyra could feel the great energy running underneath. She glanced at Edward to see if he felt it too. He looked back at her. And he understood. He nodded, signifying he felt it too.

'She's using her amulet' Edward deduced. 'I can see it glowing from here'

Flyra turned to look. She saw Erieka, but she could not see her face that clearly. What more see her hidden amulet.

'How can you see?' Flyra asked.

'Oh, I forgot to tell you, I can see very far with my magic, it's a natural trait' Edward said. Flyra smiled feeling very impressed.

The snow started to melt very quickly. The field was now visible again, except without the grass. It was just soil. The snow on the trees also melted. Green was starting to show in the woods. With one final blow, Erieka breathed out, a wave of air full of energy radiated from her in a circle. The air wiped out completely every last bit of snow. Even the water that came from the melted snow was mostly wiped out as well. Only a few puddles and wet soil left here and there.

'That's better. Marvelous Erieka' Marcala said happily. 'Send the third group forward'

Erieka glanced at Lydia and Pertum who had been waiting. She signalled them that they could move already. Lydia and Pertum grinned excitedly. Finally it was time for them to shine.

'Charge!' Pertum shouted. The third group ran forward very fast, eager to spill some blood. Lydia, Pertum and some of the avengers transformed into black birds. They planned to land in the centre of the battlefield and continue from there. Some of them got shot by the archers.

'On me, charge!' David shouted. He led his army forward. The Arstar soldiers charged into battle, they headed towards the third group.

'Archers, after me!' Nathaliya shouted, following behind the last men of the Arstar army. Some of them were very good. Like Nathaliya, she shot an arrow while running, hitting a beast right in its eye from about ten metres away. When a target was harder to aim, she stopped for a while, shot her arrow and continued running. David and his army clashed into the third group. The beasts and avengers were overwhelming. The Outland soldiers joined and the numbers just got worse. David used both of his skills, sword fighting and his Sprite power. Nathaliya fought fiercely. She shot her arrow when the enemy was far away or a good guy was in danger of the enemy. Those who came at her, she struck them twice with her bow which knocked them out.

'Tankers, forward!' a soldier who was in charge of all the tankers shouted. The tankers moved in one line at first. Then they split up. One joined the third group battle, one joined the second group battle, and the last one stayed in between, offering help to both sides. The soldiers moved very quickly. The moment they had pushed the tanker to a good spot, they got to work. One soldier took care of refilling. They have a wheeled-crate of barrels filled with water for refill. A soldier controlled the valve. Two soldiers held the hose, one as the aimer, the other as a supporter. The last soldier led them, and checked the tanker occasionally in case it needed maintenance. The tanker was switched on and water sprayed out of the sprinkler very strongly due to the piston's push. They aimed at the enemy. A lot of them were thrown backwards. It was better than having one SHAW using normal powers to keep on sending forcefield. The battle went on. A lot of casualties on both sides. The battle seemed fair at this moment. However, the evil guys still have one more group that were not involved yet. And they have Marcala and Erieka in that group. The good guys only have Edward, Flyra, Lillain and her team, and Oliver and his animal friends left. All of them could not even match with the might of the avengers from the first group. What more an entire group.

There were casualties everywhere. Those of the good guys that survived an attack, are mostly badly injured. And the lucky ones among them, their mates noticed them and carried them to the tent. Dewi and Darleen were already very busy even though it was just twenty minutes since the war started.

'We should join in and help them' Edward said restlessly.

'We can't! Remember the plan. We cannot join in until Marcala does. We have to pay very close attention to her and Erieka. The amulet has to be taken away from her. Then we'll have the chance to stop the war' Flyra replied. Edward understood, but he couldn't help his thoughts. How many people had died while he was just standing there, watching.

'Okay but I'm sending the rest of our forces in' Edward said. Before Flyra could stop him, he signalled for Lillain and Oliver to join in. They charged.

'Edward, we discussed this!' Flyra scolded. This was the first time she was really mad at someone.

'We're losing Flyra! We're losing!' Edward argued. Flyra was speechless for a few seconds.

'What is this about?'

Edward gave her a look like he had no idea what she was saying.

'The war. What is this about? For revenge?'

'Oh my Flyra, you're putting words in my mouth?!'

'I did not say that!'

'You mean that!'

'No I didn't! Stop being such a fool!'

Flyra was very mad.

'We're doing this for the good of Inland. Not for winning. Winning is a good thing, an extra thing that comes out of it. But if we lose, at least we did our best. According to what we had planned and agreed upon. We are in this together after all. Stay strong Edward. I know Master Nvago gave you some good advice. Because he advised me too. Take them' Flyra said, before walking forward a few steps, just to get away from Edward for the time being. It was clear she wanted the conversation to end there. Edward knew she was totally right. He thought of it all. He needs to find the bright person he once was. Nvago was right. The child Edward would have been much more of a help than an adult Edward now, in terms of emotion. Aside from that, he really needs to bring back the intellect he once had as well. Edward concentrated hard, he felt the energy underneath. His sister's magic, flowing very strongly. He focused on his patience, pushing his rage aside. He reached down into the ground and grasped the energy as much as he could. It was full of rage and hate. He transferred his calmness into them. The energy beneath him turned pure and innocent. And at the same time, snow started falling again just at the area. He looked around him. The surface area where the snow was falling centred around Flyra. She was causing the temperature to fall. But it only happened when Edward cleansed the area from Erieka's energy. They could help the Ocean Masters to get back their sources. Because right now, they solely depend on releasing water from their hands. They need a real source of water to get the upper hand over the avengers. He hurried to Flyra's side and told her what happened.

'I will clear Erieka's energy around the Ocean Masters, you'll let the temperature down around them' Edward said.

'I can do better' Flyra said, smiling. They nodded in agreement. Edward reached out again underneath, feeling for Erieka's energy until he reached both battlefields. He diluted the rage with his calmness. He breathed in deep, then reached out again. He was using a lot of his energy to do so. At that moment, he recalled the moment he first felt Erieka's strong energy. He was very excited about it. He ran to tell his mother, Queen Dorothy. Her kind beautiful face warms him.

'Do I have that energy?' Edward asked. Queen Dorothy shook her head gently. Edward's face saddened.

'But I've never seen anyone with so much spirit before except you' Dorothy said.

'I don't quite understand the difference between energy and spirit' Edward said.

'Energy you can feel it, but spirit, you have to see it. I see and know your spirit since the day you learn who your parents are. Yes energy will seem powerful and intimidating to anyone. But spirit is the real reason that someone is very powerful. Because of spirit, all the great masters you know master a more complicated magic such as Gratultyn magic and those with higher spirit master light magic or if the opposite, dark magic'

He remembered the conversation he had with his mother. Her explanation about spirit and energy. Even Master Nvago saw the greatness in him even though he had unintentionally buried them for many years. He felt a sudden burst of motivation. He was feeling stronger than ever. And he did not realise, his eyes turned sapphire blue. Frost grew on every part of his skin. He was focusing very hard on diluting Erieka's energy to realise what was going on around him. Flyra was very surprised. She stared with her mouth open a little for a few seconds. She then blinked her eyes many times, Edward's magic was kind of luring her to a trance.

'I guess that's the sign then' Flyra murmured. She spread her arms in front of her. Snowflakes exited her hands very quickly and continuously. The snowflakes travelled a few metres in front of her before going down. The moment they touched the ground, they started spreading around the battlefields at very fast speed. Soon the two battlefields were covered in snow. Soil was no longer visible at the side of the good guys. Flyra stopped her magic. The Ocean Masters got back to their style. They made use of the snow elegantly. Flyra glanced at Edward who was still doing his thing.

'Edward, it's done' she said. But Edward did not give any response. 'Edward!'

Edward was getting deeper into his magic. At this moment, he was already unable to control himself, he was in a trance. The sky above got darker than before. The clouds clouded over the battlefields. He slowly raised his hands up, palms facing the sky. Water flowed out in between his fingers from both hands. The water swirled around in the air, moving towards the enemy. Flyra could only stare, she didn't know if this was a good thing or otherwise. But the dark sky worried her. She touched Edward's frost-covered skin. She felt a cold bite for a second, then it was like a normal feeling of holding his arm. The frost did not affect her at all. Then she saw the area of contact her hand has with Edward's skin. Her hand was protected by a barely visible layer of shield. Just like what happened all those times before with magic. The dragon's fire could not kill her. A shield formed up when that happened. And many other times she remembered when she was younger. She was never hurt by any magic. She couldn't be hurt by any magic. Only non magic weapons hurt her. It must be something to do with the seed of Gratultyn. Everyone looks at a child of the seed very respectfully. Though maybe only a few knew the true power, everyone respects a child of the seed. Master Nvago himself spoke highly of it. Darleen also mentioned to her before they came to war, she is the key to defeating Erieka's amulet. She let go of Edward's arm. The water he was controlling was now swirling around the Outland soldiers and avengers. Some were distracted by it and the good soldiers took the opportunity to kill them. There was a huge amount of water now. It made its way towards the first group which was still standing and enjoying the show.

'This won't stop me' Marcala said. The water swirled past her to the avengers behind. Marcala used her power to take control over the water. But it wasn't as easy as she thought it would be. The water was still fully under Edward's control.

'No!' Marcala exclaimed. She tried all she could. Erieka saw her struggling and decided to try and control it. The water stopped swirling, it stayed, the particles moving only among themselves. Erieka grinned with satisfaction. She then tried pushing the water back assuming the water was now under her control. But the water did not react to her command. She tried again but nothing happened. Edward was still in his trance. Erieka had managed to only stop the water from moving further. He was now trying to break past her magic. Flyra saw what happened and helped. She shot blue light rays from her hands to the water. The light travelled at the speed of a calm river along the water towards the end. The water, the whole of it, was now glowing light blue. The water resumed swirling towards the avengers and soldiers of the first group.

'He's in his ultimate state, stop him!' Marcala ordered.

'Avengers, in five!' Erieka shouted a command. She transformed into a black bird. Four other avengers followed her. Her command was easily understood. Five of them, including Erieka as one of them, will go. The special thing about the amulet Erieka was wearing, it was enchanted to take the shape and size of the person who wears it. The amulet hung around her bird neck, small and light. They landed around Edward and Flyra and transformed back to their human or animal selves. Flyra stopped her magic. But Edward was not aware of anything going on.

'Make him stop or he'll die' Erieka warned.

'He's your brother!' Flyra argued. She couldn't believe anyone would kill their family member to get what they want.

'That won't stop me' Erieka said. She lit a fire on her palm. For the next few seconds they stared intensely at each other.

'Kill them both' Erieka told the avengers. The avengers obeyed, they conjured fire or whatever elements their specialty is on their palms.

'No!' Flyra shouted. As Erieka and the avengers threw their powers, a translucent shield grew in the shape of a sphere, protecting Edward and Flyra. She now knows for sure, she couldn't be harmed with magic. The powers hit the shield and disappeared. And that was the first time Erieka showed a surprise reaction to anyone. It takes great power for a newbie to conjure such a big and powerful shield.

'You can never hurt me or Edward or anyone else! Stop the war now! Surrender Combination back to your brother' Flyra said firmly.

'Combination is mine too, I am also an heir to the throne!'

'Then stop this. Marcala is using you. You can come back with us. Your family wouldn't have wanted you to do this'

'I have a family! And that is with the avengers'

'Your real family is right in front of you! Your brother who loves you!'

That sentence took Erieka by surprise. It made her speechless for a while. Deep inside, she could feel the love. But her mind kept telling her, duty is more important. And she's doing this for Majuza.

'No, Majuza is my family. She deserves justice' Erieka replied stubbornly. Flyra had no idea what else to say. She just stood there, hoping that help would come. But for now, she will defend herself and Edward, and fight for Inland as much as she can. Erieka and four avengers can't stop her from trying.

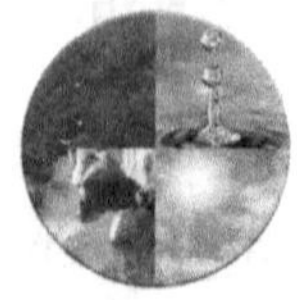

THE WAR PART 2

Before you start reading the next chapter, finish what you're supposed to do first. Done? Carry on!

The avengers had just left for the war. Combination was very quiet at this time. It was more silent than the times they had farewells. Many dead bodies and injured men who had not been attended for, for days, were lying about the streets. Some buildings were in bad condition. No one could possibly know where they could find signs of life when they walked about the streets. It was like the whole city was abandoned. Only a few Outland soldiers stayed behind, especially at the castle. The dungeons contained many of their enemies they cannot leave unattended. The people in the cells are all standing or sitting quietly. Most were actually fidgeting. They know the avengers had left for the war. And here they are trapped. Finally Master Mousy broke the silence. She couldn't stand any longer. Especially when King Henry's dead body was still lying in front of her. If Mousy had not casted the preservation spell, the dungeons would have been filled with the stench of a dead body.

'That's it, we need to do something' she said.

'What can we do, magic can't help us' Prince Nathan replied from another cell.

'I know that. But it's all I've got' Mousy said with full confidence. She shrank herself to the size of a thumb. No one could really see her clearly now.

'What are you doing?' Nathan said. 'The anti-magic will wipe your spell clean, you'll grow while you're under the bars. It'll kill you! And besides, you can't leave'

Mousy returned to her original size.

'I can't, but one of you can' Mousy said, pointing at those in her cell that are not magic-abled.

'They'll still grow when they move under the bars. It'll kill them' Nathan reminded her.

'We have to try Nathan. There's no other way!' Mousy said. 'Now, which one of you is very fast? I promise you, if you move out of this cell fast enough before you're turned back to your original size, you'll get us all out of here. I won't force you if you refuse'

One king's guard stepped up.

'I'll do it master. For King Henry. For the good of Inland' he said.

'Thank you brave soldier' Mousy said. 'Now, once you're about to cross below the bars, just run. As fast as you can'

She swiped her hand downwards over him. The king's guard shrank to the size of a thumb. Mousy could see a small figure making its way towards the bars. Few seconds passed. Nothing. She was starting to worry. She feared that the soldier is going to grow through the bars any second. It won't be a pleasant thing to see. Suddenly, the king's guard grew in size just a few centimetres away from the bars. He was lying on his front. He was rolling out from under the bars just in time before the anti-magic changed him. He passed the bars safely. There wasn't any injury. They heaved a huge sigh of relief.

'Now get the keys and get us out of here' Mousy said. The soldier ran up the stairs. Few minutes later, he ran back down with a keyring filled with many keys. Ten of which will unlock all the cells. It took at least ten minutes to get everyone out. The cell door opened, opening the circuit of anti-magic, allowing everyone to escape.

'Prince Nathan, it's your decision' Mousy found Nathan and said. He understood what she meant. There is a war going on. Between their family, friends, and all of Inland, against the avengers. They need to help them. And the first step is to reclaim back Combination. There were only less than a hundred Outland soldiers left in the city. Hundred men can easily take them down. Afterwards, they have to find and regroup back all of Combination's forces that had scattered or fled when the avengers attacked. There were some who hid in the forests, some were tortured in the encampment district. They managed to kill all the soldiers who saw them and tried to fight. Those that ran away in fear, they ignored. Altogether they managed to gather about two hundred men. Mousy also managed to gather some animal friends from the forests. They got a hundred animals who volunteered. An army of three hundred as a reinforcement. They didn't even know if the war had already started or yet to. The only information they have was that the war is going to happen at the field of Alhora.

An impromptu meeting was held at the city square. Prince Nathan, Master Mousy, Master Asher, Master William, Master Danny (a brown dog), Annie, and Laura were having a discussion on what's their next course of action.

'We can't just charge onto Alhora field with only three hundred men' Nathan said.

'Why are you always lacking in faith?' Mousy argued. She on the other hand was quite careless.

'I'm not lacking in faith. I'm speaking sense. It's suicide if we just attack now'

'But we know our friends are there as well. We'll not be only three hundred men'

'May I say something?' Danny interrupted. He dislikes arguments especially in times like this. Both looked at him like he had just spoiled both of their moods. But they didn't say no, so they were waiting for what he intended to say.

'Barenge is not far from here. Maybe it wouldn't hurt to try and convince them to join us back again?' Danny said.

'Danny! Are you the only one who always received information late? Barenge had fallen. And so had Silverside' Mousy said, irritated that she was interrupted for nothing. Danny was very shocked.

'Yes, we'll let you process that' Mousy said bluntly.

'I suggest we just move in now!' Mousy said. Nathan thought about it thoroughly. One of the king's guards suddenly came up to them.

'Your highness, masters, there is an army approaching Combination from the southeast direction. They'll enter from village district two'

'An army?!' Mousy exclaimed alarmingly. She immediately marched off towards the southeast direction. Some king's guards and SHAW masters followed her. Ten minutes later they came back with the army mentioned. A man dressed very smartly in a uniform just like the rest of the army. He was the leader. He was the only one with a grand looking headgear on his head. The Combination sigil was sewn into the centre of the headgear on the front side. If anyone or anything were to have that sigil, it always has something to do with royalty. But they had no idea who that person was.

'Morning your highness. Sir Everos, head knight of The White Keep. Army of White Woods at your service' the man said, getting on one knee. He drew his sword and pointed the sharp edge on the ground. Both his hands on the sword's grip.

'White Woods? When is there such a place?' Nathan said. He was extremely confused. Mousy went to him.

'They are actually a town under Combination' she explained. 'I didn't know either. Apparently King Henry built this town in secret after the incident and the only people who knew about it were himself, Bobby and Master Jenny'

'Our fathers were very poor people of a very obscure town in The Outlands. Seventeen years ago, King Henry found us while he was searching for Prince Edward and Princess Erieka. He took us in, built a whole new town southeast of Combination just for us. We vowed to serve him and Combination as long as our family is still living under his amenities. We owe it to him. So he decided to keep us a secret. If the avengers found out about us, they would have attacked White Woods after Combination. We also have SHAWs among us, that is how White Woods is until now hidden under the dimensional barrier. We have spies around who updated us about events going on. We got the message late however. Unfortunately one of our spies was killed when the avengers made a sudden attack on Combination. We sent another, and he found out that there was already a war coming. We waited for the avengers to leave, knowing there were still forces in Combination trapped and needed assistance. So here we are, offering our services. White Woods is at your command, your highness. We have two hundred men with us, one hundred and fifty knights and fifty SHAW warriors' Sir Everos said.

'I am still overwhelmed with amazement. My father was never a selfish man. He cared for others even when he was having problems himself' Nathan said. Everos smiled.

'I heard what happened. I'm sorry for your loss' he said.

'Thank you, thank you for coming. We will move off to Alhora now. Get ready our men' Nathan said. They all prepared to march off. The castle servants stayed behind to watch over the city and find surviving citizens and those in hiding.

At around eleven, they were already making their way north through the Combination Border Woods.

Thirty minutes later was the time when Prince Edward and Princess Flyra were surrounded by Erieka and four other avengers. Edward was in his trance, controlling the water swirling at the first group. Marcala was still trying to take control of the water. Some avengers were helping her but they failed as well. Erieka and the four avengers had attempted to kill them both but failed too. A sphere shield had protected them from their attacks. And now Erieka was getting angrier. Her pupils turned crimson. Her skin was also turning more red. She was filled with rage. Even some of the avengers took a step back in fear that she was going to explode her powers at them. She shot both of her hands out towards the shield. Like Flyra's light blue ray of light, Erieka's was red. Red light rays shot out of both of her palms, continuously and rapidly hitting the shield. The contact it made with the translucent forcefield formed sparks around the area. But the shield was not showing any sign if it's getting weaker or not. There were no cracks or anything. Erieka would die of exhaustion and the shield would still be there. Erieka gave up.

'This is not your magic! Impossible you can do this at a very young age. Even Marcala can't!' Erieka exclaimed. She was gasping for air. The rage she used drained most of her energy. 'You're just an ordinary princess!'

'That's where you're wrong. Word of advice from a princess to a princess, never underestimate someone you thought is lower than you. I am a child of the seed of Gratultyn. As long as I'm alive, you won't, I repeat, you will never achieve victory' Flyra said with sass. If

Erieka still had all her energy, she would have been more angry than before.

'I guess I have to find other ways to kill you!' Erieka exclaimed. 'Keep her busy' she told the four avengers.

She transformed into a black bird and flew towards Marcala to report.

The avengers watched Flyra very closely. The shield was still there. Even if it turned invisible again, it is still there, forever protecting Flyra and those around her from any magic that wants to harm.

'Perhaps weapons can hurt her' one avenger said, forming a sword out of the soil beneath the snow. He threw it at the shield. Her experiment failed. The shield deflected the dirt sword.

'That weapon is still magical. You craft it with magic' another avenger said. The avenger drew a sword of her own.

'That's enchanted. You casted a spell on your sword for it to be sharp remember?' a third avenger said.

'Coward princess! Drop the shield. Fight us!' the last avenger said.

'It's not a fair fight, four to one' Flyra replied.

'Face it, it's a war. Fight us, coward!'

Over at the first group, Marcala was commanding the first group to move away from the water. In the end she decided to just deploy them onto the battlefields.

'Kill them all!' Marcala shouted. The first group charged, splitting into two, some went to the first battlefield, the others went to the second. But before they could reach, water hands shot out of different spots on Edward's water line, grabbing many avengers, Outland soldiers, and beasts, by their legs. The water hands lifted them up high in the air and swung them around. They let go and the victims were thrown out of the battlefields. Most crashed into the trees of Combination Border Woods. Marcala showed a reaction that she was very irritated. She looked very ugly doing so especially since she was very old.

'I don't care what you're reporting, just kill everyone!' Marcala shouted at Erieka. Erieka turned her attention to the nearest good guy and cracked his neck.

The water turned to snow and dropped onto the ground, adding up to the layer of snow that was already there. Edward fell out of the trance shortly afterwards. Flyra caught him and helped him up.

'What happened?' Edward asked, looking around, his face full of worry.

'You got so deep into the magic. You were in a trance. It happened to me before' Flyra said, remembering the wingless dragon. Then Edward saw the four avengers and the shield. He understood what happened. He then realised he did not need Flyra to explain to him more. He understood what was going on with his own mind. His intellect. He was making progress with it. "Just keep on going" he thought. His brain will react accordingly.

'Let down the shield. We can do this together' Edward said reassuringly. Both of them made eye contact. There was the same feeling again, the funny feeling when someone is around their crush. Flyra's face was very flawless and beautiful. Her dark green scarf covering her entire head made her look innocent. She gave him the look of "are you sure?".

'We can do this' he said.

The shield had appeared without Flyra intending it to. So she had to take control over it to bring it down. The shield went down easily. The avengers grinned with satisfaction.

'Finally!' the first avenger said. Edward and Flyra stood back to back. Two avengers on Edward's side and the other two on Flyra's.

'Now let's play' the fourth avenger said. She lit fire on both of her palms. The first and fourth avengers were facing Flyra, whereas the second and third were facing Edward. All four avengers released their powers at the same time. The fourth avenger threw the two flames at Flyra. The first blew wind, increasing the fire's speed and size. The second and third avengers sent fire at Edward. Flyra's intelligent shield appeared again, deflecting all the attacks. The fire conjured by the fourth avenger burnt the first to death before he could wipe them all out.

'Fight fair!' the fourth avengers shouted. She drew her sword. Edward drew his own he had been keeping by his side.

'Take this' he told Flyra.

He passed to Flyra while still standing in the back to back position.

'Now fight!' the fourth said.

Flyra moved forward, the first avenger's body lay on the ground. She could see his skin full of burns and scalds. Her attention went to focus on the fourth avenger. The avenger smirked. Flyra held her sword in a defensive stance. The avenger went in and made an aggressive strike with her sword. Flyra parried and darted to the side. She was no longer with Edward. He was busy with the other two avengers. Edward was still dueling magic with the two. There were fireballs, water magic, soil lifting, and force-pushing and pulling. The two avengers died when Edward let out a strong quick water attack. The water exited in a small radius around Edward. Which the two avengers were inside. The water was like swords jabbing out of Edward. Every part of his body let out the water. In a second it jabbed the two avengers, and another second went back into his body. The two immediately dropped dead. Edward turned to check on Flyra. She was now continuously blocking the fourth avenger's aggressive strokes while retreating backwards. Edward ran to help. As he came closer, a sudden zap of electricity shocked him, flinging him away. He recovered as quickly as possible to find Marcala walking towards him. He held up his hands in a defensive stance. Marcala stopped when she was about six arm lengths away from him.

'Hello Ned. No, it's Edward once again!' Marcala said with a tone like she wants to find fault.

'You won't be able to stop me this time' Edward replied, staring angrily at her.

'Ooh, love that anger in your voice! I had just zapped you, you don't know that kind of magic. The only way for you to defeat me is to use your anger little boy'

Edward wanted to strangle her. But he calmed himself down. He let the anger go away and welcomed back the calmness.

'No' he said.

Marcala released her current again. This time

Edward dodged it by rolling to the side and standing back up with fast speed. Marcala did not wait to continue. She tried zapping him a few times. Edward managed to avoid them until he was tired. The next one flung him backwards. They were moving closer towards the battlefields and further away from Flyra and the fourth avenger.

The battlefields were still intense with magic, attacks, and pain. Prince Jake and Bobby were already on their feet. Their horses ran away when a fire almost hurt them. They both stayed close together, helping one another with their swords, attacking and defending against the avengers and soldiers. Most of the beasts were already dead. At the second battlefield, King David was all out striking every enemy around him. Nathaliya stood nearby, covering David and every good guy around her. She shot her arrows at any evil person coming at them when they were busy with an enemy. Her quiver was now empty. She placed her bow on her back and grabbed a sword from a dead person near her. She joined in the close combat. The animals led by Oliver were making themselves very useful as support troopers. Wherever there's a good soldier in need, at least two animals paired together to help bring the enemy down. But overall, many good guys were dying. The evil guys were winning. Their numbers were far greater than the good guys.

Suddenly those who were closer to Combination Border Woods heard a loud shout. It was more than a loud shout. It was like an army shouting. A motivating call. The ground trembled a little. And they saw the reformed army of Combination combined with the new army they had no idea where they came from, charged out of the forest. Leading in front were Prince Nathan, Master Mousy, Master Asher, Master William, Master Danny, and Sir Everos. Combination soldiers wearing green and White Woods soldiers wearing white. The evil guys nearer to the forest were surprised with the sudden appearance. Many were defeated immediately. The avengers were overwhelmed for a while longer as green and white mixed with black. The battle continued like before as the avengers adjusted to the change. And all the beasts were successfully killed. Annie and Laura were guarded by a few soldiers as they made their way to the other side where the tent was. They will be providing assistance in medical issues for Dewi and Princess Darleen.

The battle raged for another few minutes when suddenly, the worst shake the ground has ever made happened. Almost everyone stopped fighting. Flyra parried the fourth avenger's blow and rolled away until she was about three metres away. Then the avenger steadied herself, trying not to lose balance from the shake. Flyra remained in the lying position. And she realised this is not some magic conjured by a Sprite. It was something big approaching the field. She glanced sideways to the medical tent. Dewi and the rest ignored the shake and kept themselves busy with the wounded. About a hundred metres to the left of the tent, she saw a giant figure coming out of the Alhora forest. Then there was a loud roar. And the wingless dragon that Flyra had encountered before and froze it, came out of the forest, more angry than ever. His body was partially glowing red, because of the fire and heat inside raging. Every step it took, snow changed to water, and soil let out smoke. Flyra got up, shocked and afraid. She never expected to see the dragon again. This time, he is much stronger than before. His steps now made the ground shake worse. And he wasn't even glowing at The Valley of Sorrows. At first, everyone on the field was being very cautious. Suddenly, the dragon surprised Flyra even more. He did something he didn't do before, something Flyra thought he couldn't. He spoke.

'Avenge Majuza!' he bellowed. And the evil guys went into a frenzy and they became more aggressive than before. The dragon stomped towards the battlefields. The Ocean Masters went to focus their full attention on the dragon. Mainly they worked on cooling his body, so as to prevent him from breathing fire. While the good soldiers nearby, drove their swords into the dragon's feet. There were only about ten Ocean Masters left. For the time being, they managed to prevent the dragon from breathing fire. The only attacks the dragon could do now, were killing people with his jaws, claws, or stepping on them with his large feet. Flyra ran towards him. Intending to stop him for good this time. But the fourth avenger wasn't done with her. However, she cheated by using magic. She force-pulled Flyra by her feet. Flyra was flung backwards and landed a few steps in front of her. The avenger went in immediately to strike. Fortunately Flyra was faster. Flyra rolled away and got up. She had lost grip on her sword when she was force-pulled backwards. So she only has her magic to help her.

'We can use magic on you after all. Disarming magic' the avenger said. 'This will be much easier'

She attempted force-pulling Flyra again. But Flyra cut the force and force-pushed her. The avenger was thrown backwards. She recovered and got back to her stance. Flyra was already closing in. The avenger tried force-pushing this time and Flyra cut the force again as she went closer. The avenger was starting to get scared. Panicking, she sent fireballs continuously. But Flyra wiped them all out very easily. The avenger raised her sword to strike her as she came very close. Flyra conjured an invisible force to resist the sword. Every time the avenger tried bringing the sword closer to Flyra, it pulled away like magnets repelling negative sides. The avenger dropped her sword eventually as the mass became heavier when it pulled back. Flyra force-choked her immediately. The avenger rose from the ground as both her hands went to hold her throat.

'Don't push me again' Flyra said very firmly. Flyra turned her choke to a push. The avenger was flung backwards. She landed a few metres away unconscious. Flyra did not waste any more time. She turned back to join the fight. The dragon was directly in her view. She rushed to help the others fight it. But then she saw Edward at the side of the second battlefield struggling to fight back Marcala's blue current. She rushed towards him instead. Flyra ran until she was a few steps behind Edward, she sent a massive flow of ice out of her hands towards the current. The effect was very quick. Flyra's ice made its way up the current towards Marcala's hands. Marcala pulled the current back immediately. But the ice wasn't finished. It pushed Marcala backwards. Although she was very old, her bones were still very strong to keep her from falling from the impact of the ice. Marcala's feet only slid on the ground, she was still able to balance herself. Flyra quickly helped Edward to stand. By then Marcala was ready to strike again. She sent her blue current again. Flyra held her left hand up, her palm facing the current. A shield formed in front of her palm, surrounding her front and Edward's. The current collided with the shield, creating sparks and smaller currents around the surface area of the collision. They stayed that way for almost a minute.

'Flyra, this is too long, you'll lose your energy assuming Marcala doesn't stop' Edward said, full of worry. Flyra didn't respond. But it was obvious, she was getting tired. Marcala however wasn't showing any sign of exhaustion. Her face was full of determination to drain Flyra's energy and hence bring down the shield. Flyra motivated herself.

'If she can do it, so can I' Flyra said confidently. She used more of her strength. Her hand started glowing faintly, the colour of her pale skin. The shield glowed the same colour. And the glow seemed to outshine the light of Marcala's current. But then, Marcala pushed her hand forward strongly, exerting her last effort into her current. A wave of high voltage made its way towards the shield and shattered it. It continued its way to zap Flyra but another shield grew in a spherical motion out of Flyra, deflecting the last of the current to other directions. Edward watched in amazement.

'You can never hurt her' he said. Part of him was enjoying Marcala's angry and disappointed face.

'Then we shan't use magic' Marcala said, removing her black cloak and just letting it fall onto the ground. A sword was hidden underneath the cloak all along. She drew it. Edward felt for his sword on his right. Flyra no longer has hers. She dropped it earlier. Edward drew his as Flyra remained standing beside him, intending to participate as well.

'You are weaponless, princess. No magic is allowed. And it won't be a fair match if two versus one' Marcala said in a mean tone. 'Now step closer Edward'

Edward walked in front. He and Marcala were now two arm lengths apart. Marcala was holding her sword at an at-ease position, the tip touching the ground. Edward held it up in a defensive position.

'Your move' Marcala said. She was being old-fashioned this way. A sword fight that is done fairly and respectfully. Unlike the current way, anyone can just strike without warning. Edward pulled back his sword and swung it forward. Marcala moved very quickly. From the ease position, she arched her sword upwards and blocked Edward's blow in time. One second pause, she arched her sword downwards and outwards, attempting to hit Edward's thigh. Edward pulled his sword down and blocked the attack.

'Faster' Marcala said. And she made another swing to the head. Edward parried. He also made an attack which Marcala blocked and attacked again. The sword fight went on smoothly. But Flyra watched in agitation.

Across the two battlefields, many of the good guys

were dead. The good guys were losing even after the reinforcements. The dragon has the most kill counts for this round. They managed to cause bleeding on the dragon's feet. But nothing more. The dragon was still standing strong. And with only a few Ocean Masters left, he could breathe fire once again. Fire burnt continuously at the area around him as he kept breathing to prevent anyone from coming near. The medical tent at the front of Alhora Woods was getting overcrowded with casualties. Dewi, Princess Darleen, Annie, Laura, the other assistants were getting more busy by the minute.

'We're losing out there' Dewi said, observing the battle occasionally.

'Their numbers are overwhelming. And the dragon has to be stopped' Darleen replied, observing as well.

'You can help them' Dewi said to Darleen.

'I am helping you!' Darleen replied.

'Not anymore Darleen. They need you more than we do' Dewi said. 'Go alright? Go help them'

Dewi got busy with another patient. Darleen glanced at the battlefields, then at her bow on the table beside the medicines and aid equipment. Her quiver was there too, full of arrows waiting to soar. She relived the memory of the battle in Barenge. It wasn't a pleasant memory. But she grabbed her bow and quiver anyway. Ignoring her fears, she ran into battle with determination. The sight of everyone fighting for the good side motivated her. After a few seconds, many Outland soldiers had become victims to her arrows.

As the battle goes on, two things are for sure. One,

Erieka was already using her amulet to cause the dead evil soldiers, avengers, and even the beasts to stand back up and fight as the undead. Secondly, the good guys are clearly losing.

THE WAR PART 3

Before you start reading the next chapter, finish what you're supposed to do first. Done? Carry on!

M arcala and Prince Edward's duel was still going on very intensely. But now, Princess Flyra has interrupted the fight. She used her magic to form ice around Marcala's shoes so that it will be slippery for her. Marcala was very furious about that. But she was so focused on Edward's movements, she struggled to find time to get back at Flyra. Edward knocked Marcala's sword out of her hand with ease and pointed the tip of his sword at her neck.

'Your move' Edward said.

'You didn't fight fairly' Marcala said with rage. Her eyes stared angrily at Flyra. Flyra responded by showing an 'I don't care' face. Marcala released her current at her. But Edward shifted his sword a little so that it is in the way of the current. The current found interest in his sword and decided to stay there instead of going to the initial target. Blue electricity moved randomly around the iron. Edward pointed the sword back at Marcala.

Marcala released her current again continuously and defensively. The currents collided on the sword. Edward was steadily holding it. Trying his best to not lose his grip. The sword is currently the point of interest for the current. Something bad or worse will surely happen if he drops it. Flyra did not wait to do her magic. She made the area of the ice at Marcala's shoes bigger. And Marcala slipped. The electricity when in every direction, electrocuting nearby soldiers, both good and bad. Some managed to duck or block with their shield. Edward took the opportunity to move in and made sure Marcala could not do anything for good. He pointed his sword at her neck.

'For my mother' Edward said.

'So all this anger is all because of the queen? For revenge?' Marcala scoffed. Flyra put on a disbelief expression. She went through about this with Edward earlier.

Suddenly, Marcala started laughing. She just pushed the sword away with her bare hands. There was no blood or cut. She pushed it with such strength that the sword went flying out of Edward's hand. She force-choked him and continued doing so as she stood up. Flyra was getting nervous. She attempted to stop her but her force only came out a little. Marcala used her other hand to force-push her backwards. Flyra got up to see Edward was already in mid-air, his throat getting choked by Marcala's force. Flyra ran to assist. But Marcala froze her in her place. She could only see and listen to what was happening.

'This is how anger is used!' Marcala exclaimed,

feeling very satisfied. 'You think you can let anger live with light magic? You're wrong Edward. Anger lives in darkness. Your puny revenge is not gonna work if you think light magic will help. Now taste the true power of anger!'

Marcala hardened her grip on Edward's throat. He struggled frantically. Flyra could only watch in horror as Edward's neck turned red from the force. A forcefield suddenly threw Marcala a few metres away. The grip on Edward's throat was released and he fell to the ground, touching the red marks on his throat. Flyra was also released from the freezing spell. Marcala got back up to see Master Mousy standing defensively in front of Edward and Flyra.

'Master Mousy!' Marcala exclaimed in a sarcastically happy way.

'Master Widow' Mousy said.

'How nice of you to join us. Though I did not invite you'

'I don't need an invitation to destroy you'

Marcala laughed. She let water flow out of both of her hands. Mousy rubbed her hands together. Sand fell out from the gap between her hands and stayed in mid air. Mousy pulled her hands away, a huge amount of sand continued flowing out of her hands. Marcala scoffed. The idea of sand wanting to defeat water amused her. Edward and Flyra were already busy with other soldiers who suddenly found interest in attacking them. Mousy has to face the old avenger alone. Marcala attacked with the water. Mousy blocked with the sand. Mousy had to make the sand very thick as most of it became wet. The water and sand were treated like weapons. Like swords clashing. The water was clearly the better weapon. But Mousy was very smart to multitask. She parried the water strike with the sand. At the same time, she summoned some of Marcala's water to join her side. The fight went on for a while.

Suddenly, a friendly war horn could be heard throughout the entire field. A war horn which no one would expect to hear anymore. The war horn of Silverside. The said to be one of the fallen cities of Inland. From the southwest direction, a huge army of Silverside soldiers came running into the battlefields. But that was not all. Running in with the Silverside army was the army of Trisnarim. Many times bigger than the amount that followed Princess Flyra originally. There were more tankers and Ocean Masters. And riding on a huge strange white creature that looks like it is more comfortable living in water, was Queen Lady Lith herself. The creature was all white, just the same colour as what Lady Lith was showing. It's like a whale mixed with a seal. That is how it is able to move on land. Lady Lith has a staff in one hand. Which she used as a weapon. When the whale-like creature reached the nearest enemy, Lady Lith jumped off its back and knocked the soldier out with her staff as a landing style. The whale then got busy attacking as well. Lady Lith fought stylishly. She used both her staff and water magic. And her movements were more gracious than all the Ocean Masters. One soldier charged at her, she parried the sword's strike with her staff. She then turned the staff around like a wheel, cold wind swirled around the soldier, freezing him to death before vanishing. After that she dealt with another soldier. King Harold, the king of Silverside, was leading his men. His two young princes, around the ages of Princes Nathan and Jake, were by his side. The fight went on excitingly. The tables have turned. The good guys outnumbered the evil plus the undead by a few hundred.

Marcala and Mousy's fight were now being interrupted by other SHAWs joining in to help Mousy.

The wingless dragon was now face to face with Lady Lith. She ended him very easily. The dragon was already very badly injured from all the sword attacks on his feet, and the magic from masters and Ocean Masters on his body and face. Lady Lith surrounded him with icy mist and froze him inside and out. She then caused the frozen dragon to burst into a million snowflakes.

Erieka watched in horror and went into rage mode. Her whole presence, from the top of her scarf to her shoes, glowed red. Her iris glowed very bright red. More dead soldiers got back up to fight. This time they were even more aggressive. They attacked without mercy. Erieka herself was more aggressive. She made sure every strike would immediately kill the victim.

Marcala too was very angry. She pushed the enemies in front of her, in a semicircular motion, with forcefield. She reached her palm up facing the sky. This time it wasn't any normal electricity. Lightning zapped the areas around her. Some hit the masters who died instantly. Marcala's eyes were blue in colour. She continued summoning lightning, occupying a huge surface area on the ground every time it zaps. Mousy and the other masters couldn't fight that, they ran away. Mousy did not intend to let it go. She planned on returning back to Marcala to finish their fight.

Mousy stumbled upon Master Kitty and Edward who were fighting a troublesome undead beast together. Edward struck with his sword and Kitty caused the wound to spread wider with magic. The undead fell but only for a few minutes. Just like all the other undead, they'll get back up a few minutes maximum after every attack that was meant to kill them.

'We need to stop Marcala and Erieka first. That's the priority' Mousy said.

'Yes master' Edward replied obediently. He was eager to do anything to finish this war, so he was open to any good idea.

'It's good to see you again Edward' Mousy made a quick comment. She missed him so much.

'Later' she said quickly. There'll be time for this. She turned her attention to Marcala.

'We'll need Flyra's help as well' Edward said. 'She's the key to stopping the amulet's power'

'Who? Well never mind then, where is she?' Mousy said. Edward did not remember that Kitty had told him before that Mousy had been stuck in another place all these years. Hence she has no idea who Flyra or Jake were. She had only met Nathan back at the castle dungeons. Edward looked around for Flyra but could not find her. And the duels happening around him were distracting.

'We have to do something first until we can find her' Mousy said. She raised her hands, her eyes turning green. Edward remembered the last time he went into the vulnerable state. Both times, just earlier during the war and when he was a small boy. Both times he couldn't control himself. Well he could control a little when he was eight but now he couldn't. Even not many grown ups could. Mousy, Marcala and even his sister seemed to be able to control. He wants to help as much as he could but for now, he fears the vulnerable state and is not intending to enter it. Kitty's eyes turned silver in colour and he zoomed past Mousy to where Marcala was standing. The lighting was still actively zapping the areas around. Kitty was in a suicide mission. If he is not careful, he'll be dead. There were disturbances along the way, evil soldiers or undead blocking both masters' way. Mousy destroyed them. Their bodies literally turned to soil and fell back into the ground. Kitty managed to avoid all the obstacles until he was a few metres away from Marcala. The lightning zapped the grass patch a few steps away from him. Edward could see Kitty's fur stood for a while from the static current. Kitty surrounded himself with a shield as he waited for Mousy to get closer. Edward immediately continued to look around for Flyra when an avenger suddenly came up to him with a sword. Edward parried just in time. He force-pushed him away. Then he saw Flyra. She was dealing with three soldiers at once. Edward rushed to her aid. He took one opponent. The two soldiers fighting Flyra charged at the same time. Flyra formed huge ice spikes around both of them. The third soldier swung his sword at Edward. Edward parried his strike and drove the sword into the side of his chest. His sword pierced the armour. The soldier dropped. Edward turned to Flyra who nodded her head in respect and thanked him for helping.

'We need you. Marcala and Erieka overpowered' Edward said. Flyra did not question further, she followed him immediately as he led her to where Mousy and Kitty were. There were some avengers and soldiers who blocked their path. They got rid of them easily, with a sword and magic.

Mousy was already fighting Marcala's lightning. Every lightning strike, Mousy tried her best to send as many rocks up above the trees level. The next lightning was about to zap in a few more seconds. Mousy formed huge rocks from the ground, sent them all up wherever Marcala was conducting. The lightning still managed to pass and hit the ground, but the rocks did minimise the damage.

Edward and Flyra reached the two masters. Flyra immediately pointed her right palm up at the sky. Like she was expecting the lightning to zap her.

'What are you doing?' Edward asked, full of worry.

'Trust me, magic that can kill can't hurt me' Flyra said confidently. After all that she had experienced before, she was determined. The next lightning came seemingly quicker than before. The two masters and Edward watched in horror as the lightning zapped Flyra. But, they were then relieved to find what they thought would happen did not happen. The lightning stopped a few centimetres away from Flyra's palm and it was still moving in its place, as how currents would zigzag on the spot. Flyra was taking over the lightning.

Marcala through her glowing eyes, it was obvious she was shocked. Flyra looked like a lot of her energy was drained from doing that. She pushed herself to continue the fight. What happens next is only partially her intention. Flyra absorbed the lightning current into her palm. The current flowed to other parts of her body. Her whole presence was now crackling with electricity. She directed the current towards Marcala. Marcala was not prepared for this. Her eyes glowed a brighter blue as she tried to stop the current. The current hit Marcala, causing a great explosion. Sparks of electricity hit many different spots. A deafening sound for a second. Fire started burning the few grass patches on the ground. Smoke came out of other areas that were earlier covered in snow or just plain soil. Marcala was nowhere to be seen. Her whole body couldn't be found, the explosion had probably disintegrated her into ashes. They watched in amazement. The avengers and soldiers that saw the whole thing were startled. Most of them got killed after the distraction. Edward looked over to praise Flyra. But he saw her already lying on the ground. Her face was less pale.

'Flyra!' Edward exclaimed. He kneeled by her side. Flyra opened her eyes instantly. But Edward could see clearly, she had lost a lot of energy. The power she used had drained her.

'Mousy!' he called. Mousy and Kitty rushed immediately.

'She'll be fine, that was too much for her. She's not used to controlling such power' Mousy said in a praising tone. She was proud of what she saw. She still hasn't gotten to know who Flyra is but she already likes her very much.

About fifty metres away, Erieka was going mad with her undead army, killing everyone that was opposing her.

'Erieka is still standing strong' Edward said.

'Do you still wish to help her' Flyra asked softly. She was still extremely tired.

'I have to do whatever to bring peace to the land. For the good of Inland. I have to stop her. Kill her if that's what's best' Edward replied. Flyra smiled weakly.

'You have a good heart. I'm sorry it has to come to this' Flyra said. Edward understood what she meant. She was referring to his family. First his mother was killed. Then his father died from a heart attack. Now he has to kill his own sister. Edward felt a sudden sense of motivation. His intellect was recovering. He was able to understand phrases without many questions.

'I'll need help. When you're ready, join me' Edward said. Flyra nodded. 'Take care of her' he said to Mousy.

'Master Kitty, stand with me' Edward said again.

'Of course my prince. To my death I'll serve the king or future king of Combination' Kitty said, smiling.

ALPHAGA, BALE, CAPTAIN, MASTER ASHER, AND OLIVER

Before you start reading the next chapter, finish what you're supposed to do first. Done? Carry on!

Alphaga has always been a lone wolf. He loves doing things alone. And that's what happened in the war. He faced Captain, Bale, Oliver and Master Asher all by himself. Although only the master and Oliver have powers, it's still two against one. No one should underestimate Master Asher's powers. In third place after Masters Jackenzie and Mousy, Master Asher was someone Marcala found a challenge to defeat.

Alphaga threw fireballs at Captain, Bale, and Oliver. Master Asher was not there yet. Captain and Bale dodged the attacks. Oliver sent the ground in front of him up to block. Alphaga ran with high speed towards Captain who was the nearest. And they got into a no-magic combat. Alphaga was winning. But fortunately for Captain, Bale and Oliver interrupted. Bale kicked

Alphaga on his rabbit foot. Oliver pushed him away with a rabbit-sized rock. Alphaga turned furiously and sent a forcefield at them. Captain and Bale were thrown back. However, Oliver blocked the attack with a shield that shattered as the two forces collided.

'You're hitting on three innocent forest creatures?' Master Asher's voice came from the side. Alphaga looked to his left with his mad eyes.

'The wolf has decided to make his appearance' Alphaga said.

'And the rabbit looks like he's gonna get beaten real bad' Asher replied. Alphaga released flames from his bunny ears angrily. He targeted them in a semicircular direction in front of him. Oliver and Asher rolled and moved back respectively out of reach. Captain and Bale showed up beside them again.

'You two are very brave to fight a strong avenger without magic' Asher said proudly. 'Now we end him together for good'

Asher sent the wind to blow the flames away in another direction. A small opening could be seen on Alphaga's right side. Captain threw soil he picked up from the ground before at that opening. It hit Alphaga's right shoulder. The flames stopped. Alphaga force-choked all four of them at once. Asher however escaped the force. He created a forcefield around his neck that helped him to be released from the grip. Asher sent water out from his body towards Alphaga, attempting to trap him in a water ball. Alphaga hopped out of the way, at the same time losing his concentration on the choke. The three animals were released. Oliver sent the ground breaking apart in Alphaga's direction. Alphaga couldn't counter both attacks. He couldn't counter one of them. If he did, he'd be attacked by another. He had no choice but to just hop out of the way. When Alphaga was about to go very far away, Asher force-pulled him back. The water stopped for a while as he did that and resumed charging at Alphaga when his concentration was back on it. Oliver changed the course of the small quake to wherever Alphaga is. Alphaga couldn't take being overpowered, he madly released a few waves of forcefield out of his body. The three animals were thrown on the first wave. Asher was thrown on the third. After that Alphaga was nowhere to be seen.

KING DAVID, LILLAIN, LORD MORGAN, PRINCE JAKE, AND PRINCESS NATHALIYA

Before you start reading the next chapter, finish what you're supposed to do first. Done? Carry on!

In between both battlefields, Lord Morgan was slaying every soldier and SHAW. He used his magic to weaken them before striking with his sword. There were more than two handfuls of Outland soldiers by his side. Because of that, every of his victims would feel at least three times, swords slashing on their body.

Princess Nathaliya was the first to not run away from the intimidation. She nocked an arrow to her bow and aimed at Morgan.

'Oh this is no ordinary soldier. She's royalty! Look at the fancy way her outfit was made' Morgan said mockingly. Nathaliya just stood tall and confident while the soldiers laughed at her. King David came up to her right side. He was no longer on his horse and had no idea even where it might have gone to. He stared at Morgan with determination.

'Oh I'm so scared now' Morgan continued mocking.

Suddenly the ground where the evil guys were standing became weaker. It was like it changed into quicksand all of a sudden. Most of the soldiers sank very quickly. Morgan used his magic to prevent himself from sinking. Some fortunate soldiers who happened to be SHAWs managed to avoid sinking as well. Lillain made her appearance by the left side of Nathaliya. It was her that was doing her all time favourite trick. A second later, Prince Jake also stood to Lillain's other side.

'That's enough' Jake said. Lillain stopped.

'Ha! You think four of you, only one has magic, can stop me?' Morgan laughed. His few remaining soldiers followed laughing, but they were more cautious this time.

'All the soldiers you see here are also SHAWs' Morgan said.

'Who says only she has powers?' Nathaliya replied. She hasn't made a single movement since she nocked her arrow earlier. Morgan digested what she meant for a few seconds.

'You?' Morgan mocked.

'And me' David added. He made a half twirl with his left hand. A man-sized tornado formed in front of him, and made its way towards Morgan. Halfway it split into a few different same-sized tornadoes and charged at the soldiers. Morgan absorbed the tornado charging at him into his hand. The others got caught up in the whirlwinds. For the next few seconds all of them continued moving round and round on the same spot. Morgan conjured fire on his hands, bigger than the size of a head. The wind died down and the bodies of the soldiers fell down dead. Morgan was alone now.

'You shouldn't have done that' Morgan said.

'This is war' David replied.

Morgan sent fire from both hands at all four. The fire grew in size as it reached them. Morgan conjured another fire on both hands, ready to attack again. Jake and David were ready to deflect the fire away with their sword. But Nathaliya was quicker. She lowered her bow and arrow and concentrated using her eyes. The fire changed behaviour. From charging, it became static for a moment, before making its way back at Morgan. Morgan watched with mad wide-eyes and sent the fire on his hands at the first fire. A continuous flow of fire came out of his hands and hit the first fire. The two fires joined together to form one large fire and stayed static for a while. Morgan sent them charging again.

'We split, attack him from every angle' Jake said. The rest nodded in agreement. Jake and Lillain moved to their left. David to the right. Nathaliya stayed in the same position. She dropped everything in her hands, and countered the huge charging fire with both hands. Large amount of water exited her hands and collided with the fire. Steam came out at the top rapidly. Morgan stopped the flow. Nathaliya extinguished all the fire that was left and stopped the flow as well. Now the four were on equally different sides of Morgan.

Morgan did not dare say anything else. He knows

he is outnumbered. He just stood his final stand, still holding on to his values and mission as an avenger. He let fire flow out of his hands and dropped them on the ground around him. He raised them and split them into four, like whips made of fire. He attacked all four, all at once, or sometimes one by one, with the whip. One for each of the four. Jake blocked the attack with his sword. David did the same. Nathaliya used water. Lillain used the ground to block, sending the soil up every time. Morgan wasn't going to just keep this up. He planned to stop them starting with the weakest. While still doing his fire-whip trick, he sent a wave of fire at Jake. His attention was occupied by the whip that he did not notice the fire coming. The fire burnt his left side, the side that was further from his sword. He dropped to the ground, trying to endure the pain. The whip attacked him on his back. Jake cried out. David was the first to see, he rushed to where Edward was, the whip that was meant for him followed. Jake's whip now focused on David as well. Both whips attacked. David blocked successfully. He couldn't find time to help Jake. Nathaliya and Lillain saw that there were three of them left who were still able to fight. Nathaliya and Lillain made a quick glance of each other. Lillian signalled with her eyes to the water that was flowing out of Nathaliya's hands. Nathaliya did not understand, she just ignored and focused on dealing with Morgan's whip. Lillain just went with her plan. What she meant was to use Nathaliya's water as well to fight since she can't conjure herself. Lillain took some of Nathaliya's water and increased its amount.

Nathaliya noticed what she was doing and understood everything. She let water flow out of her hands more rapidly. Morgan sent another wave of fire at David and Jake. With two whips and the third fire, David will lose as well. Lillain directed the water she was controlling towards the wave of fire. The water wiped the fire out and ended with a little amount left. Lillain increased the amount again. If the water had completely finished, she would have had to take some from Nathaliya again. Morgan sent a more impressive wave. This time, it was like the ripple of water, him being the centre. The wave of fire shot out of his body around him. Lillain wiped out the fire on her side and David's. Nathaliya wiped it out on her side. There was no water left for Lillain. She took some again from Nathaliya. David decided to abandon his sword just like Nathaliya abandoned her bow for now. He sent the wind around him to blow out all the fire including the whips. But there were still some stubborn ones. Morgan conjured more fire and sent another wave. All three blew and wiped out the fire. Coincidentally, all three were thinking the same thing. They attacked Morgan at once while he was not doing anything else. Nathaliya shot a continuous flow of water directly at Morgan. David blew a continuous flow of wind directly at him. Lillain used the amount of water she had left to wipe out the remaining fire for good. Then sent a mini-quake towards where Morgan was standing. Morgan could only conjure a shield to protect himself from all three elements. But the impact was too much for him to hold for long. His shield broke and he was devoured by wind, water and soil at the same time. It was a messy combination, the elements mixed together and formed a ball that engulfed Morgan for a few seconds, pushing and pulling his body in itself. All three pulled back their magic. The small line in the ground joined back together. Morgan's body lay still and totally covered in dirt. He was dead.

THE AMULET AND THE SEED

Before you start reading the next chapter, finish what you're supposed to do first. Done? Carry on!

Prince Edward and Master Kitty fought their way through the undead army towards Erieka. There were so many of them, newly fallen soldiers stood back up slowly while the senior ones jumped up like savages. There were so many deaths. Mainly the weak ones became the victim. Edward was determined to finish this. The thought of giving up came to his mind but he quickly pushed it away. The next three undead came. Edward defeated them and there were a few more left to Erieka. Erieka's whole self was still glowing red. Since she was surrounded by her undead army, she has nothing much to do. No one could pass the ranks and get to her. So the only thing she was doing was summoning newly fallen soldiers and avengers to join the undead. Her powers reached to the edges of the battlefields. Now the undead was more than the bad guys who were still alive. In total, they're starting to outnumber the good guys all over again. Edward and Kitty found extreme difficulty to get past the remaining ranks. It was like the closer they get to Erieka, the stronger the undead are. Since they're all closer to the source of the magic. Edward tried his powers. While fighting the undead with his sword, he focused his energy on Erieka. There must be some way for him to connect with her. She's his sister. They have the same blood. But it was tough. Kitty on the other hand was busy himself releasing powers on the undead around him. Before they could get tired, Master Mousy joined the fight. She came and froze a lot of the undead in their tracks before sending them sinking into the ground. Princess Flyra came looking bright and powerful again. She released a great power like that was normal for her. But it was actually even way beyond Marcala's league. She just held up her left palm. An abnormal forcefield, lighter than how any forcefield was supposed to react, came out of her palm. It passed through every undead for about three ranks. They all instantly dropped and did not make any more movements. Flyra had cleared the way. There was only one rank left before Erieka. Erieka's glow disappeared. She glared at them and tried to reverse Flyra's magic but did not work. Erieka sent all the undead around her charging at them. Flyra did the same thing again before Edward, Mousy, and Kitty could do anything. The undead dropped again and Flyra changed her magic into a force-grip. She pulled the amulet away from Erieka's neck. Erieka's headscarf tilted up a little as the amulet made its way out. It was no longer glowing. And immediately afterwards, every single undead fell down and remained dead as they should. Erieka smiled like she knew that was going to happen. A second later, the amulet glowed again. And everyone around could see dim lights coming out of Flyra's body at very high speed and into the amulet. Flyra winced tragically. The amulet was absorbing Flyra's power and energy. Edward attempted to help her. But Kitty bit him to it. He sent a forcefield to push the amulet away but the forcefield turned against him. And after a few more seconds, the amulet had sucked everything it wanted out of Flyra. Flyra no longer has pale skin. That's the only difference they could see on her that was openly shown. Flyra fell down unconscious. Erieka summoned back the amulet to herself and laughed evilly.

'Not so fast' Edward said in a low, anger-controlling tone. He shot out his hand and force-grabbed the amulet as well. The amulet stopped in its path as both Erieka's and Edward's force tried to win over the other. Mousy helped and force-pulled the amulet towards them. However, Erieka was very determined to win. She sent fire at them with her other hand. With them distracted, she grabbed hold completely of the amulet and fixed it back around her neck underneath the scarf. She grinned, ready to start back where she last stopped. But her powers did not work. The amulet started glowing but it wasn't red in colour anymore. It was white. Erieka was getting worried. She attempted to send an attack at them again but instead, her body became stiff. Like she was being controlled. The amulet fell down from her by itself. As it touched the ground, the ground started humming. Erieka seemed to be drifting away. Like she was turning to dust. With a final scream, she exploded into a cloud of dust. The amulet stopped glowing and got back to its original colour red.

'The successor's dead! Retreat!' someone shouted. The reaction was slow at first. Then all the evil guys fell back. Some were still reluctant to leave, and some left immediately because of fear. Pertum and Lydia were not far away from Prince Nathan. He stopped them with his magic. He was planning to bring them back as prisoners. These two are very capable to rebuild the avengers if they were allowed to roam free. Within five minutes, all the evil guys had fled. Only Pertum, Lydia, and some other avengers and soldiers who were held captive were left.

Prince Edward rushed to kneel by Flyra's side. Masters Mousy and Kitty stood there as well. Soon, Captain, Bale, Oliver, Lillain, and many others gathered around. They lost a lot of people today. And they lost Flyra. Queen Lady Lith made her way to the front of the crowd, she handed the amulet over to Edward.

'I'm sorry' she said. 'I thought she couldn't die'

Edward took the amulet, appreciating the respect.

'No Flyangel!' Captain cried. The three animals cried. They huddled around Edward. Seeing them in tears made Edward cry as well. He had never felt attached to anyone like this before aside from his family. Flyra was special to him. Even Mousy was close to tears. She hadn't had the chance to get acquainted with Flyra properly which she very much wanted to do since she started liking her. Everyone stood still, respecting the moment for a while. All across the battlefields, different soldiers, masters, people, stood in respect to their friends or family.

'We have to do a farewell here, bury those who had passed' Edward said after a while. He got a grip over his emotions. He was the heir to the throne. The future king has to show that he's strong and is capable of carrying out his responsibilities even when it's hard.

Just then, white sparks blinked continuously all around Flyra. White dust flowed out of her rapidly and vanished into thin air as the sparks disappeared as well. Flyra opened her eyes.

THE PEACE

'Flyangel!' Captain, Bale, and Oliver were the first to exclaim with joy. Princess Flyra sat up and acknowledged their presence. Then she realised that many people were watching. She awkwardly stood up. Prince Edward was very surprised and was not showing how elated he was.

'Flyra… you're, you're alive' Edward was lost for words.

Flyra smiled. She suddenly gave a short speech.

'I'm still wearing the same thing from the outside. But inside, I'm very much different. I feel different. I'm not the same Flyra you used to know. The power of the seed is no longer in me. It died when it had reached its full potential when battling Erieka. Now it's just me. Simple Flyra. No more immunity or extreme powers'

'So you really cannot die when you were still the child of the seed' Queen Lady Lith said, impressed.

'In fact, new me, new name. I think I like the name you gave me, Captain' Flyra said.

'Princess Flyangel!' Captain exclaimed.

'You are different. You're much bolder' Edward said, noticing the different way Flyra was behaving. She was usually a soft-spoken person. Now, she just spoke whatever was on her mind.

'Nice to meet you Princess Flyra' Mousy said, eager to finally talk to her. 'Mousy here'

'I know you, Master Mousy. I've heard your name being mentioned quite a few times' Flyra replied.

Mousy blushed.

'And please, Flyra is no longer my name. Call me Flyangel' Flyra said. Her voice was still quite gentle but it was no longer as soothing as how everyone knows her before.

'Your majesty I believe, I should call you now' King David said suddenly from behind Edward. Edward turned to meet him.

'King David at your service' David said.

'King David, your majesty. I believe there's no need to call me with that title. And I'm not even a crowned prince yet' Edward replied humbly.

'Yes but you will skip that and straight to the highest in the land'

Edward laughed. He did not care about being king or royalty. He just wants good for his people.

'You'll make a wonderful king young sir' David smiled. 'And as a start, you might want to meet the other royalties of the different cities. And also get back to Combination' David gave him a short advice.

'Oh yes!' Edward said, feeling silly for not remembering that.

King Harold of Silverside, alongside his two young princes, Prince John, and Prince James. They were lining up their remaining troops to head back home.

'Your majesty' Edward greeted. King Harold upon seeing who was the person who greeted him, quickly bowed to Edward.

'My king' he said.

'Oh please you don't have to do that' Edward said shyly.

'No please, it's a Silverside tradition to bow to a higher status' Harold said. 'John, James, King Edward is here'

The two sons were busy calming down some scared horses. They turned and like their father, they bowed. Edward smiled, feeling a little uncomfortable. He wasn't expecting anyone to bow to him. He felt that that was meant for a more respectable person.

'I want to thank you for joining in the war. I heard that your city was attacked. But here you are with an army stronger than ever' Edward said, getting straight to the point.

'We received Queen Alice's letter, may she rest in peace wherever she is now, the letter mentioned the avengers taking over Combination and Barenge. We immediately evacuated everyone in the city. Yes the avengers took over our city. But there was no spilling of blood. Because when they arrived, there was no one left to fight. We set a few temporary camping grounds a few kilometres south of our city. Now we can get everyone back. I am proud to have joined you in the war' Harold said. 'Until we meet again my king'

With that, Silverside was ready to head home.

Edward went to look for Queen Lady Lith of Trisnarim. He found her chatting with Princesses Flyra and Nathaliya.

'I just have to say that I like your skills in archery. Maybe you can teach me sometime?' Flyra said.

'Sure' Nathaliya replied, beaming.

'Edward' Lady Lith said when she noticed Edward approaching.

'Your majesty' Edward greeted.

'I want to thank you for joining us in the war. We really appreciate the help since the very first fifty men to the army you led yourself. I am utterly amazed by your ways of magic'

'Thank you my king' Lady Lith said, humbled by the very nice compliment. Edward stepped back respectfully and went to look for others.

He found King David and many of his men with Princess Darleen helping out to gather the dead bodies together.

'King David' Edward said.

David looked up after placing one body with the others.

'Ah your majesty' David said. 'I'm gonna miss this

time. I mean definitely not the war. But the spirit of all five cities working together. I don't think we'll have any of this anytime soon after this'

'We can always plan a meeting' Edward said.

'It's not that simple. Every leader has a lot of responsibilities to their own people. I want to thank you for letting me fight with you. It was a great victory, your majesty'

Edward smiled. He was so grateful to have allies or friends that are very nice people.

'There's my handsome young king' Darleen said, coming up to them.

'I'll get back to helping' David said and continued helping with the bodies.

'Aunt Darleen' Edward said.

Darleen hugged him tightly. Edward's shoulders relaxed. He did not realise he was so tense before. He felt so emotional suddenly. Darleen was the only family member he had left. Darleen was not looking perfect anymore due to half of her body burnt, but he didn't care. That is not what's important. He felt stronger now.

'I love you Edward' Darleen said.

'I love you too' Edward replied.

Darleen pulled back first.

'Alright, we can talk later. I have to help them' Darleen said, smiling. Her eyes were a bit watery. Edward nodded in reply.

Then he saw Flyra coming towards him with Prince Jake and Prince Nathan.

'Edward, I want you to meet my brothers, Jake and Nathan' she said, pointing to the brothers respectively.

'We're not related at all but I'm proud to call them my brothers'

'Your majesty, I believe we have not been acquainted yet. I'm Prince… I mean just Nathan' Nathan said, awkwardly at the last part.

Edward laughed. His laughter was nothing Flyra had heard before. It sounded free this time. It was genuine. And it was contagious. The two joined in the laughter leaving Nathan confused.

'There's no need to be formal with me!' Edward laughed. Nathan smiled sheepishly.

'And you are Prince Nathan. You grew up a prince, so you are equally a prince as any other prince in Southernere' Edward said.

Edward proceeded to the medic tent next. Dewi was just finishing aiding some injured troops.

'Prince Edward. Or King Edward now?' Dewi said, grinning. She isn't a local here. But through the twenty years she had been here, one of her biggest wishes was to help King Henry find Edward once again. And she missed the young man very much. Seeing him all grown up and handsome made her very happy.

'It's just Edward' Edward said, smiling kindly. 'I can't believe you've lived here for twenty years. I'm very happy to see you. But don't get me wrong, I'm just curious. Don't you want to get back to where you came from? I mean your family?'

'I don't think my family misses me. When I came here twenty years ago, my relationship with my family wasn't good. I only missed my father. But, I can't go back now. I really like it here. And even if I want to go back, is there a way for me to return here?'

Edward understood what she meant.

'So you want to make this as your permanent home' Edward said.

'Yes Edward. I really like it here' Dewi replied, smiling with teeth. She was so happy just thinking of the idea of having her own house and starting a business. All those years, she had been living in the castle. King Henry had given her an important role, as the royal medic or generally in charge of the staff's welfare. She placed the idea of having her own house aside. Now, she is very open to that idea again.

'Thank you Dewi' Edward said, looking at all the casualties she, Annie, and Laura had aided.

'No, thank you Edward. You stayed strong even when your surroundings were bad. I don't think any normal eight year old could do that. Now we have you as our king. I really really love that' Dewi said, smiling wide. 'Inland will be in good hands now'

LAW AND ORDER

The atmosphere was never better. On every street of Combination there were people cheering and celebrating the victory of Inland. Every street in Arstar, Trisnarim, and Silverside had the same thing. However each city has an additional unique performance. Like Trisnarim came up with a magnificent water element display. Silverside has their sword duels. But Combination was the most beautiful. As night time came by, the people held hands together and sang Sofya's song as SHAW masters sent lanterns floating into the sky.

The next day arrived and it was time for Prince Edward's coronation. Letters had been sent to Silverside, Arstar, and Trisnarim regarding the event. All the royals showed up with very elegant suits and dresses. The ballroom was packed with chairs. They did not have enough time to prepare buffet style as how other occasions were done. There was only enough time to arrange chairs. All the rows of chairs faced the tall glass windows overlooking the garden. A small wooden stage was placed at the front. A long red carpet was placed in the centre aisle leading from the doors to the stage. The royals filled in the front rows. Followed by the masters and the citizens. Everyone came early. So it took only a few minutes to settle down. Bobby went up the stage dressed in a very smart tuxedo. He stood behind a stand that was by the left end of the stage and read a speech he wrote himself.

'Good morning everyone. Kings, queens, royalties, royal masters, masters, and fellow citizens and staff. Welcome to Combination Castle. On this special day, we gather to witness the crowning of our long lost prince. After emerging victorious from the recent battle with the help of all five cities. Relating to this, let's give a moment of silence in respect to the fallen city of Barenge'

A few seconds of pause.

'I'm happy to acknowledge that not all of Barenge has fallen. We have Princess Darleen with us here today' Bobby pointed with his whole hand at where Princess Darleen was sitting. Darleen smiled shyly.

'Alright, I'm not going to say more, because I'm sure the king will have a lot more to say later'

Laughter came from the audience.

'Ladies and gentlemen, please rise for Prince Edward of Combination' Bobby said formally. Everyone got to their feet as the ballroom doors opened. Prince Edward strode across the aisle towards the stage. He was dressed very magnificently. A long red coronation mantle covering a black tunic. A circle metal plate with the Combination sigil buttoning the mantle together around his neck. And the last detail was his appearance. He was looking extremely irresistible. There was a just-nice amount of powder on his face. His brown hair was neatly combed. Edward was just perfectly handsome. Everyone admired him as the musicians played soothing royal music. He stepped onto the stage and stood in front of Bobby, facing him. A servant held up a tray with the king's golden crown.

'Please remain standing esteemed guests' another servant who was also on the stage said.

'Edward son of Henry, please kneel' Bobby said out loud. Edward got on one knee, as how he was briefed just now morning during a short rehearsal with Bobby. His right foot was still stepping on the ground. He placed his right arm on the right knee. It was quite tiring and painful with all the heavy clothing. But he just endured it. It will only take a few minutes.

'Edward son of Henry. Father was the king before him. And now by the law that states the heir will be the first born son, or daughter if there is no son, I crown you, King Edward of Combination' Bobby announced loudly and clearly as he carefully took the crown in his hands and placed it on Edward's head.

'Please rise, your majesty' Bobby said.

Edward stood back up, careful not to trip and create an embarrassment for himself. He turned hundred and eighty degrees around to face the audience. Everyone watched respectfully. Some familiar faces showed how excited and proud they were.

'Ladies and gentlemen, please be seated. The king shall address a few matters' Bobby said and proceeded to join the rest of the servants standing by the side. Edward stood at the stand and looked at every single row of chairs and the faces of the people. They were all so happy to see him. It made him happy.

'Good morning' Edward started, testing his voice. His tone sounded informal. 'Alright, first thing first...'

Some of the audience were starting to laugh a little. They couldn't take it seriously that Edward sounded totally informal addressing a crowd with majority people he doesn't know just after his crowning. But Edward just went on with his speech.

'My fellow royals, masters, servants and staff, and dear citizens, and animal friends' Edward said, emphasising on the last "and".

'I thank you for coming today' he started sounding formal. 'None of this would have happened without all those that were involved in the war. And most of them are in this room right now. Applause for them'

The audience clapped.

'And, I want to mention the person that, to me, made this whole thing happen. Princess Flyangel, we thank you. I thank you, for being the bravest independent young woman I've ever met'

Another applause. Edward could see Flyra was blushing.

'On to that matter, White Woods and White Shore. These two cities were not independent. They had been under Combination since the beginning. That is why, my first decree is to liberate White Woods and White

Shore to be two separated independent cities. Projects will be carried out to rebuild White Shore and Barenge. Prince Nathan of Combination will be crowned king within a few months after the completion of White Shore project. He shall take full responsibility over White Shore afterwards. And Prince Jake will be by his side assisting his brother. Applause for Prince Nathan and Jake'

Applause. Nathan sat there looking humbled and very respected. Edward had asked every single person that he was going to announce yesterday, if they would agree to his offers and suggestions.

'Princess Flyangel, no longer shall she be running around, finding for adventures. Because she will have a lot of responsibilities on her shoulders. As she will be the future queen of White Woods. With Sir Everos as her royal advisor. Applause for them both'

Applause.

'Barenge. Princess Darleen, the rightful heir to the throne. After the completion of the Barenge project, she shall return to Barenge and be crowned Queen of the musketeers'

Automatic applause. And most were laughing at Edward's last description.

'Finally, Morgan's Kingdom. It's located in the Outlands. There won't be any project regarding it. Nevertheless, I will change the name. And to me, there's no better name than a name that appreciates the person that helped to our freedom. Flyra's Stand. A perfect name for a staycation town'

More laughter and applause.

'Now, onto roles and royal positions. The role of the royal master for Combination city. I've decided between three candidates. And there's no better person than the daughter of our beloved Master Jackenzie, Lillain'

Applause. Lillain was shocked. A very happy kind of shock. She couldn't believe her ears. She couldn't begin to describe how appreciative she was for Edward choosing her for a very important role.

'Why don't you stand up so that everyone can see' Edward said, smiling happily. Lillain stood up. She saw everyone cheering for her. And she was happy. She was proud. She believes that if her dad was still around, he would be very proud too. She looked at the other two candidates, Master Mousy and Master Kitty. They were very happy for her too. Mousy was probably the one clapping the hardest. She seemed to be clapping very quickly. Lillain sat back down and Edward continued.

'The rest of the roles will be the same. But, I'm adding a new role. We never had an official role for someone who's in charge of welfare. So I'm very glad to announce the royal welfare advisor, Dewi'

Applause. Edward had asked Dewi as well yesterday, so she wasn't shocked. Dewi smiled, grateful to be assigned an important responsibility that she is naturally good at.

'Now, last but not least. Regarding law and orders. Every individual city has their own laws and regulations. What I'm about to address to you, are laws that will govern all the united cities and kingdoms of Inland. Firstly, all capital cities to be an ally to one another in any circumstances, should anyone break this rule, the city they rule shall automatically be part of the Outlands and Inland will have every right to go to war with that city. Secondly, on this day, the first of April, shall mark the first official National Day of Inland. This annual celebration should be at least appreciated by all capitals of Inland. And lastly for now, anyone who breaks the laws of their city, shall face a minimum of two months in jail if the crime is not a death sentence type of crime. I appreciate everyone listening attentively. The new laws are to ensure that proper discipline will be carried out to avoid more unnecessary war in the future. As well as a reminder for every single one of us to stay vigilant to any possible threats from the Outlands. I'll end my speech here. Now everyone can enjoy the feast in the dining hall. Citizens and masters, kindly follow the directions by the staff. Royals, please follow me, I'll direct you to the royal lounge'

Edward stepped down from the stage. The royals went to congratulate him.

'I'm so proud of you' Princess Darleen said, hugging him straight. No formal status in between them both is going to stop her from that.

'Thank you Aunt Darleen' Edward replied.

Behind Darleen, Princess Flyra was eagerly waiting for her turn. She has a very big smile on her face. She's pretty.

'Alright, you continue talking, I'll bring those waiting to the lounge' Darleen said, pulling away. Flyra happily stepped closer, in front of Edward.

'Your majesty!' Flyra said excitedly. Edward had never seen Flyra this happy before. It made him very happy too.